The Spy Catchers of Maple Hill

ALSO BY MEGAN FRAZER BLAKEMORE

The Water Castle

The Spy Catchers of Maple Hill

Megan Frazer Blakemore

BLOOMSBURY

NEW YORK   LONDON   NEW DELHI   SYDNEY

First published in the United States of America in May 2014
by Bloomsbury Children's Books
www.bloomsbury.com

Bloomsbury is a registered trademark of Bloomsbury Publishing Plc

For information about permission to reproduce selections from this book, write to
Permissions, Bloomsbury Children's Books, 1385 Broadway, New York, New York 10018
Bloomsbury books may be purchased for business or promotional use. For information on bulk purchases
please contact Macmillan Corporate and Premium Sales Department at specialmarkets@macmillan.com

Library of Congress Cataloging-in-Publication Data
Blakemore, Megan Frazer.
The spy catchers of Maple Hill / by Megan Frazer Blakemore.
pages   cm
Summary: Hazel Kaplansky and new student Samuel Butler investigate rumors that a Russian
spy has infiltrated their small Vermont town, amidst the fervor of Cold War era McCarthyism,
but more is revealed than they could ever have imagined.
ISBN 978-1-61963-348-3 (hardcover) • ISBN 978-1-61963-349-0 (e-book)
[1. Mystery and detective stories.   2. Friendship—Fiction.   3. City and town life—Vermont—Fiction.
4. Spies—Fiction.   5. Cold War—Fiction.   6. Vermont—History—20th century—Fiction.]   I. Title.
PZ7.B574Spy 2014   [Fic]—dc23   2013039857

Book design by Nicole Gastonguay
Typeset by Westchester Book Composition
Printed and bound in the U.S.A. by Thomson-Shore Inc., Dexter, Michigan
2 4 6 8 10 9 7 5 3 1

All papers used by Bloomsbury Publishing, Inc., are natural, recyclable products
made from wood grown in well-managed forests. The manufacturing processes
conform to the environmental regulations of the country of origin.

Dedicated to
Eileen Frazer
(Code Name: Mom)
Thank you for all the stories.

The Spy Catchers of Maple Hill

Instrument Day

Hazel Kaplansky flew down the Monument Street hill with her feet held out wide from the pedals, one hand raised in the air like a rodeo rider. She coasted so fast she believed she could lift off and fly right into outer space. People would watch her through their telescopes as she shot higher and higher into orbit until she landed on the moon. She'd be the first person to walk on its silvery gray surface.

Instead she landed at Adelaide Switzer Elementary School.

Placing her bike's front wheel between the slots of the bike rack, she checked her school skirt and saddle shoes for grease, and then headed toward the door. She stared down at the cracks in the sidewalk, so she almost walked right into Maryann Wood.

Maryann's hair was long and straight and so blond it almost looked white. Hazel thought it looked like dead, bleached-out grass, and knew her own short haircut was much more practical, but all the other girls said it was *so* pretty and they were *so* jealous. Hazel would be lying if she said she didn't fantasize about cutting it off at least once a day.

Just now Maryann stood at the bottom of the stairs, spinning a long strand of blond hair around her finger. *Who would she be without that hair and her watery blue eyes?* Hazel wondered. *Would she still be Maryann?*

"Hey, shrimp," Maryann said. Now that Hazel's best friend, Becky Cornflower, had moved to Arizona, Maryann was the tallest girl in the class, and thin as a wisp. Hazel was the third shortest, practically average, yet Maryann still insisted on calling her a shrimp.

"Good morning, Maryann," Hazel said, trying to sound chipper. "Lovely autumn weather we're having here, isn't it? I simply adore the fall in Vermont."

Maryann pursed her lips. "Why are you so weird?"

Hazel decided to keep up her strategy of being overly friendly. If nothing else, it would confuse Maryann. "I prefer the word 'unique.' "

"Square," Maryann said.

Hazel decided not to point out that being square meant being boring and she didn't think someone could be both weird and boring. "See you in class," she said cheerily.

Maryann rolled her eyes.

Hazel trotted up the stairs, opened the big metal door, and made her way down the hall to Mrs. Sinclair's classroom. She walked into the room and announced, "Mrs. Sinclair, I have arrived!" Mrs. Sinclair stood at the chalkboard writing "Friday, October 23, 1953" in her perfect, curly cursive. Her white chalk letters never smeared, and unlike many teachers—especially Mr. Hiccolm in fourth grade—she did not wind up with chalk dust all over her clothes by the end of the day. She looked up and said, "Why, good morning, Hazel!" as if the same thing didn't happen every morning. Hazel hung her backpack and coat in the cubby area and then sat down in her assigned seat in the second row. She preferred to sit in the front row, but she knew that Mrs. Sinclair needed to put the hooligans there to keep an eye on them.

Hazel took out a piece of paper and began drawing a diagram of a human cell. This was not part of the regular curriculum. Hazel much preferred things that were outside of the usual school program.

Before Becky left, Hazel and Becky would stay by the cubbies until the last possible second, getting each other up-to-date on all the things that had passed since they'd parted the afternoon before—Becky's cat's hairballs and what they looked like (Becky thought her cat was trying to communicate through them), Hazel's adventures in the graveyard, and if they needed to add any total rainfall to their yearlong tally (each girl kept a jar with a ruler outside her house). All that had ended when Becky had been plucked away for a new life in Arizona, where it hardly ever rained.

Mornings like these Hazel missed Becky the most. She could always help Hazel feel better, usually by making creepy faces like pulling down her lower eyelids and sucking her bottom lip in so far it looked like she didn't have any teeth at all.

A moment later, Maryann arrived with Connie Short. The two were locked at the elbow, just the way she and Becky used to walk, only it hadn't been annoying when they'd done it. Maryann and Connie were in deep discussion of a television show they'd seen the night before. Hazel knew the name, but she had never seen it. Her family had a black-and-white television, but they hardly ever used it. All her parents liked to watch were the news and educational shows like *You Were There*. Hazel did watch the cartoons, though, when she got up before her parents on the weekend.

Connie, with her wide green eyes and bouncy brown curls, was prettier than Maryann, though no one, least of all Connie, would ever say so. She said she was plain because she had a dusting of freckles across her nose. Pretty as she looked, she was also pigeon-toed, which made her waddle when she walked.

Sometimes Hazel wondered if Maryann had built Connie like some sort of Frankenstein-type monster. Connie was a shadow of Maryann: paler, quieter, not as smart, and not as cruel. She was Maryann's echo. If Hazel hadn't known both of them her whole life, the artificial-creation theory would be hard to dismiss. They'd been best friends since forever, and both of them had a dark, solid center that made them mean. Not everyone else could see it—not all the other kids and certainly not the teachers, who seemed to think that

Maryann and Connie were just about as perfect as perfect could be—but Hazel could.

Maryann and Connie didn't even have a chance to ignore her before Mrs. Sinclair asked them all to stand to say the Pledge of Allegiance. Their words all ran together, and Hazel didn't think it was respectful. The Pledge was their way of saying they stood with their great nation against Communism and dictators and everything else awful in the world, and they just rushed through it. Hazel wondered how many of her classmates even knew what the word "allegiance" meant.

Next came music. Hazel hated music, and she found it particularly unfair that she had to start off Friday morning with it. Friday should be a day of celebration, but for Mrs. Sinclair's fifth-grade class at Adelaide Switzer Elementary, it was Instrument Day.

Hazel took her seat on the rust-colored rug knowing that today would be just the same as every other day. Mrs. Ferrigno liked to make a big dramatic deal about handing out the instruments in music class, but it always ended up the same. Big and polite Anthony got the largest set of cymbals, and his friend Timmy got the smaller ones. Another set of boys got vibraslaps. None of the boys could manage to sit still and quiet with their instruments, so as Mrs. Ferrigno kept going, her voice was accompanied by metal sliding on metal and the occasional soft *boinggggg* of a vibraslap hitting a knee.

As Mrs. Ferrigno made her way through the instruments, Hazel knew the inevitable was coming: Maryann and Connie would get the two glockenspiels, and of course they would react to this news with squeals of delight. *Just once*, Hazel thought, *I would like to get the glockenspiel. I would react with dignity and take the mallets from Mrs. Ferrigno's outstretched hand and sit behind my instrument like I was getting ready to play Carnegie Hall.*

Hazel imagined herself standing center stage at Carnegie Hall. She had never been there, but she had seen pictures. The vaulted ceiling would arch high above her head, making her look small on the stage. But once her mallets hit the glockenspiel, there would be no denying her power. In her mind she played Bach. She played Chopin. She played "The Flight of the Bumblebee," with her mallets flying over the bars. At the end of her performance, her hair would be wild around her head and there'd be beads of sweat on her brow. She would nearly collapse from the exertion of it all. And the audience would burst into applause, rise to its feet, and declare her a star.

Hazel shot her hand into the air. The time had come to set herself on the path to glory. Time to stand up to the Maryanns and the Connies of the world. Hazel knew that information was power, and she was about to wow Mrs. Ferrigno with all the information she had. She had spent hours in the library reading up on percussion instruments, in particular the glockenspiel.

"Yes, Hazel?" Mrs. Ferrigno said.

She sat up straight and sucked in her belly as she took a deep breath. "Did you know that 'glockenspiel' is German for 'play of the bells'? And that's because at first there were bells that people would hit. But then they started to be made out of metal bars instead."

"That's interesting, Hazel. Thank you for illuminating us."

"My pleasure. Also, did you know that Mozart used the glockenspiel in his work? Perhaps we could challenge ourselves to do one of his pieces."

"I'll take that under advisement."

"Great!" Hazel said. She was getting somewhere, she was sure of it. Before she knew it, Mrs. Ferrigno would be handing her the mallets, and then she'd finally have her chance to shine.

Mrs. Ferrigno reached out the hand holding the mallets. "Today let's have Maryann play first glockenspiel." She hesitated for a moment and glanced at Hazel, who could feel her heart beating faster in anticipation. "And Connie play second glockenspiel."

Squeals of enjoyment from Maryann and Connie.

Hazel slumped as Mrs. Ferrigno said, "So, Hazel, that leaves the triangle for you."

Fallout Shelter

Saturday morning, the glockenspiel snub of the day before still stung. Hazel tried not to let it bother her. True, Mrs. Ferrigno was keeping her from reaching her full potential as a percussive instrumentalist, but Hazel had other ways to shine. In fact, that very day she had big plans. Plans she had been working on for weeks. It all depended on being able to open up one of the mausoleums in the cemetery behind her house. These were small stone buildings that held a number of bodies, but tucked into drawers so it wasn't like there were skeletons hanging about. Or so she thought. She had never actually been into one before, since they were off-limits. But she knew that when the Russians attacked, her mom and dad would forgive her the minor rule breaking since she would have saved their lives by turning the mausoleum into a fallout shelter.

Like most parents, hers claimed they didn't need a shelter.

The chances of the Russians attacking their small town in Vermont were slim. Only Connie Short's family had one in their backyard. Connie made a big show of keeping a list of who would be allowed down in the shelter with her. She claimed there would only be room for three of her friends. Maryann Wood had a permanent spot on top of the list, of course, since Connie couldn't even breathe without Maryann, it seemed. Other girls rotated on and off the list with alarming frequency. Hazel herself had never been on the list and didn't hope to be: Connie Short had hated her ever since the second grade when Hazel found her trapped in a bathroom stall blubbering hysterically. Hazel told her to just crawl under, but Connie didn't want to touch the bathroom floor, so Hazel went and found Mr. Potter the janitor to let her out. Connie's face was blotchy red and tear soaked and she told Hazel never to tell anyone. Hazel hadn't, but that didn't seem to matter to Connie.

Anyway, Hazel needed to take matters into her own hands. There were three mausoleums in the cemetery. The first was grown over with vines. The second was still in regular use. She stood now in front of the door of the third. She pushed gently. Nothing happened. She blew the bangs of her pageboy haircut out of her eyes and wiped her clammy hands on her dungarees, then pressed harder against the cool, rough stone door. After looking over her shoulder to confirm the graveyard was deserted, she bent her knees and pushed again. The door started to slide with a creak, and a rush of cold air came out to meet her. Dead air. She peeked in: dry dirt floors and she shimmied farther along it. She would like the tree to work like it did in the *Loony Tunes* cartoons: she'd crawl out to the end, and the branch would droop down and deposit her gently on the ground. Instead she took the branch in her hands, swung down, then dropped to her feet with a crunch. Leaving the rake resting against the tree trunk, she made her way down into the knoll behind the tree.

Beyond the knoll was where the poorer people were buried. Her father said they were the more practical ones who recognized that the view didn't matter when you were dead. The graves were close together, and she liked to hop from one flat headstone to another. As she hopped she sung a tuneless song, since tunes were one of the few things that Hazel was not good at. Hazel was good at many things, and exceptional at others, so she figured it was only fair that there were some skills that eluded her. Though, she argued in her mind, she was not as pitiful as Mrs. Ferrigno made her out to be.

A sharp clang rang out, and Hazel looked behind her to see Mr. Jones digging a fresh grave. The muscles in his arms tensed like springs with each stab of the shovel into the hard Vermont ground. He dug each new grave into a perfect rectangle, all smooth angles and sides, no roots or stones sticking out. Mr. Jones had Brylcreemed hair that shone like black river rock. He kept a barbershop comb in his back pocket, and he took it out to smooth down his hair when he thought no one was looking. But Hazel was always looking and writing down her observations in her Mysteries Notebook. So far she hadn't come across any real mysteries, but she figured it was only a matter of time and of being observant.

Mr. Jones was the closest thing Hazel had to a true investigation. He'd started working there only the month before. He just showed up on their doorstep with his hat in his giant hands asking if there was any work. He was tall, over six feet, but didn't stoop down in their small doorway. Hazel had peeked at him from around the stairs. Their old gravedigger had just gone to an early grave himself, so Hazel's parents were glad to have him. In fact, Mr. Jones's first duty was to dig Old Lou's grave. Hazel, of course, had watched him do it, and the whole time he'd had a small twist of a smile on his lips.

Each morning when Mr. Jones rumbled into work at the cemetery in his old blue truck, he wore a moth-eaten wool sweater. He shed this by midmorning, and he worked in a white T-shirt. His jeans had creases on the front, but Hazel just could not picture Mr. Jones standing above the ironing board each evening smoothing out the denim. By the end of the day his clothes had dirt and sometimes blood smeared across them. But each morning he came back in a snow-white shirt and pressed jeans.

He strode king-like through the graveyard and it sometimes seemed as if Memory's Garden was his, and not the Kaplanskys'. So comfortable was he in the cemetery that he would sit right down sometimes with his feet hanging into a freshly dug grave and eat his lunch. He cut slices of apple with a penknife and pulled them into his mouth with his teeth. She had diligently written down all these observations in her Mysteries Notebook, but she couldn't make them amount to much of anything.

Her father, who liked to talk to anyone who wandered by about the weather or sports scores or the proper placement of Christmas decorations—small talk, he called it—even he never said much to Mr. Jones beyond "Good morning" and "Fourth plot in the third row for Wednesday." Her mother rarely spoke to him at all.

At school she'd heard the other kids call him Grim Reaper Jones. They said the scar on his hand was from wrestling alligators in Florida. They said he ate raw squirrel every night for dinner. They said he slept with his eyes open. Hazel knew that all of these were implausible, but still she wrote them down in her Mysteries Notebook. She had her own theories about him. "Paul Jones" sounded like a made-up name to her, and she felt certain that he was an ex-convict, maybe even an *escaped* convict, and she steered clear of him.

So she continued to skip until the headstones stopped and the ground gave way to a large pond. She hopped up onto a bench and walked across it with her arms held out to the side as if it were a tightrope. As she neared the end of the bench, she pretended to wobble and drop.

She made her way around the pond to a cluster of three statues. They were the Three Graces, she knew, but she called them Tabitha, Abitha, and Babitha. "Why, hello there, ladies, lovely day, isn't it?" she asked. "And Babitha, that is a glorious robe. Where'd you get it?"

The kids at school said that she talked to the dead people, that those were her only friends now that Becky was gone, but that wasn't true. She didn't talk to the bodies, only the sculptures. Hazel had long ago accepted that she would not ever be considered normal by her peers at school, but even for her, talking to dead people would be beyond the pale.

"Why, yes, Abitha, I did get a new pair of sneakers. You like them?" She held out her foot, which was clad in the same old pair of canvas sneakers she always wore. She brushed a bit of dirt off her dungarees. "I would love to chat, girls, but I've got quite a busy day ahead of me. Quite a busy day."

She started up the hill toward the oldest part of the cemetery, and as she crested the rise, she heard voices and froze. A blue Packard automobile was idling on one of the roads that ran through the cemetery. Mr. Jones was talking to someone, but Hazel couldn't see who. She crept through the cemetery to try to get a better look. She found a tree and climbed right up, but she nearly fell out when she saw Connie Short's father hand a box to Mr. Jones. Mr. Short was a foreman over at the Switzer Switch and Safe Factory. What on earth could he be giving to Mr. Jones?

Mr. Jones nodded, took the box, and went toward an old gardening shed. He unlocked the padlock on the door—since when had the gardening shed been locked?—placed the box inside, and relocked the door. Mr. Short drove off, pulling his hat down low as if he didn't want anyone to see him.

What was in that box?

Hazel sat in the tree chewing on her lip. Something was not on the up-and-up. Last year she had read every single one of the Nancy Drew mysteries, and just like Nancy always did, she had a hunch, but you didn't need to be a young sleuth like Hazel and Nancy to know that when a person locked something up, he was hiding something. And just like that, Hazel had her first *real* mystery.

Thorns

Hazel's mother made egg salad sandwiches for lunch, and they sat outside at an old picnic table that was out of sight of the cemetery. Hazel had her Mysteries Notebook open and balanced on her lap, and she chewed on the end of her pencil.

Her Mysteries Notebook was an old composition notebook of her mother's from college. She'd found it the previous spring in her parents' office, and only one page had any writing on it, so Hazel had figured it was okay to take. "Doctoral Dissertation Ideas" was the heading, followed by a list that made little sense to Hazel. She had torn out that page and tucked it into the bottom of a pile of her mother's work. Then she took the notebook back up to her bedroom, where she crossed out her mother's name on the front and wrote her own. In the place where it said "Subject" she wrote Mysteries.

Sometimes she thought it should be called her Questions Notebook, since she had a lot more questions than mysteries.

Why does Timmy only write on the bottom of his left sneaker, but not his right? Where does Miss Angus hide that pencil in her hair? Who has been drawing chalk outlines of people on the street outside the cemetery? That last one she had an answer to: little Trudy West from up the road had received sidewalk chalk for her birthday and spent most of the month of July tracing all eight of her siblings. At Becky's insistence Hazel had also written: Just what is Becky's cat trying to tell her with all those hairballs? Hazel never planned to answer that one. She was being a good friend, just like Becky was a good friend and read all the Nancy Drew and Trixie Belden books with Hazel even though she preferred Louisa May Alcott. Really, though, Hazel thought that Becky got the better end of that deal. Nancy Drew taught real sleuthing techniques, and Trixie Belden taught you that you should always trust your hunches, but Hazel couldn't think of one single, solitary useful thing she had learned from *Little Women*.

The page with the most writing was the one that said Who is Mr. Jones? Really??? She had written:

Why does he iron his jeans?

Why does he eat the same thing every single day?

Today Mr. Jones sat by a fresh grave with his feet hanging in, whistling that song from Gone with the Wind, the one about the house. That's strange, isn't it? (Aside: Who names a house? Second aside: Why is the Strand Theater so intent on showing Gone with the Wind every Sunday? Can't they go ahead and show something new already?)

Now she added:

What does Mr. Short have to do with Mr. Jones?
What's in that box?

"Eat your lunch, Hazel," her mother said. "You don't want the egg salad to spoil."

"Sure," Hazel said, and took a bite. Her mother put pickles and onions in, both of which Hazel felt did not belong in egg salad. Becky Cornflower's mom made hers with Miracle Whip, and Hazel thought that was just perfect. One more thing to miss about Becky.

Her parents nattered on about what kind of roses would be best for a new hedgerow along the back end of the cemetery. "There's the mermaid rose, of course," Hazel's father said as he chewed on his sandwich.

Hazel's mother shook her head. "But we'd have to put a fence up for that. I thought the point was to have a natural barrier. I was thinking fairy roses."

Hazel realized she had not been very good about writing down all that she knew about Mr. Jones. She tried to remember more details. It wasn't much. Once Otis Logan had told a story about seeing Mr. Jones at the A&P filling his whole cart up with steaks and ground beef. "It was like he's a werewolf or something," Otis had said. "There's no possible way one man could eat all that meat, not unless he wasn't really a man at all." Hazel had thought that was very silly at the time—after all, there was no such thing as a werewolf—but Otis was right that someone filling a grocery cart with red meat likely had some unnatural tendencies. She wrote down: *Strange appetites.*

When her father had asked Mr. Jones where he was coming from, he'd hesitated and then said, "A bit of here, there, and everywhere." Her mother had told him she was glad that he'd made it back to Maple Hill. His truck's license plates were from New York, so Hazel supposed that was the last place he had lived. It wasn't a for-certain, but it was an educated guess. He was a drifter; that was the best she could come up with. If she were a drifter, she wouldn't drift into Maple Hill, that's for sure. Still, she wrote down: Drifter. New York?

Hazel picked at a splinter of wood on the picnic table. The whole thing needed to be sanded down and repainted. She pictured both of the men in her head. Mr. Jones and Mr. Short. Try and try, she just could not bridge the gap.

She knew a little more about Mr. Short than she did about Mr. Jones. Hazel had met Connie's father once, two years before. Connie's grandmother had died, and her father had come to make arrangements. He was a handsome man, sort of like Spencer Tracy. He'd brought Connie along and suggested the two girls play together. They'd gone into the sitting room and sat on opposite ends of the couch while *Howdy Doody* was on television. Connie's father had been nice, though, even if he had been oblivious about how terrible his daughter was. He was well respected in town, jovial, always ready for a laugh. He was, in point of fact, the exact opposite of Mr. Jones. So what could they possibly have in common? "No one in the Shorts' family has died recently, have they?"

"Fairy roses? The thorns aren't big enough. What about Othello?"

"We don't want anything too large. It might seem disrespectful." Her mom patted her lips with a paper napkin. "Just who are you trying to keep out of the graveyard, anyway, George? I was thinking of rabbits and the occasional teenager. The prickers on the fairy rose should be fine for that. We could get them in a nice pale pink. They'd be subtle but lovely."

"You never know who might want to come in. All sorts of new folks are moving to the area."

"What kind of folks?" Hazel asked, looking up from her notebook.

Her father kept talking to her mother. "And I'm not sure the fairy roses would stop a rabbit, anyway. Maybe we should just keep the fence."

"A fence won't stop the real threat, and neither will the biggest prickers you can find," Hazel said.

"What's the real threat?" her dad asked.

"You know what I'm talking about. The Russians. No thorns are going to keep them back. We need a more secure place where we could weather a nuclear attack." Hazel figured she should give her parents one more chance to build a proper fallout shelter. They didn't go for the bait.

"Don't worry, Hazel. If Senator McCarthy is to be believed, all the Communists are down in Washington and New Jersey."

"New Jersey?" Hazel asked. New Jersey was far away, but

not stupendously far away. You could get there in a day's drive. She certainly didn't like the thought of danger being so near.

"Don't encourage her," Hazel's mom said.

"At the Fort Monmouth Signal Corps," her dad explained. "McCarthy says that the Rosenbergs were just the tip of the iceberg and there's a whole ring of spies down there. At least twenty."

"George," Hazel's mom said in a warning tone.

"Really?" Hazel asked.

"That's what they're reporting, but we don't know for sure because Senator McCarthy insists on holding all the hearings behind closed doors so no one can see what he's up to."

Closed-door meetings made sense to Hazel. The investigators couldn't give away what they knew.

Her father reached out and tousled her hair, and she pulled back. "I've always loved the Othello rose," he said to her mother.

"I just think if we go for those big flowers—lovely as they are—well, who would want big fat roses behind them as they say good-bye to their loved ones?" She leaned her head back, and the kerchief on her head fluttered in the breeze. With her sunglasses on, she could almost look glamorous, like Elizabeth Taylor or something. "Now, if we could have a proper English garden, that's where we should have the Othello and the mermaid roses. Wouldn't that be nice? But for a graveyard, nothing so big."

Hazel sighed. This conversation was going round and round. "Why don't you just get small roses with big thorns?"

Her dad looked at her with a mix of excitement and surprise that she seemed to care about the flowers. "Well, Hazel, you can't get big thorns without a big flower."

"Bigger flower, bigger thorns, stronger smell," her mother explained.

"So the biggest, best-smelling roses are the most dangerous?" To Hazel, that sounded like it could be something from an Agatha Christie novel: *The Case of the Thorny Rose*. It would be about a beautiful woman and all the men who loved her. They would leave roses by her door, but she would ignore them. One day there would be the most beautiful rose she had ever seen, and even she couldn't ignore it, so she'd bend over and pick it up and be pricked by the huge thorn that the murderer had covered with poison. She'd drop dead, or maybe into a deep coma like Sleeping Beauty. It would take Miss Marple all of ten seconds to figure out it was one of the girls in town who was jealous of the woman's beauty. And smarts. The beautiful woman would be smart, too, and that's why she wouldn't have the time for the suitors.

Hazel was getting quite caught up in her own story when her father said, "Would you like to take a look at some of the catalogs? Perhaps you'd like to choose the rose for the back hedge."

"Is there a type that has a thorn that could serve as a poisoned dart?"

Hazel's mother rolled her eyes, but her father said, "Well, now, I don't suppose I know just what it would take to make a poisoned dart. Why, is there someone you want to poison?"

He laughed, but in truth there was a whole list of people Hazel wouldn't mind giving a touch of poison to. Not enough to kill them, of course, or even to send them into Sleeping Beauty la-la land. Just enough to make them reflect on their actions. "I can think of a couple," she said.

"Oh, Hazel." Her mom sighed. "Are kids at school giving you trouble again?"

Parents always asked the most ridiculous questions. And even if she answered truthfully, what would her mother be able to do about it? Before she had a chance to answer, her mom said, "I'll just go ahead and order those fairy roses. I want to get them in before the frost."

"So what about the Shorts, anyway?" Hazel asked.

"The Shorts?" her dad asked. "Now, why on earth do you think they'd be sneaking into the cemetery?"

"I asked if anyone in their family had died recently."

"What would make you ask a question like that?"

Three crows in the pear tree started cawing at one another, and it was like a warning to Hazel to zip it. "Oh, something Connie said in class. I must have misunderstood her."

"Connie's a nice girl," her mom said. "Shame about the pigeon toes, though."

Even her mom noticed the pigeon toes, and her mom didn't notice anything.

Ghost Boy

Monday morning meant music again. Surprise, surprise, Hazel was given the triangle, while Connie and Maryann played the glockenspiels.

After music, they all went back to class. Hazel sat down in her second-row seat and then arranged her pencils on her desk.

When she lifted her head, she was surprised to see a boy standing there. He had a shaggy haircut, poorly done, so his bangs fell down into his eyes. He wore old-fashioned glasses, perfectly round with wire frames. His clothes were not usual, either: brown pants, a button-down shirt, and suspenders. He looked like the pictures in their history textbooks of folks from the Civil War. His skin was so pale it was almost blue, and he had deep, dark circles under his eyes. He seemed to shimmer, he jittered so much, like he was wavering between this world and the next. He looked for all the world like a ghost; that wasn't possible, of course, or so she had thought, but there he was, there but not. A ghost! She had lived all her life in a graveyard, and at school was where she saw her first ghost. It had to mean something. Something special. Something different.

Mrs. Sinclair cleared her throat. "Boys and girls, we have a new student. I'd like you all to welcome Samuel Butler."

There were a few murmurs at the name, a ripple of excitement that washed over the class. Hazel, though, couldn't help but be disappointed. He was just a regular kid. Well, not regular regular. He stood with stooped shoulders next to Mrs. Sinclair. His hair was mussed and his glasses looked smudged.

His presence after music class raised a number of questions, though. Why, for example, had he not arrived at the beginning of the day? Or maybe he had arrived, but had spent the entire time meeting with the principal in the front office—a prospect that raised many more questions. She even allowed herself the fantasy that he had some condition that prevented him from being able to attend music class, and if he could get such an excuse, then, maybe, so could she.

He joined the row behind her, on the other side of the room. In fact, he took Becky's seat. She couldn't see him, but she glowered. How could Mrs. Sinclair give away Becky's seat? There was still a possibility that she would return, and then she would be faced with this small, strange boy sitting in her chair. That would not be much of a welcome. Becky would probably cry—Becky was quite a crier—and then she'd run out of the room, maybe all the way back to Arizona.

"Why couldn't we get someone normal?" Maryann whispered from her seat behind Hazel.

"Seriously. Look at those glasses," Connie replied. "So square."

Hazel tried to look over her shoulder, but didn't want the other girls to notice that she was taking any interest in him. She just wondered how they had made their judgment so quickly. It was the clothes, she decided. His old-fashioned clothes were what made them shun him. In her case, she often wondered if it was because she lived in the cemetery. She feared, though, that it was something about her, something that emanated off her like sweat, and they would sense it even if she lived in one of the brick houses on the hill.

"Today we begin our study of ancient Greece," Mrs. Sinclair announced. "Let's start by listing the things we know."

Hazel waited a moment to raise her hand. This was something Mrs. Sinclair had asked her to do in order to give the other students a chance to process the question and come up with their own answers. Hazel was an awfully fast thinker, and it frustrated her to have to wait, but Mrs. Sinclair had explained that Hazel should have pity on her classmates and their pea-sized brains. She hadn't used those words, of course, but that was the gist. Hazel was excellent at picking up what adults really meant when they spoke to her.

"Yes, Samuel, how nice of you to volunteer on your first day."

Samuel stood up next to his desk with his hands folded. "There are many interesting things about the ancient Greeks, but to my mind the most interesting part of their culture is their form of government. It is the predecessor to our own democracy."

There were general rumblings around the room. "He talks like a grown-up," she heard Anthony say to Timmy in a low voice.

"That's right," Mrs. Sinclair said. "Thank you." She wrote "Democracy" on the board.

"At the same time," he went on, "the civilization was grounded in war and had some of the most ruthless soldiers of the time. Most notably, the Spartans."

"Soldiers?" Timmy asked. "Like the army and the navy?"

"Well, it was the Romans who had the first standing army," Samuel said. "But the Spartans were highly trained and organized. Boys left the home early and trained all their lives to be soldiers."

"I wish we could do that!" Anthony exclaimed. "I'd go right now and get trained and then the Commies wouldn't know what hit them."

"Me, too!" came a chorus of boys.

"Gentlemen," Mrs. Sinclair said, and waved her hands downward like she was calming a pack of wild dogs.

"The way the Spartans fought actually might appeal to the Russians," Samuel said. "They did it in a group called a phalanx. All together as one."

The boys grumbled at this. Hazel shifted in her seat. She

could feel Maryann and Connie staring at her. It was one thing to be an outcast, and quite another to be an outcast with something special about you. Hazel was an outcast, but at least she wasn't like Ellen Abbott, who sat in the back row and never spoke. The only thing Hazel knew about Ellen was that she liked horse books. Hazel hated horse books.

Hazel was smart. The smartest. This fact was acknowledged by the whole fifth grade. Now here was some new boy trying to challenge her place at the top. She shot her hand into the air, and before Mrs. Sinclair could call on her—or not—she began speaking. "They are also well known for their mythology. It was a complicated system, and the gods and goddesses weren't well behaved. They were always getting jealous of one another and interfering with the humans. My favorite goddess is Athena. She sprang fully grown from Zeus's head."

Connie and Maryann made retching noises behind her.

"Yes, that's right, too," Mrs. Sinclair said. "Anyone else?"

"Also," Hazel added, unwilling to be outdone, "it wasn't just about politics. Their art was spectacular, especially the painting and sculpture, and it's still around today and is valuable and I once went to Boston and saw all these sculptures made out of white marble. They were beautiful, and people still learn from them today."

"True, Hazel. Let's see what anyone else knows."

No one moved. Then Samuel raised his hand. "In the time of the ancient Greeks, those sculptures were actually painted.

To our eyes today, they would seem gaudy, but that's how they liked them."

Hazel looked down at her hands on her desk. They were shaking. This was a nightmare. It had to be a nightmare. She heard a titter, and then she raised her eyes. Maryann, in a singsongy voice, whispered, "Samuel's smarter than Hazel. Samuel's smarter than Hazel." And she knew then that it wasn't a dream. Not at all. This was all too real.

Impossible, Hazel thought, shaking her head. There was no way that any other fifth grader—or sixth grader for that matter—could be smarter than her. Maybe Samuel was just super super interested in ancient Greece. Like Ellen with her horse books, or Anthony with different kinds of cars.

Her stomach dropped as Samuel raised his hand again.

Free Air

As she rode her bike to the library after school, Hazel listed all the ways that she was probably smarter than Samuel. True, he had shined in math and science and even knew the name of the painting that the art teacher held up, some strange portrait where the parts of the face were all misshapen and put together wrong, which turned out to be by a man named Pablo Picasso. Hazel had been thinking, *I could do that*, but then Maryann said, "It doesn't even look like a face. It looks like something a baby painted." So she'd clamped her mouth shut. Out at recess he pulled a big book with a brown leather cover from a bag that could only be called a satchel and sat on the wall and read. Even Hazel didn't read at recess. She walked the perimeter of the playground and occasionally went on the swings.

Back to her list. She felt certain she knew more about plants.

She knew a lot about bees and how they pollinated different fruits in a special order, and about famous swimmers, and the names of small parts of the body like the philtrum or the uvula.

Her bike started to wobble a little, and she noticed her front tire was low on air. Wall's Garage was just up the way, so she pedaled a little farther. There was an air pump with a sign that said in big letters: FREE AIR. That always made Hazel smile: as if people would try to charge for air.

Her bike tire had what her dad called a slow leak, and he'd promised to fix it, but he hadn't yet. So she kept filling it up. Nancy Drew knew how to change her own car tires, and Hazel expected she would learn herself when she had a car. But even Nancy preferred assistance sometimes, so Hazel didn't mind going to the garage for help.

Mr. Wall was pumping gas for Mrs. Logan, who wrote the gardening column in the *Maple Hill Banner* and who was married to the pastor at the Protestant church in town. They had four noisy boys who were wrestling in the backseat of the car. Otis was in Hazel's class at school even though he was a year older than her, because he'd gotten polio two summers before and missed a lot of school and now walked with a limp. Hazel had thought that having a life-threatening illness would make you thoughtful and strong, but that didn't happen to Otis. When he saw her, he stuck out his tongue, and soon all four boys had their faces pressed against the glass in grotesque contortions. Mrs. Logan acted like she didn't even notice, chatting merrily away at Mr. Wall, who didn't get a chance to say a word. She spoke at such a rapid clip, all he could do was nod his head. People said with four boys and blabby Pastor Logan at home, well, Mrs. Logan had no choice but to get all her words out when she was out and about.

Hazel couldn't hear much above the whirring gasoline pump, but she thought she heard Mrs. Logan saying something about Communists "right here in Maple Hill!" But that couldn't be possible, because her wide, toothy smile never left her lips.

As she drove away, Mr. Wall took his hat off, scratched his head, then tugged his hat back on. Seeing Hazel, he gave a hearty wave.

"Hello, Mr. Wall," she called.

"Hello there, Hazel," he said. "What's the facts today?"

He always asked her that, like she was a walking encyclopedia. At least someone recognized her genius. She hoped that Samuel Butler would never have any reason to go to Wall's Garage. "Well, today I learned about this painter who made millions of dollars by painting faces with the eyes on the chin and the nose off to the side and everything stretched out and squished like a fun house mirror. Isn't that bizarre?" she asked.

"It sure isn't sane," he replied. Mr. Wall wore coveralls with his name sewn onto a patch over his heart. There was no Mrs. Wall, so Hazel wondered if he'd done it himself, or if he'd been able to order them with the name tag. She thought that coveralls would be a useful garment to have. She could play all day in the graveyard and then pull off the coveralls and be perfectly clean underneath. All she would have to do was wash the dirt from under her fingernails.

Mr. Wall's fingernails were black underneath, and all around the cuticles, too. She imagined his hands smelled like his garage did. Maybe his whole house smelled that way. Hazel liked the mix of gasoline, tar, rubber, and tobacco. It smelled like a job well done.

"What was Mrs. Logan saying about Communists?" she asked.

"Oh, you know Mrs. Logan," Mr. Wall said as he took off his hat and rubbed his head. "Half is gossip and the other half is nonsense. You shouldn't worry much about what she says."

"If you say so." Hazel kneeled down next to a spot on the pavement slick with oil. She thought the way it shimmered purple and green was one of the most beautiful things in the world. People like Connie and Maryann would only see it as dirty, but that's because they weren't creative and individual thinkers like Hazel was. While she unscrewed the cap on her tire, Mr. Wall uncoiled the air hose and passed it to her. "Mr. Wall, you seem like an unusually perceptive adult."

"Why, thank you, Hazel." He winked at her. Hazel thought his eyes looked just like pennies that were starting to oxidize (something else she probably knew more about than Samuel Butler did). She'd even found a penny once that was a perfect mix of green and copper, so she'd given it to him and he'd kept it right on top of his cash register. He said he would only spend it in case of emergency.

"You're welcome. That's why I like talking with you. You don't just see me as a kid. You see me as a person."

"I suppose kids are people, aren't they?"

"Exactly," Hazel agreed. Not so many adults thought so. Like Mr. Jones in the cemetery. She once came upon him working on some sort of little device. He had a soldering iron going and a wire pinched between his teeth and sticking out one side like a fuse on a stick of dynamite. She'd asked him what it was and he'd hissed, "Radio transmitter." She'd crouched down to watch what he was doing. She'd never seen anyone using a soldering iron, and she leaned in close even though the smell of burning lead made her nose twitch. But instead of keeping on with his business, he'd stopped and stared at her, then pointed the hot tip of the soldering iron right in front of her nose. He'd stayed just like that until she'd said, "Okey-dokey, I suppose I'll be moving along, Mr. Jones." That night her father had told her to give Mr. Jones his space because some adults just didn't feel comfortable around kids, especially not curious little girls, only he had used the word "pestering," which Hazel hadn't thought was very kind.

Mr. Wall, though, was different. The sun was bright in the blue sky, and she had to squint up at him and he looked almost like an angel. "And in your line of work, you must meet all different kinds of people."

"That's true." Once again, Mr. Wall took his hat off and scratched his head, and then placed the ball cap back on his head just so. Mr. Wall was a particular person, which Hazel thought was probably what made him a good mechanic, but she also wondered if all that scratching was what gave him the shiny bald spot on the top of his head.

"When you meet so many people, it means you must be a good judge of character. So, I would like to ask you a question that requires your heightened skills of perception and character judgment."

"Okay, Hazel."

"What are the first three words that come to mind when you think of me? Don't think, just answer."

"Oh, um, well—"

Hazel held up her hand to shield her eyes. "Don't think, Mr. Wall. I'm looking for the impression that comes from the very core of your being."

"The very core. Well, let's see. Obviously you're a well-spoken young lady." He leaned over and checked the pressure in her tire.

Hazel nodded eagerly. "You might even say that I speak like an adult, right?"

"Sure."

"What else?"

"Not at all shy."

"What's the point of being shy? That's what comes to mind first?"

"Yes, the first two."

"And the third?"

"Well, um, I would say that you are very, ah—"

"Yes?" Hazel prompted.

"Bright. You're a bright girl."

Hazel sighed in relief. "And maybe, if you were going to

rank them, my intelligence, that would actually be the first thing on the list?"

"Sure, I suppose it could be."

"It could be or it is?"

"Inquisitive," Mr. Wall said. "Relentless."

"Relentless," Hazel repeated.

"It means you'll never give up."

"Oh, I know. And that's definitely true." She had never actually thought of using this word for herself, but it fit. She liked the way the word sounded. *Relentless.* It made her sound like a warrior.

"Where's all this coming from?" Mr. Wall asked.

"I just think it's good for people to know how they're perceived in the community. For example, you are perceived as honest and reliable. Isn't that nice for you to know? Incidentally, there's a new boy at school and he's also bright," Hazel said, using Mr. Wall's word.

"Someone else's being smart doesn't make you any less so," Mr. Wall said.

Hazel thought about that as she squeezed her thumb against the tire to make sure it was full enough. "But what if, and I'm not saying this is the case, but what if he actually is smarter?" She unhooked the hose from her tire.

Mr. Wall extended a hand and helped her to her feet. "There's always somebody smarter, Hazel. Somebody smarter or faster or more talented. Somewhere there's a better mechanic than me. But I'm still a good mechanic."

"Of course you are," she said.

"And of course you're still smart."

Hazel used her toes to lift her kickstand. A car pulled up to the gas pumps, over the hose that made the little *ding* noise. Hazel thought one of those would be a useful thing to have. Actually, she thought it might be nice in general to own a gas station, to see the people come and go. Although by the time she was a grown-up, maybe they would have hovercrafts. People would float right in, and she would lift her hat in greeting, just like Mr. Wall did. While she fueled their hovercrafts with hydrogen, they would talk about the events of the day and everyone would tell her their problems because she was so good at solving them.

She kicked her leg back over her bike and started riding away. As she passed Mr. Wall, he looked over his shoulder at her and said, "Don't go down that road, Hazel, comparing yourself to others. You'll only end up driving yourself crazy."

It was good advice, Hazel had to admit. The only problem was, whenever someone told her not to go down a road, she couldn't help but sprint ahead.

Red Scare

The library was an old stone building just up the street from Mr. Wall's garage, right in the center of town. This geography made sense to Hazel: the library, seat of knowledge, at the center, while the cemetery was on the outskirts. The building had big windows with leaded panes, and a wide set of steps that led up to a heavy wooden door. Hazel wrapped her hands around the metal door handle and pulled. She liked that the door swelled when it was humid, which made it a little hard to open, like you had to work for the bounty that was inside.

It should come as no surprise that Hazel loved the library. She loved everything about it, even the smell, like paper and paste, and sometimes, when old Richard Begos was there, a little bit like pipe smoke. This gave it a dignified air, she thought, though Miss Angus, the upstairs librarian, complained about it. Hazel and Miss Angus didn't see eye to eye on many things.

On the way in, she stopped and looked at the newspapers. Even though Mr. Wall told her not to worry about what Mrs. Logan said, the idea of Communists in Maple Hill was still niggling her. She scanned the headlines. A story about Earl Warren, the new chief justice of the Supreme Court. Something about President Eisenhower and farmers. Still more about the Yankees winning the World Series. Boring, boring, boring.

There it was.

Her heart just about stopped when she saw the headline on the front page of the *Burlington Free Press*.

McCarthy Searches for Reds at Maple Hill Factory

She snatched up the paper and tucked it under her arm, then cut across the reference area, feeling Miss Angus's eyes upon her. Miss Angus was the only aspect of the library that Hazel did not love. She was taller than any other woman Hazel knew, with bright blond hair and bright white skin. Hazel couldn't help but imagine that she looked a lot like the bodies buried in the cemetery. She had no-nonsense glasses and no-nonsense shoes. Hazel always hurried by her as fast as she could, eyes down, but this time Miss Angus stopped her. "Hazel Kaplansky," she hissed. "Was it you who rearranged the Chronicles of Narnia?"

Hazel shifted the newspaper so that Miss Angus would not see it. Series books were a long-running feud between herself and Miss Angus. Hazel felt sure they should be arranged on the shelf in the order they were to be read. How else would you know what was next? Miss Angus claimed that they needed to be shelved by title, in accordance with proper cataloging and shelving rules. And while it was true that Miss Angus had her master's degree and was the expert, Hazel knew that in this case Miss Angus was just plain wrong.

"Did you know that there are seven books in that series? And that C. S. Lewis and J. R. R. Tolkien were friends? They met at a faculty meeting at Oxford."

"I was not aware of that, Hazel, and while it is an interesting bit of trivia, it is not pertinent to our conversation." Miss Angus stamped the back of a book and put it on a shelf. "I believe I have made myself perfectly clear on the issue of shelving series fiction."

Hazel slumped against the reference desk. "But, Miss Angus, how will people know what order to read them in? Especially with a series like the Chronicles of Narnia. Most people think *The Lion, the Witch, and the Wardrobe* is first, but it's not; *The Magician's Nephew* is. So by putting them in the proper order, we've kept readers from making a horrible, terrible mistake."

Miss Angus looked down her long nose, and Hazel stood up straight. When she gave Hazel that look, Hazel felt like Miss Angus was growing even taller, like one of the plants in the cemetery. Hazel wanted to stand strong, to be relentless, but under that gaze she felt herself shrink. Miss Angus snapped a book shut. "If you wish to lodge a complaint, take it up with the Library of Congress."

"I just may do that, Miss Angus. Thank you for the advice." Hazel backed away and ran down the pocked marble stairs before Miss Angus could say anything else.

The downstairs of the library was a different world. It was the domain of Miss Lerner, a kind woman with warm eyes and red hair who always had a bowl of fruit on her desk and a stash of candy beneath it. She wore pretty dresses with tight waists and full skirts, and her hair was always just perfect. Hazel thought she was all kinds of glamorous, and though she herself abhorred wearing skirts and dresses, she thought that if she looked like Miss Lerner, it might not be so bad.

Miss Angus said that children were only welcome on the lower level, unless accompanied by a responsible adult, which Miss Lerner said was *not okay* and that they could go wherever they wanted as long as they were respectful. But all the other kids were too afraid of Miss Angus, and Miss Lerner made things so nice that most kids just stayed on the lower level. Except Hazel. She ranged all over the building.

The downstairs was carpeted in broad orange and brown stripes, and so Miss Lerner had adopted a tiger theme. Hazel patted the head of the stuffed tiger that lazed at the bottom of the stairs. "Hello, Miss Lerner," she called as she crossed the room. You didn't need to whisper in the downstairs library.

"Why, hello there, Hazel, how are you?"

"Peachy," she said. Her heart was still beating quickly after her run-in with Miss Angus.

"Did I see you riding through town over the weekend? That's one smart bike you have."

"Thanks, Miss Lerner."

Hazel found a chair in a secluded nook and slipped the newspaper onto her lap. She took a deep breath. Hazel was not afraid of much, but she was afraid of Communists. The Russians had been American allies in the Second World War, but after the war, things had soured and now the Russians were turning all the countries around them Communist, and they wanted to do the same thing to America. They were just waiting for the opportunity to come over and make all the people here exactly like them: no choices, no freedom, and no ice-cream floats from the soda fountain in the drugstore, even if you'd been on your best behavior all day. Samuel had been right that the Greeks had started democracy, which meant that the people got a say in how things worked. Americans had those rights, and the Communists wanted to take that away. And now there was a chance that there were Red spies right in her town!

She smoothed out the front page and began reading the story. Senator Joseph McCarthy, whose mission was to hunt out Communists, had sent a team of investigators to the Switzer Switch and Safe Factory. It seemed that the factory had been working on fabricating some sort of switch related to the launching of a guided missile. This was all very exciting to Hazel, and she wished she had known about it sooner, but she was rushing through the article to find out more about why

McCarthy thought Russian spies might be there. It turned out that several of the union bosses had at one time been members of the Communist Party, and so McCarthy wanted to make sure they weren't stealing secrets. He had people investigating at the General Electric plant in Schenectady, New York, too.

Hazel leaned back in her seat. Communists. Right here in Maple Hill. This was worse than she could have imagined. Not only could someone she knew be telling secrets to the Russians, but also those secrets had to do with making weapons. Those spies could have bombs raining down right on her town.

"Hazel?"

Hazel jumped in her chair, but it was just Miss Lerner.

"What are you reading there?"

Hazel hesitated for a moment, but she knew that Miss Lerner was a good listener. "It's about Communists, Miss Lerner. Russian spies right here in Maple Hill, working at the Switzer plant and stealing all our secrets."

"Says who?"

"Senator McCarthy."

Miss Lerner gave a slight frown. "Far be it from me to question a US senator, but it seems to me that Senator McCarthy points fingers first and asks questions later, if at all."

"What's that mean?"

"It means he makes a big fuss about other folks being un-American, but the way he goes about it, well, it's like Senator Margaret Chase Smith said, the way he's doing it goes against some of the basic freedoms of being an American."

"But the article says they're building missiles there. Did you know they were building missiles? I sure didn't."

"I had heard that," Miss Lerner said.

Hazel remembered then that Fred Bowen, one of the foremen and the union boss at the factory, was courting Miss Lerner. "What does Mr. Bowen say about all this?"

"Hazel, I don't think you need to worry about spies. The folks that work at the factory, they're our neighbors."

Hazel narrowed her eyes. She trusted Miss Lerner, but maybe she was blinded by love. Love could do that to you, and so Hazel had promised herself to never fall in love. Mr. Bowen could well be a Communist and maybe even a spy. "That's the thing about spies, Miss Lerner. They live among us. They hide. Anyone could be a spy. Why," she said slowly, as if it were just occurring to her, "I suppose even Mr. Bowen could be a spy."

Miss Lerner laughed at that. "Mr. Bowen is as American as apple pie. Don't let your imagination get the best of you, Hazel."

Hazel folded the paper and smoothed the crease. "All right, Miss Lerner," she said. But she didn't mean it. If there were spies in Maple Hill, Hazel wanted to be the first to know.

"Good. Now, how was school today?"

Hazel thought about telling Miss Lerner about Samuel, or about music class, but instead she said, "Okay. I need to bone up on Greek history, though. Starting a new unit in school."

Miss Lerner's eyes lit up and she waved her hands like a little bird. "We just got a new series in. You take some home and read them and tell me if you think they're any good. If you don't like them, I'll send them back!"

Hazel beamed. Sometimes Miss Lerner called her "librarian-in-training" or her "unofficial assistant."

Miss Lerner went behind her desk, the little gate swinging to and fro behind her. Hazel desperately wanted to get behind that desk and see all the secrets there, but Miss Lerner had never asked. Hazel figured it would happen when her assistantship moved from unofficial to official.

Hazel liked to imagine what Miss Lerner's house was like. She pictured it as just like the library, full of books with neat labels on the spines. If her parents were ever to die in a horrible, tragic accident, she hoped that Miss Lerner would adopt her, and they would catalog books all the time.

Miss Lerner lifted a stack of books: *Daily Life in Ancient Greece, Government in Ancient Greece, Warfare in Ancient Greece, Mythology in Ancient Greece.* Hazel felt pretty solid on mythology, but she took the other three.

"Thanks, Miss Lerner," she said as she tucked them into her backpack.

Samuel Butler wouldn't know what hit him.

The Rat

The books made her wobble a little as she pedaled up the Monument Street hill and then coasted the slight decline to her house. She had planned to go right inside and start studying ancient Greece, but as she rode up the circular drive in front of her house, she decided it was too nice out, and soon it would be cold and rainy, and then winter would come, so she ought to take advantage of all the nice, sunny days she had left. She shrugged off her heavy book bag and left it in the mudroom before heading back to the cemetery. She didn't bother to change from her school clothes into play clothes since she just planned to walk around the cemetery and take in the fresh air. The people in the books she liked to read were always taking strolls in the fresh country air to clear their heads and their lungs, and so it made her feel grown-up and European to do it.

When she stepped outside, Mr. Jones was leaning against a tree smoking one of his odd-smelling cigarettes. "Oh!" she said, surprised. "Good afternoon, Mr. Jones."

Mr. Jones dropped his cigarette and squished it down with the heel of his work boot. Bending over, he scooped it up and dropped it into a tin can that he left by the tree. He looked her up and down. "I've seen what you do to those graves," he said. "Hopping and skipping from one to one. That's not right."

"Well, I . . ."

Hazel's heart beat as fast as a wind-up toy. Was Mr. Jones trying to tell her something? Was it a warning or a threat? He'd had a sneer across his lips like she was a skunk he'd found dead in the road. She thought of what Otis had said about Mr. Jones and the cart full of meat, and the gravedigger's words seemed all the more menacing. She almost ran inside to get her Mysteries Notebook so she could write down what he had said just as he had said it. But today she had a lot to contemplate—this new boy, Red spies in Maple Hill, ancient Greece—and as soon as Mr. Jones moved on, she was lost in her own head.

Most of the town worked at the Switzer Switch and Safe Factory, but she'd never given much thought to what they did there. As the name implied, there were two parts: safes and switches. The safes were famous. They were even advertised in *Life* magazine: "Your Secret's Secure with a Switzer Safe." But if there were Red spies, they would probably be on the switch side trying to get secrets about the switches being made for the missiles. She supposed there was a slight possibility there were safes on the missiles, or that secrets about the missiles were kept in a Switzer safe down in Washington, DC. This was a small possibility, but she knew that good detectives like Nancy Drew or Sherlock Holmes always considered all possibilities and she ought to do the same.

A little ways off, she could see Mr. Jones had begun work on a grave; a new cigarette dangled from his lips and sent smoke swirling around his head. She made sure to go in the other direction, back toward the Three Graces. "No, Babitha, I'm not in a bad mood. I've just got a lot to do." Concentrating on the potential spies was difficult, as she couldn't get Samuel out of her head. Leaning over, she brushed some dirt off the base of their statue. She heard a clanging noise and looked up and saw the top half of Mr. Jones sticking out of the open grave. He lifted his shovel and jammed it into the earth. It must have hit a stone to make such an awful noise. She watched him work. He drove the shovel into the ground over and over again.

That there were spies in America was more or less a certainty. What else could explain how quickly the Soviets had developed their own atom bomb? They must have had someone passing them information. And just that summer Julius and Ethel Rosenberg had been executed for passing information back to the Communists. But Maple Hill seemed so far removed from that sort of thing. Miss Lerner was right: the people at the factory were their neighbors. Hazel didn't like the idea of one of her neighbors spying on her or anyone else in town.

It *couldn't* be someone from the plant, someone from Maple Hill. If there were spies in the town, they had to have come from outside. She sat on the Graces' bench trying to make sense of it all.

From the pond came a sluicing sound. Hazel watched as a rat crept out of the Graces' pond like an old man from a bathtub. It stopped at the edge, turned its head right and then left, and then waddled onward. It was a fat rat with long whiskers and a tail that dragged behind it like a dead snake.

Hazel held still. These were the things Hazel knew about rats: they bit you with sharp teeth and they had rabies, which would make you froth at the mouth and go on a rampage, biting everyone you saw before collapsing in a trembling heap on the ground. Moving slowly, since she wasn't sure about a rat's eyesight or its sense of motion, she turned her head. No one. She looked the other direction. Coming over the rise was Mr. Jones carrying a shovel. She couldn't very well go and ask Mr. Jones for help.

The rat stopped its progress and lifted its nose up into the air. Hazel held her breath. Then, as if it had forgotten something, the rat turned around and began waddling in her direction. She lifted her feet off the ground, but as the rat got closer, she thought that if it lifted itself up on its hind legs, it could grab her shoelaces with its tiny claws and heft itself up onto her foot, then scurry up her leg. It would bite her, and the mouth frothing would commence.

She stood on the bench, but the bench seemed perfectly

climbable, so she stretched her leg over to the base of the statue of the Three Graces. She wrapped her arm around Babitha's waist, mumbling, "Sorry, ladies, desperate times call for desperate measures." She shimmied up Babitha's torso, then hooked her leg up over Abitha's arm. Pushing on Babitha's head, she pulled herself up so she was sitting on top of them, looking as if Abitha and Babitha had hoisted her up on their shoulders after she scored a home run to win the World Series.

From her perch she could see the rat sitting at the base of the statue. It sniffed the air, but there was no way that fat rat could get to the top of the statue. Hazel stuck out her tongue.

"What are you doing up there?"

Hazel swallowed hard at the sound of Mr. Jones's voice. She looked down and saw his shiny hair glinting in the sun. She couldn't speak, and instead lifted her arm and pointed down at the old rat, who had curled up at the base of the statue, waiting for her to come down so it could infect her and then be on its way.

Mr. Jones bent down for a closer look. After a moment he stood up straight, raised the shovel above his head, and brought it down with a dull *thwack*.

The rat lay motionless on the ground. Easy as you please, Mr. Jones scooped up the carcass in his shovel and began walking toward the end of the property. It didn't bother him at all, as if killing rats and disposing of their bodies was an everyday occurrence for him, as common as digging. It took a certain kind of person to end a life so easily—even if the life belonged to a rat. Cold. Calculating. Like an automaton, or Gort, the robot in *The Day the Earth Stood Still*, which she had snuck in to see at the Strand Theater and then she hadn't been able to sleep for two days. That robot had been mission-minded. Shoot first and sort it all out later. She just knew that rat wasn't the first creature Mr. Jones had killed. Was that his secret? Was he a murderer on the lam?

As soon as Mr. Jones was out of sight, she scrambled down the statue and began running in the opposite direction. She kept running, up the hill and through a part of the graveyard where bodies were buried in tight, neat rows. With each footfall, the word pounded in her head: *robot, robot, robot.* She thought of Gort and how he didn't have a choice in what he did. *Robot, robot, robot.* It was just like what the Communists wanted to do to Americans: program them to be all the same. *Robot, robot, robot.* Program them so they couldn't think for themselves or make any choices or ever do anything fun like eat lollipops that turn your tongue green or skip over gravestones. *Robot, robot, robot.*

Spy!

Looking over her shoulder to see if he was following her, she tripped, tumbling forward, feet over head the way Mrs. Warsaw was always trying to get her to do a somersault in gym class. She landed on her butt, legs splayed out in front of her. There was a grass stain on the sleeve of her school blouse, and her saddle shoes were scuffed.

"Are you okay?"

Hazel screamed and closed her eyes, sure that this was it, her very last moment, and she wished it had come in a more dignified way.

The voice screamed back. Hazel opened her eyes, and there was Samuel.

"Why are you screaming?" she demanded.

"Why are *you* screaming?" he replied.

"Because I just watched a Red spy kill a rat."

If this were a movie she would have fainted and it would have been a big dramatic moment. There would be a hero to rescue them all from the spies. All she had, though, was another ruined school outfit and Samuel Butler staring down at her with his wide, sad eyes.

The Gravedigger Is a Spy

"A Red spy? What do you mean?" Samuel asked.

Hazel widened her eyes. For a smart boy, he didn't know much about the world of the here and now. "The Reds? The Communists?"

"Sure. What about them?"

"They've infiltrated Maple Hill. Senator McCarthy sent up an investigative crew to the factory to smoke 'em out. And what I've just figured out is that the leader of their cell isn't working at the factory. That would be too obvious and too dangerous. No, he needed to find a nice, quiet job where no one would notice him. A gravedigger. And I just figured it out, and now he's going to have to kill me to keep me quiet. He's going to put me into the sausage grinder. That's what Communists do, you know."

"You told him?"

Hazel shook her head. "Do you think I'm crazy or something?"

"Well, then, maybe he doesn't know you know yet. How are you so sure he's a spy, anyway? Because he killed a rat?"

"It wasn't just that he killed a rat—it was the *way* he killed the rat: like he was programmed to do it. And that's just what the Communists want to do to us: program us so we're all the same and we're an army of robots to destroy the world."

Samuel scrunched up his lips, and Hazel could tell he wasn't quite convinced.

"Also, Paul Jones is for sure an alias. And just look at the way he dresses. The perfectly creased dungarees? Nobody here irons jeans, but I bet in Russia they get inspected twice a day just to make sure their creases are straight." It was true that Hazel did not know a whole lot about Russia. Just what they'd learned in school about it being a poor country and the fact that the people on the farms worked and worked and the women wore scarves on their heads. Still, she felt certain that if any people were going to iron their dungarees, it would be the Russians. "On top of that, he hardly ever talks and I bet that's because he's trying to cover up his accent. Sure, he thinks he's hiding, but he didn't count on someone as clever as me being here."

Samuel remained unswayed. "If he's a spy, why's he working as a gravedigger? There are no secrets here."

"I told you, he's trying not to draw attention to himself." She gasped then and grabbed Samuel's arm. He flinched back, but she didn't let go. "I bet he's burying secrets. His spies at the plant bring him the plans and other things they find and he buries them to keep them safe until he can smuggle them out and no one notices it because that's his *job*. I bet that's what he was doing, and we interrupted him and—" She shook her head. "We are dead as doornails."

"I think you may be rushing to judgment."

Hazel frowned, but part of her knew that Samuel was right. She needed to make a report to the Senate Permanent Subcommittee on Investigations—the long name for Senator McCarthy's group of Communist catchers—but she couldn't go to them with just a gut feeling. She would need to find some hard evidence. That's what detectives like Nancy Drew did. "Well, since you asked, I can tell you that I'm just beginning my investigation. But I'm already compiling quite a bit of information."

"Like what?" Samuel asked.

"For starters, he just appeared out of nowhere. He's got no family to speak of, and he wouldn't even tell my parents where his hometown was. His diet consists solely of red meat. And apples that he eats with a knife. He just killed that rat like it was nothing. Practically cut its head clean off. I bet he learned how to do that in the Russian army."

"Go on."

Hazel didn't have anything else to add. She scratched at a mosquito bite that was left over from the summer. "A radio transmitter! He has a radio transmitter so he can send the secrets back to Russia!" That, she knew, was the real reason he hadn't wanted her watching him fix it. He knew she could be the one to figure out his dastardly secret.

"It still seems like a bit of a stretch."

Hazel stood up and brushed the dirt off the knees of her tights: another pair ruined. It was clear that Samuel was going to be no help at all. "What are you even doing here?" she demanded.

"I came to do some grave rubbings."

She jutted her hip out. "That's illegal, you know, unless you have permission."

"I know," he said. He opened up his bag and produced a piece of paper. It was from the town and had a raised notary seal and everything.

She had never actually seen one of the permits before, as no one ever had them. Still, she read it over, nodding her head and squinting at parts as if she were examining it. "This looks legitimate," she said.

"It is," he said. "I assure you."

"And why do you want to do the grave rubbings, anyway? I know it's not for a school project."

"I like to think about the people's stories. I have a book. I collect them and then I try to find out information if I can."

This, to Hazel, did not actually seem like such a bad answer. "All right, then. I suppose that's okay."

"What would you have to say about it, anyway?" His question was challenging, but he kept his eyes on the headstone, as if he were afraid to look at her.

"Only that my family runs this place, and even with a permit, if I don't think what you're doing is up to snuff, then I can kick you right off the property."

He nodded. "I see."

"You're okay for now. So, what, this is your hobby?"

"It's a good way to get to know a new place. And if all your friends are dead, it's not so hard to leave them behind." He chuckled like he was making a joke, but Hazel didn't get it.

"How many places have you lived?"

"Seventeen."

"Are you for real?"

"My mom always said you know when you're home, and she never felt it."

Hazel shook her head and said, "Seventeen places. I've always lived in the same one."

"You're lucky," he said.

But Hazel didn't feel lucky. Seventeen new places meant seventeen new chances. She looked up toward Pauper's Field, an old part of the graveyard that wasn't used anymore. Mr. Jones was there, crouched over a headstone just inside the gate. There was no reason for him to be up there; it was the place where people who couldn't afford a plot were buried, and no one had been interred there since the Civil War. "Now, what's he doing up there?" she asked more to herself than Samuel.

"Up where?"

"Mr. Jones is in Pauper's Field, but he doesn't have any work up there."

Hazel got a buzz of excitement. She wasn't sure what he was doing there, but she felt certain it held a key to proving he was a spy. She had her first clue, and as soon as she could, she would investigate it, and Samuel was going to help her.

Mr. Jones stood up and left Pauper's Field, closing the gate carefully behind him. Samuel shifted his satchel on his shoulder. "If it's all right with you, I'd like to get back to my work."

"Hold your horses. I've got a stone for you."

"What do you—"

"Just wait."

Mr. Jones got into his truck and drove out of the graveyard and back toward town, where he rented a house.

"Okay, Sammy—"

"Samuel," he interrupted.

"Sure," she said. "Whatever you want. I have a proposition for you."

"A proposition?" he echoed.

"How would you like a challenge?"

She couldn't be sure, but it looked like his ears actually pricked up a little bit, like a dog when you call its name. "I relish a challenge."

"I mustard a challenge," she said back.

"What?"

"Nothing." She shook her head. No one ever laughed at her mustard joke. "Are you in or out?"

"I don't even know what you want me to do yet."

"I need some help finding out a story behind a headstone."

This seemed to catch his interest, but he said, "Is this about the gravedigger?"

"Yes, but you don't need to worry about that. He was just up there looking at a headstone. I need you to look at it and tell me what you think. You're my expert witness. You can stay out of the spy thing if you want. I can't pay you right now," she continued. "But I bet there's some sort of a reward and I'll give you, say, five percent. What do you say?"

Samuel didn't answer at first, just chewed on the inside of his cheek. "This isn't the type of thing I normally get involved with."

"Well, me neither, but it's not every day when the world drops a big fat mystery in your lap. And I for one believe that if you're given a mystery, you should solve it, but if you're not up for it, I can find another expert," she said, though she wasn't sure where or how.

"Show me the grave."

"Follow me," she said, and started to lead him up to Pauper's Field. "Pauper's Field is where all the people who didn't have enough money to pay for a proper plot are buried. Most of the stones just have a name on them, and no dates or any message or anything. My dad says there are probably hundreds without stones at all."

"If there's nothing on the headstone, what can I do to help you?"

"I thought you were an expert."

"I am."

She stopped walking and raised her eyebrows. "Oh, okay, sure. Listen, I just thought that since you're so good at this whole investigating the histories of people in graveyards, and it's your passion, you might be the person to help me out here. But if you're not up for it . . ." She let the words hang in the air.

"I didn't say I wasn't up for it."

"I'm just giving you a chance to get out now, honorably, I mean. I won't tell anyone."

She wouldn't tell anyone no matter what happened, as she had no one to tell, but if he hadn't picked up on that already, she wasn't about to point it out.

"I'm in."

Hazel pulled open the gate with a loud creak. Even though she knew Mr. Jones was gone for the day, she still looked over her shoulder.

She wasn't sure if she'd be able to find the stone he had been crouched near, but it was clear as soon as they opened the gate. There were chrysanthemums freshly planted around the stone, the soil from the pot still visible above the dirt of the ground. Hazel brushed a stray leaf off the stone, which was cool and shiny. Unlike the other stones, it was a perfect square. The font was simple, but soft. All it said was:

ALICE
TEN YEARS OLD

"Well, then, what I need you to do is find out who Alice is."

"That's more than a challenge," he said, but he dropped to his knees and pulled out a piece of paper and a crayon. He laid the paper carefully over the square stone, lining up the sides.

"What are you doing?" she asked.

"Grave rubbing."

"Why are you bothering with that? It's just a name and an age. Just write it down and let's go." She looked behind her, expecting Mr. Jones to return at any moment. With a shovel. She could still hear the sound it made as it came down on the rat. She wondered what kind of sausage she would be turned into: the sweet breakfast kind, or maybe the spicy kielbasa that her father liked.

"It's part of the process," he said. "If we're going to solve this mystery, we need to follow the process."

"I thought you said this wasn't the type of thing you got involved in." Hazel kicked at the ground. She regretted bringing him up here in the first place. If he was going to approach everything in this slowpoke sort of a way, they'd never get anywhere.

"All I'm going to do is find out who she was," he said. "We're going to find out Alice's story."

"We?"

"This was your idea," Samuel said. He pressed his hand down flat on top of the paper, holding it in place. "I'll help you figure out who this Alice girl was, but you have yet to offer me any substantial proof to support your claim that he's a spy," he told her.

Hazel frowned. She looked at some of the other stones, which were tilted at odd angles like something out of a Halloween greeting card. "Why else would he be up here?"

Samuel shook his head. "He doesn't look like a spy."

"He wouldn't be a very good spy if he looked like one," Hazel said. "If every spy looked like a spy, Senator McCarthy and his crew would just gather them all up off the street and we wouldn't have to worry about a Commie invasion."

Samuel finished his rubbing and stood up. "You asked me to find out the story of one of these graves, and I'll do it. If you want to help, I'll be going to the library tomorrow. You can meet me there."

He hitched his satchel up over his shoulder and then left Pauper's Field. The squeaking gate stayed open behind him.

A Regular Family

The Kaplanskys' kitchen table was shiny new Formica, but you couldn't tell since it was piled with catalogs and magazines related to horticulture. Her parents would flip through the magazines during dinner, and typically left Hazel to her own thoughts, and that was okay with Hazel. That night in particular she had a lot to think about.

She served herself peas and mashed potatoes. She liked to make a well in her potatoes and fill it with gravy, then float the peas in it, but her mother said that was uncouth, which was another way of saying no. So instead she swirled the gravy into the potatoes and thought about her mysteries. After dinner she would write everything down in her notebook, but in the meantime she could contemplate.

If Mr. Jones was a spy—The Comrade, as she decided to call him—then what possible connection could he have to a ten-year-old girl? She puzzled over this as she lined up her peas and slid them onto her fork.

"And how was school today?" her mom asked.

"Fine," Hazel replied before shoveling one forkful of potatoes into her mouth after another.

"Manners," her mother said. She snapped out her napkin, then spread it across her lap.

In the detective stories she read, the detective always had someone to bounce ideas off. Hazel, though, didn't have anyone. She told herself it wasn't a problem. After all, Nancy Drew was alone for the first four books—her friends Bess and George didn't show up until the fifth book, *The Secret at Shadow Ranch*—and she solved those first four mysteries just fine without them. Anyway, Bess and George weren't as smart as Nancy—or Hazel for that matter—and they sometimes got in the way instead of helping.

Becky would have been good at this mystery, Hazel knew, and she was sad to have to solve it without her. Maybe she could copy over her notes and send them to Becky, and Becky could write back with her ideas. Of course, that would take a long time, but she liked the idea of receiving a package with a mystery in it, and thought that Becky would, too.

Anyway, she refocused herself, the most obvious option was that the person buried there was not in fact Alice, Ten Years Old, but perhaps someone who had figured out who Paul Jones was. She shivered; she didn't want to end up buried in Pauper's Field.

On the other hand, by planting flowers by a headstone in Pauper's Field, Mr. Jones was practically putting up a big sign saying that something was going on.

Maybe there isn't a body there at all, she thought. *Maybe it is simply a hiding place.*

"Did you learn anything?" her dad asked.

She knew she couldn't just come out and tell them that she'd learned that their gravedigger was spying for the Russians. "We're studying ancient Greece."

"Ah, ancient Greece," her dad said, nodding, as if he had his own fond memories of the place. "I made a scale model of the Parthenon when I was your age. I bet I have it somewhere."

"Greek mythology!" her mom said, pleased as could be. Her parents stank at this talking-to-their-kid thing.

"Yes," Hazel said. Her parents' sudden interest in traditional family dinner conversation seemed scripted to Hazel, as if by playing the parts they could become a different kind of family than they were. Hazel kept lining up her peas and spiking them onto the tines of her fork. She decided to throw them a bone. "Did you know that the Greeks were the founders of our modern form of democracy?"

"Well, something *like* our modern form of democracy," her dad said.

"Sure." Hazel pushed another large bite of potatoes into her mouth, and her mother raised an eyebrow, so the next time she took a smaller scoop. She was saving her chicken for last since she didn't like it and hoped she could fill herself up with peas and potatoes.

Her parents exchanged a glance and her father cleared his throat and then her mother gave him a pointed look, and finally he said, "We saw you by the pond today. With a boy."

"Oh, that's the new boy," she said.

"That might have been the type of information you could have shared when we asked you what happened at school today," her mom said.

Hazel shrugged. "It's no big deal." Though, in fact, new students were pretty rare at Adelaide Switzer Elementary.

"So what's his name? Where's he from?" her mom asked.

"Samuel," she said. "And I don't know where he's from. He said he's lived seventeen different places."

"Samuel?" her mom asked, putting down her fork. "What's his last name?"

Hazel tried to remember if Mrs. Sinclair had said his last name. "I'm not sure—"

"He's not Samuel Butler, is he?"

"Yes! That's it!" Hazel looked from her mother to her father and then back again. They were communicating in the wordless way of parents: raised eyebrows, twitches of lips, and intense stares. "What?" Hazel asked.

"Nothing," her dad said. "His mother used to live in town, a long time ago."

Hazel shrugged. "Yeah, well, he's in my class now and he's smart and kind of strange."

"And what were you two doing by the pond?" her mom asked.

Hazel bit her lip to keep herself from spilling the whole story about Mr. Jones and the spies in town and Alice. She'd already been warned more than once to just leave Mr. Jones alone. "He was doing some grave rubbings and I told him that he needed to have a permit, and he did. I've never actually seen one before. They're pretty boring."

Hazel's mom picked up her fork again. "Well, you be sure to be nice to him."

"Why?" Hazel asked.

"You should always be nice to people, Hazel."

"I know that. So why did you specifically tell me to be nice to him?"

Her parents exchanged another look before her mother spoke. "Well, Hazel, because he's new, that's why. You don't know what it's like to be the new kid at school, and I imagine it's difficult. It can be hard to make friends."

Hazel didn't need to be told it could be hard to make friends. "He seems all right," she said. "But strange."

"You mentioned that already," her mom said.

"If someone is a little different from the norm, that just means they're more interesting. More going on upstairs," her dad said, tapping his head. He leaned in and spoke in a stage whisper. "Some people think your mother and I are weird."

"You *are* weird," she said.

"Point proven," her dad replied.

"Just try to be a little kind," her mother told her. "Some people are more fragile than others."

Hazel imagined Samuel shattering like a vase. Then she wondered how her mother would know if he was fragile or not.

It was a little odd to think that he was actually from Maple Hill, or his mom was anyway, and that she'd never met him. He was like a mystery all to himself. True, a far more boring mystery than the gravestone they'd found in Pauper's Field, but a mystery, nonetheless. Maybe he had a strange illness, and his mom had it, too, and that's what made him fragile. Or maybe he was actually not from Maple Hill at all and it was a big charade that all the adults were in on, or at least some of them, because actually he was a prince from some small European country whose king (his father) had just been deposed and he needed a safe place to hide. That squared up with his clothes and his strange way of talking.

"Kind, but no kissing," her dad said.

"Yuck," she said.

"Good," he replied. Then he reached over to the counter and picked up a seed catalog. Family time, it seemed, was over. Now Hazel could get on with her investigation.

As soon as she finished clearing the table, she raced up the stairs to her bedroom and took her Mysteries Notebook out from between her mattress and box spring. Now that she had a real mystery to solve, she had decided to keep it hidden. She began by writing down everything she knew about Mr. Jones, Communist spies, and Alice. For Alice all she had was that, if she was a real person, she was ten years old. For Communist spies, she knew that they were suspected to be at the Switzer Switch and Safe Factory, so she felt she could write down "In Maple Hill." Mr. Jones was also in Maple Hill, so she wrote that under his name and then put a star next to each entry to indicate a connection. Samuel would probably call it a loose connection, but Maple Hill was a small town, and if spies were in the factory, it stood to reason that they would be elsewhere in town. That's what Hazel thought, anyway.

There were a number of other facts she could write under both "Mr. Jones" and "Communist spies": secretive, potentially violent, keep to themselves.

Next she decided to make a list of all the questions for which she needed an answer:

What is Mr. Jones's real name?

Is Mr. Jones from Russia?

Did Mr. Jones have previous experience as a gravedigger? What did he do before coming here?

When Communists infiltrate, do they all go to work in the same place? Wouldn't it make sense for them to have a leader outside the company that they reported to?

How do spies get their secrets back to Mother Russia anyway?

Who is Alice?

She looked over her list. She wasn't sure how she was going to find out all these things. She supposed there might be information about Communists in the books and magazines

in the library. Hazel wished she had a little blue sports car like
Nancy Drew. Then she could drive herself to the library to do
more research, though the library was probably closed. While
it was true that Nancy Drew had managed just fine on her
own for four mysteries, Hazel wasn't sure if she was ready for
this one. She was smart, smarter than anyone, but for this case
she was going to need backup. After all, even the great Sherlock Holmes needed Watson. Though she didn't want to admit
it, she needed Samuel.

Hazel crouched at the bottom of the stairs like the gargoyles in
the graveyard. She listened to her parents in the living room.

" 'In any weather, at any hour of the day or night, I have
been anxious to improve the nick of time, and notch it on my
stick too; to stand on the meeting of two eternities, the past
and future, which is precisely the present moment; to toe that
line,' " her father intoned.

They were reading Thoreau to each other, something they
did like normal parents played bridge or swirled cocktails in a
glass. Of all the people in history, Thoreau was the person
Hazel would least like to spend time with. The whole world
was open to him, and he had chosen to lock himself away in a
little cabin in the woods.

The living room was off the hall that led to the kitchen.
The kitchen was where she needed to go to get the lemon

juice and toothpick in order to write her secret message to Samuel.

When she was a grown-up, and a real detective, she would probably have a special watch that also served as a communicator, and she could send information to the other detectives that way, but for now she had to use another method to let Samuel know what she had found out. She had begged and begged her parents for a Super Spy Kit that she had seen advertised in the back of an *Amazing Detective* comic book. It had a special notebook, and a pen that wrote with invisible ink, and a magnifying glass, which is what she wanted most of all. Her parents had told her no, of course, so she was going to have to make her own invisible ink to send a note to Samuel.

"Read the bit about simplicity, about the marrow of life," her mother said.

Hazel heard a shifting as her father moved in his chair. Her mother would be sitting at his feet, perhaps with her eyes closed, while he read. If Hazel timed it right, to move while her father was speaking, perhaps both would be too distracted to hear her go by.

"Here we are," her father said.

Hazel started moving catlike down the hall. She closed her eyes as she passed the living room, as if this could somehow ward off their seeing her. Three more steps and her hands were on the door to the kitchen, pushing it open. She held it by the knob and let it slowly shut, with not even a click as it fell back into place.

She let out her breath like the slow leak from her bike tire. Her heart was racing. She liked adventure, might even say that she lived for it, yet in the moment, it made her feel rather ill.

The lemon juice was easy. She took a small, chipped cup from the back of the cupboard and filled it from the glass bottle in their refrigerator. The toothpick was harder to locate. They were not much of a toothpick family. Her father did not drink martinis with olives when he got home from work. They didn't have people over for hors d'oeuvres that needed to be spiked on sticks. Once Hazel had been to a party at Becky's, and they'd had tiny hot dogs wrapped in dough that Hazel thought were the most astounding things ever, but the only people Hazel's parents ever had over were other horticulturalists, and she guessed they weren't the tiny hot dog kind of crowd.

So the toothpicks were kept on a high shelf of the pantry. She went to the table and lifted a large, heavy chair and carried it over to the pantry. Normally she just dragged the chair, which her mother hated because she said it would scratch the linoleum, but that night she couldn't risk the scraping sound on the floor.

When she climbed onto the chair, her knee hit the bag of King Arthur flour, tipping it forward. As she reached down to catch it, a small white cloud emerged, dropping tiny snowflakes onto her nightgown. She carefully righted it, imagining the flour spilled all over the floor and the absolute disaster that had just been averted.

Her hand closed around the small box, and she took out

two toothpicks, just in case, and tucked them into the corner of her mouth. Mission accomplished, she climbed down from the chair and lugged it back to the kitchen, trying to make sure it was at just the same angle it had been when she'd retrieved it. It was true that her parents were not detectives like she was, and thus not trained to notice such things as a chair slightly out of place, but they had an uncanny way of knowing when she was on a mission or, in their words, "up to no good," which she thought was an unfair characterization, as everything she did was for good.

She eased open the door and heard her mother's laughter tinkling like the wind chime above the garden. *It's now or never,* Hazel thought, and scurried by, more mouse-like this time. She took the stairs two at a time, sloshing a bit of the lemon juice onto the green carpet.

At her desk, she placed the cup of lemon juice next to a clean sheet of paper. She took one toothpick from her mouth, and left the other in, hoping she looked as smart as Mr. Wall, who sometimes chewed on a toothpick while sitting outside his garage. She thought it made him seem contemplative and wise, like John Wayne. She dipped the end of the other tooth-pick in the lemon juice and then held it over the paper. One single drop fell and landed on the paper.

Then, nothing.

She needed to ask for Samuel's help in figuring out who Alice was, and to break up the spy ring, but of course she couldn't just write that down in a letter, even one written in secret ink. Once Samuel held the letter to a lamp and the message was revealed, well, then anyone could read it—including Mr. Jones—so she didn't want too much information on it. Secrets had to be kept. They would have to develop a code to send each other messages. In the meantime, she would be brief.

The drop of lemon juice spread out, making a translucent dot before disappearing altogether.

Finally, she wrote We need to meet. It took her longer than it would to write with a pen, scratching each letter out on the paper, and she imagined this was what scribes had felt like. She left the paper on her desk. In the morning she would fold it into a simple square, write Samuel's name on the outside, and slip it into Samuel's cubby.

Triangle People

Hazel made sure no one was watching when she slipped the folded square into his cubby where it wouldn't be obvious to anyone walking by but would be seen by Samuel when he was putting his things away.

To her surprise, Hazel found a note in her own cubby. It was an office slip, telling her she should report to the main office, with the box next to "Immediately" checked. Normally these slips were for when kids needed to leave early for a dentist appointment or something like that. When "Immediately" was checked, though, it meant something was up.

Mrs. Sinclair was busy talking to Otis Logan about multiplication tables—he was still stuck on the fours and he blamed the polio, but Hazel knew that was just an excuse. So Hazel left without saying anything. Surely it was Mrs. Sinclair herself who had put the slip in Hazel's cubby, and so she would know that Hazel was at the office. Hazel headed down the hall against the rush of students hurrying to their classrooms before the bell rang to start the day.

Hazel tried to imagine why she was being called to the office. In her highest flying fantasy it was because Senator McCarthy and his investigators had found out about her work and were coming to offer support and give her a medal. She knew that was unlikely, as she still had a long way to go in her investigation.

When she arrived in the office, Mrs. Dunbarton, the secretary, had a phone cradled under her ear and a line of students waiting. When it was Hazel's turn, she handed the office slip to Mrs. Dunbarton, who was still on the phone. She glanced at the slip and shook her head while speaking to the person on the other end of the line. "Got it. Out at one thirty p.m. Yes." Pause. "Yes." Another pause. "Mrs. Mitchell, I can't make any guarantees as to whether Lucy will remember to bring her lunch box home today. Take it up with her teacher."

She sighed as she hung up the phone and then looked at Hazel. "Where'd you get this slip?"

"It was in my cubby."

Mrs. Dunbarton pressed her index finger onto the slip so hard the tip turned red and white. "There is one person in this school who writes the office slips. That person is me. This is not my handwriting."

Hazel felt herself flushing, though she hadn't done anything wrong.

"So where'd you get it?"

"I told you, Mrs. Dunbarton. It was in my cubby when I got to school."

Mrs. Dunbarton held the slip up to the light and examined it closely. "This is the real deal, no counterfeit. Someone stole an office slip!" She looked at Hazel through narrowed eyes over the top of her cat-framed glasses.

"It wasn't me. I swear."

"I'm going to hold on to this. You get back to class."

Perplexed, Hazel made her way back to her classroom. When she opened the door, the class was in the middle of the Pledge of Allegiance. Hazel walked to her seat, joining in for the last line. After everyone was seated, Mrs. Sinclair said, "Hazel, where's your tardy slip?"

"I don't have one," she replied.

"You were tardy, so you need a slip."

"There was an office slip in my cubby, so I went to the office—"

"Hazel, please hurry and get your tardy slip so you won't be late for music."

Heaving a sigh, Hazel stood up. Connie and Maryann were smiling like cats, and Hazel instantly knew this was their doing. She also knew she had no proof. So she went back to the main office.

"You again?" Mrs. Dunbarton said.

"I need a tardy slip."

Mrs. Dunbarton pulled out a small pad. She tucked a piece

of cardboard under the carbon copy slip. "Hazel Kaplansky," she said to herself as she wrote. "Reason?"

"Excuse me?"

"Your reason for being tardy."

"I was here. With you."

"Don't blame me for your tardiness," Mrs. Dunbarton snapped.

Hazel thought about telling her that it was Connie and Maryann who had swiped the office slip, but instead she said, "Is miscommunication a choice?"

"I'll just mark 'Other.'" She tore off the top white piece of paper and stuck the yellow piece in a stack on her desk. "Let's not have this happen again, okay?"

Hazel agreed and, tardy slip in hand, headed back to the classroom. The class was just walking out of the room in two parallel lines, one for girls and one for boys. Hazel slipped into line next to Samuel. She spoke without looking at him so as not to draw attention. She was worried that he hadn't found the paper. "Did you read my note?" she asked.

"You left that paper in my cubby?"

As if anyone else would leave a note for Samuel. "Yes. Did you read it?"

"It was blank."

"It's a secret message," she said.

"But it's blank," he said again.

She turned to look at him now, incredulous. "It's a secret lemon juice note. You hold it up to a light and the letters come out."

"How was I supposed to know that?"

"Everybody knows that."

"So what did it say?"

She sighed. If she had been him, she would have gone straightaway to the bathroom and held the note over a light there, even if it meant standing up on a toilet to do it. But Samuel was not her, so she would just have to tell him. "We need to get working on gathering intel on the Red situation." She tried to sound as cool and matter-of-fact as Sergeant Joe Friday on *Dragnet*. She loved that program and almost always used her allotment of one show a week to watch it. It covered every detail of how the police solved cases, even if it could be a little boring at times.

"Intel?"

"Intelligence," she whispered. "It's time to do some sleuthing." Nancy Drew was always referred to as a "young sleuth," and Hazel thought that was a good word. *Hazel Kaplansky, the young sleuth*, she imagined her own adventure being told, *had long harbored a hunch about Mr. Jones, and now she was going to prove his dastardly nature. Other girls might be afraid but not our heroine!*

They all sat down in a circle, and Mrs. Ferrigno began the ritual of passing out the instruments. Mrs. Ferrigno stopped near them to hand Anthony the big cymbals and Timmy the smaller ones. Next she delivered the vibraslaps. Hazel was so wrapped up in the mystery that it didn't even faze her when Maryann and Connie got the two glockenspiels. She was barely even paying attention until she heard Mrs. Ferrigno say, "Samuel, you may play the triangle."

When Hazel looked up, she saw Mrs. Ferrigno with her hand to her lips. "Oh my! Hazel, what shall we have you play?" She went to a small closet and began rustling around. Hazel wondered what she might pull out. A tambourine, perhaps, or one of those sticks with all the bells on it. "Ah, here we go!" Mrs. Ferrigno exclaimed, and she pulled out a second triangle, smaller than the first and with a decided bend in one of its legs. "Go sit next to Samuel. You'll play as a couple, which in music we call a 'duet.'"

Connie turned to Maryann and mouthed the word "duet" and giggled. Hazel felt herself getting pink and uncomfortable as the teasing laughter rippled around the room.

With little fanfare, she took the malformed triangle and sat back down next to Samuel. "I always got the triangle at my last school, too," he said.

"I always miss the cue," she confessed.

Mrs. Ferrigno began to teach them a new song: an all-percussion version of "Yankee Doodle," which sounded, to Hazel's ears, like a closet full of pots tumbling down a set of wooden stairs, but Mrs. Ferrigno clapped and said "Lovely, lovely" as they practiced each section. When the class could play the piece the whole way through, Mrs. Ferrigno turned to Hazel and Samuel. "And the grand finale," she said, trilling out the *e*.

Hazel and Samuel dinged their triangles at the same time. "Satisfactory."

While the class worked through the song, Hazel looked at

Samuel and thought of her mother's advice to be kind to him. Her mother had never gone out of her way to give Hazel social advice of any kind, and Hazel wondered what made Samuel so special. If her parents had known his mother and she was from Maple Hill, maybe they had all been friends.

"Hazel!" Mrs. Ferrigno said, exasperated.

"Sorry," Hazel replied. "I was caught up in the beauty of the music."

Mrs. Ferrigno rolled her eyes and said, "From the top."

She wondered if Samuel's mother was as annoying and particular as he was. Everything had to be logical and reasonable for him, but when you were dealing with mysteries, things weren't always logical. She bet even "just the facts" Joe Friday would admit that.

The class kept playing, and when they got to the final ding of the triangles, Samuel elbowed her in the side and she came in right on time. Mrs. Ferrigno almost smiled. "Will wonders never cease."

"Does that mean I can get a glockenspiel next time?"

"I think you're more triangle material."

This got Maryann and Connie laughing, and Mrs. Ferrigno didn't even tell them to stop.

On the way out the door, Connie called, "Hey, Hazel!"

Hazel turned around, and there were Maryann and Connie with their hands up on their foreheads, fingers in the shape of triangles, snickering at her.

The Priest Knows All

On the bike ride over to the library, Hazel planned the investigating she and Samuel would do. They'd start by canvasing
the neighborhood to see if anyone remembered a girl named
Alice. Then they could come up with a list of persons of interest.
They'd have to interview each of them, and for that they'd
need a cover story. Maybe they could say they were interviewing people for a school project about Maple Hill's past.

Right next to the library was the big white Catholic church
that Hazel's mother had attended as a child; she'd stopped
once she grew up and got married. The door of the church
opened and Father Paul came out. Waving, he called, "Hey-o,
Hazel." He knew her even though they didn't go to church
because the priest knew everyone.

And everything, she realized. And the whole history of
the town.

Hazel leaned her bike against the tree and trotted up a few steps. "Hello, Father Paul," she said. "How are you on this glorious day?" She had noticed that religious people often used the word "glorious."

"I am well, my dear, and how are you?"

"Very well," she replied. "Actually, I'm working on a project, and I thought maybe you could help."

"A school project?"

She didn't think it was a good idea to lie to a priest. "More like a personal project. I'm researching some of the graves in the old paupers' graveyard. With Samuel Butler. He's interested in that sort of thing."

Father Paul made a tut-tutting noise, but then he said, "It's good of you to befriend that boy."

What was it about Samuel that made people think he was so fragile? He was odd, that was for certain, but he seemed more or less sturdy. "What do you mean?" she asked.

"Oh, Hazel, it's a very long story."

Hazel looked at him and waited. She had plenty of time.

"What's this project you're working on?"

"Well, it's a bit hard to explain. I'm just wondering if you might know of anyone buried up there who maybe didn't belong here."

"Everyone is welcome here."

Hazel sighed. "I don't just mean the church. I mean the whole town." She didn't think she could come right out and ask about Alice. She didn't want to give too much away.

"Well, sure, there have been people who have drifted through, if you know what I mean."

She sure did, but for once her line of questioning wasn't about Mr. Jones. She wanted to know more about Alice. "Any girls, maybe? About my age. Maybe some who were lost under mysterious circumstances?"

"Is there something specific you're getting at, Hazel?"

She didn't want to tip her hand too soon. "I just think it can be interesting to research people who are like you but who lived in a different time. Sometimes I wish I lived in a different time."

Smiling, Father Paul sat down and patted the space next to him. So Hazel sat down, too. "Is something troubling you, Hazel?"

Hazel knew that anything you told a priest was a secret if it was part of a confession. But she wasn't sure it counted if you told a priest someone else's secret. "Imagine there was somebody you knew, and you found out they weren't who you thought they were at all."

"We all have secrets, Hazel. Even me."

Hazel tried to imagine what sort of secrets Father Paul could have. Maybe he wore a bright red T-shirt under his priest shirt or sang along with Frank Sinatra on the radio. "Me, too," she said. "The thing is, this is a really, really big secret."

"How big?"

"Huge." Hazel held her hands out as wide as she could.

"I've heard a lot of secrets in my day, and the one thing I

can tell you is that people always feel better when they share them."

"The problem is, it's not my secret."

"Ah, that's a different matter entirely. How did you come to uncover this secret?"

"I deduced it."

"Deduced it? I see. And you are certain of your deduction?"

"Ninety-nine, well, maybe ninety-eight point nine nine nine percent sure."

"That's still more than a percent of uncertainty."

Hazel nodded.

"I suggest, then, that you find out one hundred percent before you start deciding what to do about it. But always remember, if it's not your secret, it may not be yours to tell."

Hazel knew he was right in the general sense, but the identity of the spies in town was a secret that had to be told. Father Paul had a point, though—she needed one hundred percent indisputable proof before she could tell anyone what she knew. "Thanks, Father Paul. You helped a lot."

"That's my job," he replied.

Hazel stood up, ready to go, but then she looked back at Father Paul. "Have you heard they're investigating Communists at the factory?"

Father Paul's face darkened. "That's nothing you need to worry yourself about, Hazel."

"But, Father Paul, if there are Reds in the plant, they could be everywhere. They could be anyone."

"You listen to me, Hazel. These are tough times in our country. We face a real threat. But there are those who would use that threat as a way to instill fear in our communities."

Hazel wasn't sure what Father Paul was getting at. It's not like folks would just go around calling people Communists for no reason. She kicked her saddle shoe against the stone step.

"Maple Hill is made up of good people. Don't let anyone tell you otherwise."

"You're right," she said. But then again, Mr. Jones wasn't from Maple Hill. "Thanks, Father Paul. This was a good talk."

"You're welcome, Hazel. We'll be sure to do it again sometime."

"Sure thing, Father Paul." Hazel trotted down the stairs, ready to meet Samuel and keep investigating.

The Third Floor

"Come on," Samuel said, standing by the stairway on the main floor of the library. The *up* staircase. No one went upstairs. It was where all the microfilm and microforms and old newspapers were. Only the librarians were allowed up there, and a select few adults who had been specially trained on the machines.

"We can't go up there."

"Why not?"

"Miss Angus wouldn't like it," Hazel told him.

"Miss Angus? She's the one who sent me up here."

Hazel opened her mouth but could think of nothing to say, so she shut it quickly. "Oh, well, you didn't say that," Hazel said. "I wasn't sure if you'd been given permission yet. But since you have, let's go right on up."

Samuel gave her a funny look and started up the stairs.

The third floor of the library was hot and dusty and had a

funny smell, like old wood and chemicals. Hazel sat down on a wooden stool. "Smart move, coming up here. It's very private, so we can talk freely about the case. We don't need to use code words or anything." In truth, Hazel rather liked using code words.

Samuel looked around before dropping his satchel on an old table with a broken lamp built right into it. "I suppose that's true."

"I brought supplies," she said. She slipped off her backpack and pulled out her Mysteries Notebook. She had searched her house for a magnifying glass, but there hadn't seemed to be any. She had found a compass, and even though she knew every inch of Maple Hill and could never get lost, she had brought it along with her just to have something. "I also have our cover story, for when we do interviews."

Samuel took out his big leather book and turned to a page with the grave rubbing taped to it. There were no lines on the paper, but his writing was perfectly straight. "Typically I start with newspapers, to get an obituary. That's the most straight-forward path."

"The most boring path, you mean." A fly buzzed around her head and she swatted at it.

Samuel ignored her. "We only know her first name and how old she was, which means we will need to be better detectives."

Hazel perked up at the mention of being a detective. "Exactly. So we'll need to come up with a list of people to question who might know something about a girl named Alice who died when she was ten years old. Like I said, I've got our cover story for that all set. We're doing a school project on the history of Maple Hill. Once we've done our interviewing, then we can plan our stakeout. I've already started by interviewing Father Paul."

"Not that kind of detective," he said, tapping the grave rubbing. "Research. Background. Finding the story in history."

Hazel didn't know what other kind of detective there was than a sleuth like Nancy Drew. She looked up. The ceiling was open to its pointy top, and she could see the rafters, the fly dancing around them. "We already know that Paul Jones is a Communist." She opened her own notebook to show him the list of qualities that Mr. Jones shared with Red spies. "We just need a little more proof. We need to find out what he's doing in Maple Hill, and how he's getting his information back to the bigwigs in Russia. This Alice girl must be the key. Or at least a major clue."

Samuel wrote something down in his book. "We don't need to find out what a spy is doing in Maple Hill until we know that he's actually a spy. Right now we need to figure out who Alice is. If you're right and he is a spy, then figuring out Alice will give you more evidence."

The fly had swung back down and was circling her ankle. She kicked out her foot. "We're dealing with a matter of national security here. We have to be people of action." It wasn't just the country she was worried about. If someone else discovered that Mr. Jones was a spy, they might think her family had harbored him and send them all off to prison with him.

"That's your assumption," he said.

Hazel slumped onto the table, burying her head in her

arms. This was not how she had expected to spend her afternoon. She'd imagined herself on the trail of a dangerous villain, and that would show Connie and Maryann, wouldn't it? They wouldn't be able to call her a triangle person anymore if she single-handedly caught a Russian spy. Well, single-handedly with Samuel's help. She lifted up her head just in time to see the fly land on the table. She slapped her hand down but missed, and it buzzed away.

"I'm not a triangle person," she announced.

"There's nothing wrong with being a triangle person," he replied. "We play an important role in the overall composition."

"The song would sound better without it," she said.

"Perhaps," he said, without giving it too much consideration. "What we need to do is to estimate the age of the headstone, and then we can start surveying a range of newspapers, looking for stories that might be related. Surely a ten-year-old girl dying would be in the paper."

"Indomitably," Hazel replied. When Samuel looked confused, Hazel tried to give him a benevolent smile, but really she was soaring inside: she knew something he did not. "It means definitely, without a doubt."

"I think the word you mean is 'indubitably.' 'Indomitable' means that it can't be defeated or even stopped." Hazel was deflating like a balloon with a pinprick, but then Samuel added, "As in, you are indubitably indomitable."

Indubitably indomitable, Hazel thought. *Relentless.* Too bad the rest of the world didn't see her that way. "I just don't know why they think they're so much better than me. You know, they're the reason I got a tardy today. They stole that office slip and put it in my cubby. I've gotten the perfect attendance award the past three years and now I won't get it this year and it's all because of them."

"I've never gotten a perfect attendance record." Samuel wrote some figures down in the margin of his book.

"That's because you've gotten to live in seventeen different places. You really think I'm a triangle person?"

"I didn't say that. I said being a triangle person might not be so bad. I'm not sure I even know what it means to be a triangle person." He leaned his face in close to the grave rubbing to examine it.

"It means being a dud. A square."

"Oh, then you're definitely not a triangle person. So how old do you think the stone is?"

"I have no idea."

"You're the cemetery expert," he said.

The sun was filtering in through the octagon-shaped window at the end of the floor. It left an elongated shaft of light on the floor that was edging toward her toes. "Well, no one's been buried there since Civil War times."

"The Civil War started in 1861 and ended—"

"In 1865," Hazel finished for him. "Almost ninety years ago."

Hazel sighed again. The adventure of the enterprise was rapidly seeping away. Even the fly was bored. It perched on the edge of a chair, just out of reach.

Samuel got up and began reading the labels on the cabinets. "Here we are. Do you know when Pauper's Field started?"

"It's always been there."

"Well, then I suggest we start in 1865 and work our way forward in time."

"This seems like an awful lot of work," she told him.

His face, previously animated, fell. "Oh. I thought you wanted to figure out the mystery."

"I do. I want to know what The Comrade is doing in my graveyard."

"Who?"

"The Comrade. Mr. Jones. That's my code name for him."

"It's not a very coded code name."

Hazel pursed her lips. "What I'm trying to say is that an investigation is about—"

"Interviews and stakeouts, I know. First we need to get our foundation. We need to know who to interview and who to stake out." He opened one of the drawers and ran his fingers over the rolls of film. "Do you know how to use microfilm?"

"Sure," Hazel lied. All she knew about microfilm was that Adelaide Switzer had donated the machine and all the archived newspapers to the library because she wanted to preserve the town's history. It was a big honking deal, and it was just about the most excited Hazel had ever seen Miss Angus.

Samuel walked over to one of the huge books that indexed the chests of small drawers, but Hazel stayed in her seat. She spread open the latest copy of the *Burlington Free Press*, which she had grabbed on their way into the library. Below the fold was a story on the spies in the Switzer Switch and Safe Factory:

No Names Released Yet in
Maple Hill Factory Spy Investigation

The article explained that though the investigators had unearthed several leads, they were not yet ready to go public with what they had found.

"Who could it be?" Hazel murmured.

"Who could what be?" Samuel asked.

"They've found spies in the plant, but they won't release the list yet. I know The Comrade has a contact in there. At least one. It could be anybody!"

"Oh, here's something!" Samuel rushed to a drawer to get the film. He put it in the machine, which started with a whirring sound.

Hazel kept reading. "Listen to this. 'McCarthy believes that the Switzer Switch and Safe Factory is one of many companies to have been infiltrated by spies. Investigators are currently trying to determine if these groups are linked, or perhaps operating as individuals who report to an individual higher up the chain.' Did you hear that? 'An individual higher up the chain,'" she repeated. "Mr. Jones could be that individual. That could explain how he just showed up. Maybe he's going from factory to factory, collecting what information the spies there have gathered."

Samuel moved the finder around to locate the article he

wanted. "You might be on to something there. Some spies might be embedded in their factories, while others are rovers, gathering information to send back."

"Exactly!" Hazel said. The fly landed on her paper and she swatted at it.

"Still, I'm not quite ready to believe that Mr. Jones is that person." Samuel pushed his glasses up and squinted at the screen. "Drat."

"What?"

"I thought I found something, but it's about a cat. She was ten years old and missing. Reward offered."

Hazel flipped forward three pages to read the rest of the newspaper article. "Samuel, you are not going to believe this!"

"What now?"

Hazel cleared her throat and read from the newspaper. "'So far, only one arrest has been made in all the investigations. Alice Winthrop, who worked in the secretary pool at the General Electric plant in Schenectady, New York, was brought in for questioning late last week. She was charged with conspiracy.'" Hazel put the paper down. "Alice! There's our Alice!"

"If she's a secretary, she's not ten years old."

"It doesn't matter. Mr. Jones needed a place to have the secrets dropped off. He went through the cemetery and found that stone. 'Leave it with Alice.' I bet that's what he says to all the spies he has working for him. Why, he could say it right out in the open. 'Just leave it with Alice. She'll take care of it.'"

"It's not a bad theory," he says.

"Better than a missing cat."

"Most assuredly better than a missing cat," he agreed.

"Plus Mr. Jones's license plates are from New York. Maybe that was his last assignment. He's moving around, blending in, and collecting secrets."

Samuel looked up from the microfilm machine. "I have to admit that you're getting somewhere. I think you still need more proof, though."

"You know who else was a secretary? Ethel Rosenberg!" That summer Ethel Rosenberg and her husband, Julius, had been convicted of spying and sharing national secrets, and had been put to death. Hazel hadn't thought that was a good idea. She didn't suppose killing a criminal made you much better than the criminal himself. And anyway, who knew what other secrets those two might have been hiding.

"She wasn't a secretary exactly, was she?"

"Her husband got the insider information, and she typed up the secrets to be sent out."

"A bit of a stretch."

"What have *you* got?" Hazel said.

Samuel frowned. "Nothing yet."

"Exactly," Hazel said again.

The fly landed on her knee and she smacked it as hard as she could. She felt it crush beneath her hand, and a smile spread across her lips. They were making progress. She had a workable theory. She was feeling quite proud of herself until she looked down and saw the broken, crooked carcass in her hand.

Remarkable

Hazel dropped her backpack inside the front door of the cottage. "Mom! Dad!"

There was the sound of the typewriter coming from the office, and Hazel thought she heard someone yell "In here!" This was perfect: she wanted to add more canned goods to her mausoleum fallout shelter before it got dark.

From her room she retrieved a brown paper bag from the A&P grocery store that she had filled with cans of peas and mixed vegetables from the pantry. These were not her favorite foods, but she had to work with what she had. It wasn't like she could go out and buy her own. She wished she could get cans of tiny hot dogs. Becky Cornflower's dad had loved those and always shared with her when she went over. Anyway, the vegetables would be good because they would need their vitamins, locked away in the dark mausoleum.

Outside again the sky had clouded over and cast the cemetery in shadows that threatened to dampen her mood. True, research in the library was not her preferred means of investigation, but they had made a breakthrough. Even Samuel had to admit it. Alice, Ten Years Old didn't matter. It was just a front. It even explained why Mr. Jones had been taking such good care of that particular stone: so the spies could easily identify it. Though if she were Mr. Jones, she would put flowers on some of the other graves, too, as if it were part of one big project of flowering Pauper's Field. Then she would tell her spies, "Don't forget, Alice's favorite color is orange," and they would know just where to go.

Making sure Mr. Jones wasn't near, she ducked around to the door of the mausoleum. The stone was wet, as if it were weeping water. It moved a little more easily this time. The can of tuna was just where she left it. She scooped it up as she stepped inside the mausoleum. The air inside was warmer than the outside and smelled as old as dry leaves. They would need some candles. Carefully, she placed her bag of canned vegetables next to the wall. She wasn't sure how much food they would need; they would be on rations for sure, like back during World War II when you could only buy certain things with stamps and everyone had a Victory Garden to grow their own vegetables instead of buying them at the store. Her grandmother had told her about those. It was too bad that her grandparents were all the way down in Florida. She hoped they had the sense to make their own fallout shelter.

Peeking outside to make sure the coast was clear, she reemerged.

With a shove that took her whole body, she closed the door to the mausoleum. She took a deep breath of the damp fall air, and it felt just like breathing in new life. She was so close to finding the proof she needed, she could taste it.

She followed the meandering paths to the edge of the cemetery far from Alice's stone. This was Soldier's Field, where those who had died in combat were buried. Her dad had told her that not every stone had a body under it; some people were buried overseas or their bodies had never been recovered. Hazel didn't understand why they had headstones, then, but her dad explained that people liked to have a place to go to still feel like they were with the person who was gone. Hazel knew this was true because people were always coming to the cemetery and sitting and talking and crying—in fact, the Wellehans were at the grave of their son at that very moment—but it still didn't make a lot of sense to her. The grave was just the grave. Still, she did like Soldier's Field and the way the graves were dotted with tiny American flags. She liked to see the flags all in rows, like the soldiers were still standing at attention. There were two newer graves, not even four months old, for two boys from town who had been in Korea and died just before the war ended and the troops were called back home.

One of the boys was Archie Winslow, whose sister Annabelle had been in Hazel's class the year before. She'd cried for three days. The other was Bobby Li, whose family had come to Vermont from China and had a Chinese restaurant in town.

Hazel had the menu memorized because they went there at least twice a month. People said it was funny that Bobby went back home to fight against the Koreans, but Hazel knew that was wrong, because China and Korea were different countries, and anyway, Bobby had been born here just like her. He used to give her chopsticks that he'd bind together with a rubber band so she could use them like pinchers when she ate. Hazel knew it was sad that the boys had died no matter what, but it seemed especially sad that if they had only made it a couple more weeks, they'd be home and probably working in the factory or in the restaurant instead of being buried in Memory's Garden.

Someday, Hazel realized, someone like Samuel might come along and try to find out their story. She ought to write down some more information so that whoever it was could get the whole story and get it right.

Just at the turn of the fence stood one of her favorite climbing trees, and she scrambled up the trunk, reaching for the familiar first branch and heaving herself up. She kept climbing until she got to the crook, a perfect place to sit and contemplate, sheltered by orange and red maple leaves. She could see out, but others couldn't see her.

Her mind wandered to school that day. Triangle people. Maryann and Connie didn't mean that she was well balanced or pointed or the base of a pyramid. No, they meant that she was not cut out to do anything more exciting than chime the triangle at the end of the song, and they all knew she couldn't even do that well. She didn't know the words to the skipping rope songs, and on the one occasion when she'd been asked to join in—prompted by their third-grade teacher, Mrs. Messing—she'd tripped over the rope anyway. She'd asked her mom to buy her a rope, but with just her and Becky Cornflower, it hadn't worked so well. They'd tied one end to a tree, and Becky spun the other while Hazel tried to jump, but Becky got bored and Hazel never got any better.

The problem, Hazel knew, was that she was a remarkable person trapped in an unremarkable package.

If only I had a glockenspiel, she thought. *I'd show them.*

When she solved the case, then they'd know just what she was capable of. In the stories, one clue led to another so easily. She and Samuel had a theory now, but finding hard evidence against The Comrade was proving far more difficult than she'd originally imagined, especially using Samuel's methods.

A breeze blew through the tree, rustling the leaves. They seemed so fragile, orange and ready to fall, but they held on.

A snapping sound came from below her. She leaned forward and peered through the branches. Mr. Jones was in Soldier's Field straightening the flags.

This was her chance to observe him without his knowing it.

He was carrying a shovel in one hand and was using it like a cane, swinging it out in front of him with each step. The point tapped into the dirt with each long, loping stride. Hazel knew there weren't any soldiers being buried, so once again he was in the wrong place with his shovel. He looked at his watch. Maybe he had a rendezvous with one of his associates.

She could watch the whole thing go down. They might be exchanging money, or information, or maybe the associate was coming to tell him that the investigators at the factory were getting too close and they would have to call off the whole mission. Hazel didn't want Mr. Jones to leave before she had a chance to expose him as a Russian spy.

He walked a few more steps, then stopped in front of a grave. Hazel counted the gravestones to remember where it was, but just as quickly he moved on.

She held on tightly to the branch, wondering what he would do if he found her spying on him. She wasn't spying, of course. He'd come into her space, and she'd just been minding her own business, in her own thoughts. But he wouldn't see it that way.

He crouched down like a wolf, ready to pounce. Maybe he sensed her in the tree. She tried to make herself as small as possible, pulling herself right back against the trunk. She took a deep breath, then pressed her lips together to hold it in.

Mr. Jones stood up, placed his hands on the small of his back, then tilted his head up toward the sky. Then he did the strangest thing. He walked a bit more into Soldier's Field, bent over, and picked up one of the flags. He tucked it into his back pocket and started on his way. Hazel was just about to let out her breath when he stopped and looked over his shoulder, right at the tree.

As soon as he was gone, Hazel rushed into her house and took out her Mysteries Notebook. She wrote:

Stole flag from cemetery.

What, she wondered, could he be doing with it? She imagined him breaking the tiny flagpole, stomping on the flag. Maybe he would even burn it. A tiny pit of anger curdled in her stomach. He had to be stopped.

Anti-American activity observed.

She turned the page back to her questions. Next to *Who is Alice?* she wrote:

Alice Winthrop, secretary. Headstone is potential drop point. Must prepare stakeout.

Chopsticks

"Hazel!"

Hazel's mom's voice boomeranged up the stairs and into her room, where she was flopped back onto her bed reading a Kay Tracey book. Knowing Hazel liked Nancy Drew, her grandmother had picked up one of the Kay Tracey books at a yard sale, but it just wasn't the same. Nancy was a far superior sleuth and had all-around better adventures.

"Hazel, put your school clothes back on! We're going to Li's!"

Hazel sat up straight in bed. Li's was her favorite. She had to take a minute, though, or her mom would know she hadn't ever changed out of her school clothes in the first place. She stood on one foot for as long as she could, then stood on the other. When she decided enough time had passed, she skipped down the stairs.

Her mother's hair was tied up in a loose, messy bun. As the family drove into town in their old Ford that made a clunking noise whenever they turned to the right, Hazel found out the reason for their trip: the seed company had mailed the wrong kind of bulbs and they needed to be planted this week. "We didn't have enough savers last year, and if we want to expand the line all along the front edge . . ." Her mom shook her head. Her mom had spent the whole afternoon trying to get it sorted and had forgotten all about dinner. Again.

Someday people would be able to just push a button and any kind of food would appear in their refrigerators. That would actually be too bad, Hazel thought, because she loved Li's. They had dark red velvet curtains with gold pom-poms as trim. Each table had a pink tablecloth and a little white china bottle for soy sauce and a little glass jar of the spiciest relish in the whole entire world. Plus Mr. and Mrs. Li were just about the nicest people you could ever meet. Mr. Li did most of the cooking, and Mrs. Li was out front, and she always seemed to have a pitcher of water so your glass was never empty. Maybe in the future they would still have restaurants. You'd just be able to get to them by teleporting.

They parked around back and walked to the front, and it was Hazel who saw the window first. She stopped. Instead of red curtains, the window was covered with a sheet of plywood.

"Hazel," her mom said, annoyed, but then she saw the plywood, too. "What on earth is that about? There isn't a storm coming, is there?"

Hazel's father shook his head. "It's broken," he said. "See, around the edges."

They pushed open the door and Mrs. Li greeted them, but she wasn't as happy to see them as she usually was. She'd been sad since Bobby died, but this was different. This was like someone had soaked her with water, then wrung her out before throwing her on the floor still damp.

Neither of her parents said anything about the window, so Hazel spoke right up. "Who broke your window, Mrs. Li?"

"Hazel," her dad said, his voice quiet but stern.

Mrs. Li shook her head. "Just a bunch of juvenile delinquents."

Mr. Li stood by the kitchen wiping his hands on his apron. He said something to Mrs. Li in Chinese, and she shook her head again. Hazel didn't speak Chinese, but she felt pretty sure that Mr. Li thought it was something other than juvenile delinquents. His eyes sparked fire.

"That's terrible," her dad said. "Just terrible."

"We'll fix it," Mrs. Li said.

"No. We'll leave it!" Mr. Li called to her. "Leave it and let people see."

"Right this way," Mrs. Li said, and led them to their usual table.

When they sat down, they didn't pick up the menus that were cased in red leather with gold tassels; they always got the same thing.

"Why would someone smash in the Lis' window? That

doesn't make any sense. Why not the window at the drug-store? Mr. Nitz is always chasing away kids."

"That's no reason to break a window," her father told her. Of course it was no reason to break a window; Hazel knew that. But if you were the type of person who wanted to break a window, wouldn't you do it to someone who was mean to you? Not someone who made delicious pork dumplings. "I don't think it was juvenile delinquents."

"Hazel," her mom said. "Just let it go."

"It doesn't make sense, and Mr. Li doesn't think so, either. There has to be another reason."

"You don't think—" her mom began, but let her thought go unfinished.

Still, her dad seemed to know just what she meant to say. "No. Well, then again, I suppose it is a possibility."

"What's a possibility?" Hazel demanded. The candle in the tiny glass votive holder flickered.

"It's nothing you need to worry about, honey."

But Hazel *was* worried. There was a marauding band of vandals raging through her town. Their first stop might be the Lis' window, but maybe the next stop would be the cemetery. Why, they could be there right now turning over headstones and ripping out flowers.

The tinkle of chimes came from the door, letting them know that someone had arrived. It was Mrs. Switzer, the owner of the Switzer Switch and Safe Factory, and right behind her was Samuel. Mrs. Switzer's gaze flitted around the room like a butterfly in a steel plant, looking for a place to land. When Mrs.

Li came over, Mrs. Switzer shifted her eyes to the window, and then back to Mrs. Li: quick, but Hazel picked up on it.

Hazel waved her hand. "Samuel! Hey, Samuel!"

When Samuel saw her he smiled, and Hazel stood up to go say hello, and so did her parents. Her mother reached Mrs. Switzer first, extending her hand. "Mrs. Switzer, I'm not sure if you remember me, I used to babysit—"

"Lydia Tenley," Mrs. Switzer said, voice as tight as razor wire. "Of course I remember you."

Hazel thought her mom ought to be embarrassed at the way Mrs. Switzer was talking to her. It was the way Mrs. Sinclair sometimes talked to Otis when he was being particularly bothersome. Hazel's mom just said, "This is my husband, George Kaplansky, and this is my daughter, Hazel."

Mrs. Switzer gave her a quick once-over, gaze lingering on her scuffed saddle shoes. "Memory's Garden. Thankfully I haven't a need for that place yet."

"We've got your plot waiting for you when you do. Planted new grass seed just last year," her dad said.

Hazel's mom elbowed her father hard, but his comment got a sly smile out of Mrs. Switzer.

"Are you eating here, Samuel?" Hazel asked. "You have to have the dumplings and the moo shu pork. You should sit with us. We get a bunch of things to share."

"We're not staying," Mrs. Switzer said. "I was called in for a meeting at the factory, last minute, you see." She looked at Mrs. Li and then away. Hazel had a hunch. It was such a strong hunch that she leaned forward on her tippy toes. Mrs. Switzer seemed like the kind of woman who wouldn't be afraid to stare down a six-headed fork-tongued demon, but she wouldn't look Mrs. Li in the eye. "Samuel tells me he is fond of Chinese cuisine, so I told him we'd pick up some food and he can bring it to the meeting."

"Alone?" Hazel asked. That seemed like the saddest way possible to eat Chinese food.

"He's brought some books," Mrs. Switzer said. "My office at the factory is quite comfortable. There's even a settee should the meeting run late."

"Why doesn't Samuel stay and eat with us," her mother said. "We could bring him home after."

"I'm not sure just how long this meeting will last. With recent events, the board is looking for a strategy."

Recent events. She had to be talking about the spies at the factory. Hazel got a tingle of the hunch again. She rocked back on her heels. She'd been so interested in her hunch, she'd missed the obvious question right in front of her: What was Samuel doing with Mrs. Switzer?

"We can take him home with us. If the meeting goes on too long, we have a spare room."

Mrs. Switzer looked at Samuel and the Kaplanskys. Samuel gave a little nod. "If you're sure it's no trouble, I'm sure my grandson would find it enjoyable," Mrs. Switzer said.

"No trouble at all," Hazel's father replied.

Mrs. Switzer didn't hesitate. She took down the Kaplanskys' telephone number, thanked Hazel's parents, and was on her way. Hazel led Samuel right over to their table. She wished the two of them could sit together and she could tell him what she saw with Mr. Jones and the American flag and ask him why he'd never told her that Mrs. Switzer was his grandmother.

"So you're a Chinese food aficionado?" her dad asked as they sat down.

"My mom likes it a lot. She's not much of a cook."

"My mom's a great cook so long as it comes out of a can."

Hazel's father laughed but tried to make it look like a cough by covering his mouth with his hand. "Your mother is a fantastic cook," he said.

From her seat, Hazel could see the boarded-up window, the way the plywood buckled a little bit at the middle.

While they waited for their food, they sat in silence. This wasn't unusual for her family, but it felt awkward with Samuel there. Samuel was the one who broke the silence. "So, who do you like for the World Series?"

Her dad cleared his throat, and then said gently, "The Series already happened this year. The Yankees took it."

"I'm talking about the next one. 1954."

Her father smiled. "Are you asking me to predict the future?"

"Baseball is just a numbers game. Entirely predictable if it weren't for the players."

"Is that so?" Her father chuckled.

"It is. My money is on the Giants."

"The Giants? They haven't won in decades."

"Of course, it will depend on any off-season trades."

Hazel's father grinned and said, "Come this summer, we can put money on it."

Mr. Li brought their food, each plate covered with a metal dish that he ceremoniously pulled off: dumplings, moo shu pork, General Tso's chicken, and her mother's favorite: lucky tofu. They were serving themselves and starting to eat when Samuel asked, "How long have you been in the cemetery business?"

Hazel's father dropped a spoonful of pork onto one of the wafer-thin moo shu pancakes. "It's a family business for me. My father ran the graveyard, and his before him."

"What about you, Mrs. Kaplansky?" Samuel asked.

Hazel's mother smoothed her napkin. "Well, now, let's see. I met Mr. Kaplansky when we were in college. Well, I suppose we knew each other our whole lives, both of us from here in Maple Hill, but he was older than me and we never really talked. When I started at Smith, he was finishing up at the University of Massachusetts. He used to drive me back and forth to campus. I suppose it's when we were married. I married George and the business came along with it. That was thirteen years ago."

Hazel picked up her chopsticks. Bobby had tried to teach her the right way to use them. *Hold the first one like a pencil. Now lift up your index finger. Slide the other one in.* But the chopsticks slid and crossed. She didn't want to have to use a fork like her parents, though. She liked that she used the chopsticks; it was as if she belonged. She imagined someday traveling to China and sitting down at a table and everyone watching her, sure she would drop her food all over her lap, but instead she would just scoop it up and pop it into her mouth.

"I studied horticulture at Smith," her mother said. "So it turned out to be a good fit."

"Did you know that in early American society, cemeteries were right in the center of town, and often weren't well maintained? It wasn't until 1831 with the development of Mount Auburn Cemetery that we started to get the large, landscaped graveyards."

Hazel's parents exchanged a look, and Hazel didn't need a translator to understand this one. "Well," Hazel's dad said. "I guess that means we're pretty lucky to live now and not in the 1800s. There wouldn't have been a job for us then."

"Not to mention cholera," Samuel said. "I suppose once Hazel's grown, she'll inherit the business."

Hazel's dad had spiked a half dumpling with his fork, and he paused with it nearly to his mouth, the pork filling looking like it was ready to dive right out of its wrapper's doughy embrace. "Well, now," he said. "Well, I don't suppose we've thought that far ahead. If Hazel wanted to—"

"No," Hazel said. But what was shocking was that her mother said it at the exact same time. Hazel glanced up. Was her mother saying she didn't want Hazel around? Her mother's eyes, though, were flashing. "Hazel has other plans," she said.

"I do," Hazel said. "Lots of plans. And none of them involve sticking around little old Maple Hill."

Samuel rubbed his chopsticks together. "I think Maple Hill's a nice town."

Hazel sighed. How could this boy who had lived in seventeen places want to stay in a town as small and far away from the world as Maple Hill? Then she had a horrible thought: What if all the other places were smaller and more isolated than Maple Hill? What if the whole country, the whole world, was just like Maple Hill, over and over again? No, that couldn't be a possibility. "I might be an archaeologist," she said. "That's one of my plans. And then I can actually go to Greece and discover new ruins and new places and they might even name a museum after me."

"I'm not sure that's the aim of archaeology," her father said.

Hazel shrugged. She tried again with her chopsticks, but only succeeded in dropping her dumpling in the sweet and salty sauce, and it splashed up, leaving little brown dots all over the pink tablecloth. "Hazel." Her mother sighed.

Then out of nowhere, Mr. Li was there, and he handed Hazel and Samuel each their own set of rubber-banded chopsticks, just like Bobby used to make for her.

Hazel had never had a friend over to her house other than Becky. "So this is where we live," she told Samuel as they walked together into their living room. The carpet was deep blue, which Hazel had always liked, but now she could see that it hadn't been vacuumed in a long time. "This is our record player." She opened up a cabinet. "My parents don't let me get a lot of popular records, but my grandparents sometimes buy them for me. I have Perry Como and Rosemary Clooney that we could listen to. Or we could watch television. I'm allowed to watch one program during the week, and I've already used it up, but I bet my parents would let us watch one anyway. Do you have a favorite band?"

"My mom always liked to listen to Frank Sinatra. She said his voice was smooth as honey, but salty, too."

"That doesn't make a whole lot of sense," Hazel told him.

"My mom doesn't always make a whole lot of sense. Anyway, I don't like music so much. Not new stuff anyway." As he spoke, he dug into his satchel and came out with his book, which he placed on the coffee table. "Since we're here, let's strategize," he said. "What do we know?"

Hazel looked over her shoulder to make sure her mother had not come back into the room. She wished he would be a little more circumspect.

Samuel read from his notebook. "We know her name was Alice and that she was ten years old. That's a start."

"But it doesn't matter anymore. We don't need to know who Alice, Ten Years Old is. It's just a front."

"You asked me to find out about that headstone, which means figuring out who Alice, Ten Years Old was, and that's what I aim to do."

"Suit yourself," she said. "Have you ever done a grave with so little information?"

He shook his head.

"Hey, how did you know that stuff about the graveyard? About the one in 1831?"

"Mount Auburn," he told her. "It's in Cambridge, Massachusetts. We lived there for a tiny bit, and I read about it when I was doing some research."

"And you remembered it?"

"Sure. It was interesting."

"Why didn't you tell me your grandmother was Mrs. Switzer?"

He looked up from his notebook and then back at the table. "I thought everyone knew."

She had to admit that everyone did seem to know who he was. Everyone but her. "That meeting she's at, it's about the Communists, isn't it?"

Samuel nodded and wiped some dust off the book that wasn't really there.

"Did you see the window in the restaurant?" she asked.

"The broken one?"

"Right," she said. "Mrs. Li said it was juvenile delinquents, and maybe it was, but I think they chose the Lis because they're Chinese and people thought they were Communist even though they aren't." She wished her hunch was wrong, but she was pretty sure she knew why the window had been broken. It was the only thing that explained why Mr. Li was so angry, and why Mrs. Switzer seemed so uncomfortable: someone must have read the news about the Communists in town and instead of doing a thorough investigation like Hazel was, they'd gone after the Lis because they were from China, a Communist country. And if folks were willing to do that to the Lis, what would they do to her family when it was discovered that there'd been a Communist spy working right beneath their noses? The Comrade had to be exposed, and Hazel needed to be the one to do it.

Samuel said, "People jump to all sorts of conclusions."

"Precisely. And what's really stupid is that Bobby Li died in Korea, fighting the Communists. That's why this is such an important case. We need to do it right and get the facts before more innocent people are hurt. We know who the real Communist is here."

"You have a theory," he told her. "You are gathering evidence, but you still don't have any concrete proof."

"He saw me earlier. Watching him."

"You were watching him?"

She swallowed. "Not intentionally. I was up in the tree and he just appeared, and then I swear he was staring right at me. Do you think he knows we're onto him? If The Comrade knows I know . . ." She shook her head and let out a low whistle.

"Let's deal with the here and now," Samuel said.

"Well, even though I wasn't spying, I did observe something." She waited for him to prompt her, but he was busy reading over his notes. "He stole an American flag from Soldier's Field."

"Soldier's Field?" Samuel asked.

"Yep. Stuck it right into his back pocket."

"From a soldier's grave?" he asked. "Which soldier?"

"How should I know? But that's pretty bad, don't you think? You can't get more un-American than that."

Samuel frowned. "Actually," he said, "I'd like to watch television after all."

Hazel looked at him for a minute. "Sure," she agreed. "But *Dragnet* won't be on until Thursday."

"I think we have enough mystery right here," he said. "Let's find a variety show."

Hazel was not a big fan of the variety shows, but she figured Samuel was her guest, and her mother always said you let the guest choose. "Okay," she said. She stood up and clicked on the television, then turned the dial until she found Milton Berle on the screen.

It was actually pretty funny, she had to admit, and there was something about watching a funny show with someone else: even when the jokes were so-so, they still laughed. It was like their laughter was the Blob, grabbing on to them and growing, growing, growing, until they were clutching their stomachs and her mother came in to see what all the noise was.

"I made up the guest room for Samuel," she said, once they had control of themselves.

In her own room, Hazel was ready to get into bed, but then she started thinking of staying with her grandparents in Florida. She had to stay in the den, and it was dark and strange, so she didn't know what any of the shapes were. An armchair can look an awful lot like a renegade robot.

She unplugged her night-light and carried it into the

hallway, where she tapped on the guest room door. Samuel didn't answer, so she tapped again. The door opened and there was Samuel in one of her father's T-shirts and pajama bottoms. The pants were too big, and he had to hold them at the waist to keep them from falling. She held out the night-light.

"I'm not afraid of the dark," he said.

"I know. But it's hard to see, and anyway you might wake up in the middle of the night and need to use the bathroom."

"Thanks," he said, reaching out his free hand to take the night-light from her.

"You're welcome."

Hazel went back to her room and shut off the light and then she shut her eyes so she wouldn't have to see the claw of the tree branch outside her window, just ready to reach inside.

Here's the Drill

Since Samuel didn't have a bike, Hazel pushed hers while they walked to school. Hazel kicked an orangey-brown rock and it skittered ahead and then Samuel kicked it and soon they were kicking this rock down the street, seeing who could get it the farthest. One of Hazel's kicks made it take a sharp turn and it skipped off the sidewalk and into a puddle. "Ohhh," they both groaned, and then they laughed.

"Bon voyage, little pebble," Samuel said.

"Send a postcard!" Hazel called. Then she found another rock, this one smooth and gray, to kick along.

"My mom has this jar of rocks," Samuel said. "It's one of the only things she's sure to carry with us from place to place. She gets a rock in every town. We've got beach rocks and river rocks and gravel from driveways."

"Why does she do that?"

"She said it's a way to keep her grounded."

"Ha, grounded!" Hazel laughed, but Samuel didn't. "I just meant because they were rocks. From the ground."

"I know," he said.

"I wonder what kind of rock she took from here," Hazel said. "I would take a nice shiny hunk of mica."

"Mica's not a rock," he said.

"Then what is it?"

"It's a mineral that can be part of a rock."

"Then I'd find a big rock with a nice hunk of mica stuck in it. What about you?"

"Me? I guess I haven't thought about it."

"It's not a big decision," she said.

He bent over and picked up a red maple leaf and twisted it between his fingers. "I still think I need to ponder it a little more."

"That's your problem, Samuel. Too much pondering, not enough action."

"Fine. I suppose I'd take some granite from the quarry."

"There you go. Doesn't that feel good?"

They walked along a bit and then Samuel said, "I was thinking about Memory's Garden and what's going to happen to it. I could take over for you. I could buy it; I think my grandmother would give me the money. Or if you wanted to keep it in the family, you could hire me to run it for you and then you would always have a place to come home to."

Hazel could see the school up ahead of her, a yellow bus emptying its load of students. She had never given much thought to what would happen to the graveyard when her parents wanted to retire. "I don't think my parents will be quitting any time soon."

"That's okay. We still have to finish primary school and get through high school and college. And I think I would like to get another degree or two. I'm looking twenty or so years into the future."

Twenty years into the future. By that time Hazel planned to be well established in her adventure of a life as an international spy catcher and archaeologist. Still, she supposed she might want to come back to visit folks like Miss Lerner and Mr. Wall, and even Samuel himself. "Okay. That sounds like a deal. But you should probably buy it outright. I don't want anything tying me down."

"Deal," Samuel agreed.

"And hey," she said, "when I visit you, *I* can stay in the guest room!"

"If you want. Or I can keep your room for you."

"I'll have to think on that," she said.

They were heading up to school now. Hazel dropped her bike by the tree. As they went in the door, they walked by a group of seventh-grade boys. One of them let out a low wolf whistle and another one sang out, "Hazel and Samuel sitting in a tree, K-I-S-S-I-N-G." All Hazel and Samuel could do was laugh, clutching their sides and running down the hall to Mrs. Sinclair's classroom.

They had said the Pledge of Allegiance and were settling into a math lesson when the alarm went off. It *woo-wah woo-wah*ed in and out like some sort of possessed trombone and everyone knew exactly what to do. Under the desks they crawled. Hazel pulled her shoes right up to her bum and made sure her underwear wasn't showing. Once Becky had tucked herself up into a ball and didn't realize the whole first row could see her white underpants and she hadn't heard the end of it for weeks.

Hazel put her hands over the back of her neck, arms over her ears, face right down on the dusty linoleum floor. Mrs. Sinclair must have done a lot of erasing on the board, because it felt like a whole chalk stick worth of dust went right up her nose. She wrinkled her nose and even wiped it against her knees. She squeezed her eyes tight. *Don't sneeze! Don't sneeze!* They had to keep perfectly silent, which was difficult for Hazel under the best of circumstances. Becky Cornflower had once told her you could stop a sneeze if you sucked in really, really hard through your nose, and so Hazel tried this, but all she did was pull the dust farther back and then there was no stopping it. A giant sneeze erupted out of her like a cannon backfiring. It was so big and so old-man-like that she thought maybe no one would realize it was her, and then she heard Maryann laughing. "Hey, Sneezy," Maryann hissed. "You really are a dwarf, aren't you, Sneezy?"

Hazel couldn't answer because she, unlike Maryann, respected the rules of the duck-and-cover drill, even though she wasn't too sure how much protection a desk would give.

They watched the movie each September, with Bert the Turtle loping along and hiding in his shell whenever he saw a flash. Just thinking of it got the song stuck in her head: *He ducked and covered! Ducked and covered!* The movie explained how big the blast could be and how it could burn you like a sunburn. It said that most attacks would be announced beforehand, like they actually expected the Russians to say: "Watch out, we're going to drop an A-bomb on you!" Hazel didn't think that was a very good battle tactic. The narrator told them that if they ever saw a flash of light, they should assume the worst and find the safest place they could duck and cover just like a turtle.

Now that the sneeze was out of her, Hazel just had to work on staying quiet. Mrs. Sinclair had taught her the trick of touching her thumb to each finger and counting how many times she made it around. She was up to thirty-seven before the siren stopped. A minute later their principal, Mrs. Rushby, knocked on the door to tell them the drill was over.

"Good job, children," Mrs. Sinclair said. "As I am sure you are well aware, our town is in a heightened state of alert, and we must be ever vigilant. I'm happy to see you all taking these drills seriously." She gave Hazel a look. "Most of you, anyhow."

Hazel could not help but try to defend herself. "I am utterly sorry, Mrs. Sinclair, but when I was down there I breathed in a whole bunch of chalk dust and I tried to keep the sneeze in, really I did, but—"

"But Sneezy just couldn't help it," Maryann said sweetly.

"Poor Sneezy," Connie chimed in.

"Did you know," Samuel said without raising his hand and without being called on, "that an atom bomb has the same explosive power as fifteen thousand tons of TNT? On top of that is the radioactivity."

"So?" Maryann demanded.

Hazel jumped in: "So what he's saying is that ducking down under our desks isn't going to do us any good if the Russians decide to drop a bomb on Maple Hill. The whole school would be blown over and then the radiation would come and burn our skin to a crisp and all our hair will fall out and we'll be walking around here like skeletons, if we can even walk at all."

Ellen Abbott began to cry.

"Hazel, that is quite enough," Mrs. Sinclair told her.

For once, Hazel didn't argue, even though she knew she and Samuel were right. She just said, "Yes, Mrs. Sinclair." Because Samuel's fact meant Hazel's giant sneeze had been forgotten.

Push Comes to Shove

At lunch Hazel slid into her usual seat in the back of the cafeteria. When Samuel sat down, she looked with pity at his lunch box, which his grandmother had delivered that morning. She had noticed it on the first day, and thought it was just about the saddest thing she had ever seen. It was an old-fashioned one, green, made of tin and shaped like a Quonset hut. She had the Hopalong Cassidy metal lunch box she'd begged her parents to buy her for over a year. She'd dented it on the first day of school when she'd dropped it getting off her bike. He noticed her staring at his and said, "It was my dad's."

"So he got a new one and you got stuck with that old thing?" She took a bite of her cream cheese and jelly sandwich.

"He died," Samuel said.

Her sandwich lodged in her throat. "Oh," she managed to murmur. She looked at him sideways, trying not to stare. Parents getting a divorce like Becky Cornflower's was rare and exciting, but a parent dying? That was too much. Maybe that was why everyone was saying to be nice to him.

She didn't want to say anything else, because she felt fairly certain that she would say the wrong thing. So she chewed and chewed and chewed her sandwich until it turned into paste in her mouth. She should have realized something was up. He talked about his mom, but never his dad. Swallowing the lump of sandwich, she said, "Well, it's a very lunch box–y lunch box."

"Thank you," he said.

Hazel unscrewed the top of her thermos. That morning she had dumped a can of tomato soup in without heating it up. She wanted to get used to eating lukewarm food for when they were in the fallout shelter. "Is that true about the atomic bomb and fifteen thousand tons of TNT?"

"I did read that once," he said, spreading out a paper napkin and then placing on it his sandwich, cut into four neat triangles. "I'm not sure if anyone knows for sure."

"Well, anyway, thanks for the diversion."

"It's not your fault you sneezed." Samuel picked up one of the triangles and started eating from the inside point.

"Do you think someone put the chalk dust there on purpose?"

"That's not what I—"

"Of course we know who it was. It doesn't take a sleuth to figure that out." She could just picture Maryann and Connie grinding the chalk into dust as they cackled their horrible laughs.

"That theory only works if they knew we were going to have a duck-and-cover drill today."

Hazel took a bite of her sandwich and mulled over this idea. "Maybe they have someone on the inside. They were able to get that office slip, after all."

"Forget I even mentioned it." He wiped the tips of his fingers on his napkin. "Your folks are nice."

Hazel groaned. "That was them at their best. You should try living with them." She gulped some of the tomato soup. It went down her throat thick and sludgy. "It's always seeds and bulbs and grass and graves."

"I like seeds and bulbs and grass and graves."

"Really? Not just the graves, but all that other stuff, too?" Hazel took another drink of the soup, smaller than the first. It went down a little bit easier.

"Sure. I used to keep flower boxes in some of the places we lived. My mom would buy me seed packets, and I'd start them indoors in the winter and move them to the window boxes in the spring. It was always a good sign if we stayed in place long enough to make the transition. That only happened once or . . ." His voice trailed off.

Hazel felt the presence of two people standing behind her. Samuel looked up, then back down at the table. Hazel slowly turned around, then made her face into a surprised smile. "Maryann and Connie, I didn't realize you were standing there. You scared me. I mean, not that you're scary or anything—"

Maryann interrupted, but she wasn't speaking to Hazel or

Samuel. "Connie, you know what I think? I think it's just so sad that there are people in the world who are so, well, sad."

"Triangle people," Connie agreed, nodding.

Maryann put one hand on her hip. "There are some people you can help. But some are just—"

"Helpless," Connie said, aping Maryann's stance.

"That's right, helpless. And mean. Making Ellen Abbott cry like that today. Poor Ellen."

Hazel felt certain that Maryann had never before felt a single drop of sympathy for Ellen. Hazel did have to admit, though, that she did feel a little bad for making Ellen cry. She had seen the movies of the atomic bomb exploding like a mushroom, the radiation spreading out like waves at the ocean, and it had made her insides turn to jelly. Ellen was right to be scared.

Maryann switched hands on her hips, and Connie followed suit. "Really," Maryann declared, "some people shouldn't be let out with other people. They just can't behave like normal folks."

Hazel tightened her hands into fists and wondered what was different. Usually Maryann and Connie only targeted her if she wandered into their line of fire. Lately, though, it seemed like they were seeking her out. Her eyes flicked over to Samuel. There were two of them now, she realized, and that was simply too much for the girls to resist.

Maryann sighed as if the weight of the world were on top of her, squishing down her pretty blond hair. "And I try to tell myself that it's not their fault. After all, one of them has grown up in a graveyard."

"With all those dead old bodies. Yuck." Connie wrinkled her freckled nose.

"And the other, well, we all know your story, don't we, Samuel?" Maryann said.

Hazel looked over at Samuel, waiting for him to say something, to stick up for himself. His face was pinched as if he were expecting a slap, the same way it had been in the cemetery when she'd accused him of being a chicken, only tighter. She could barely see his eyes. "What are you talking about?" she demanded, standing up.

Maryann and Connie exchanged a look that made her think of her parents and the way they'd wordlessly communicated when she'd been telling them about Samuel. "He didn't tell you?" Maryann asked.

"Everybody knows," Connie said.

They were starting to draw the notice of other kids in the cafeteria now: eyes swiveled slightly at the scene unfolding.

"Everybody knows what?" Hazel asked.

"Oh, of course he hasn't," Maryann said. "If it were me—if I had his mother—I wouldn't tell either."

"You're putting me on. Samuel doesn't have any secrets. Right, Samuel?"

Samuel stayed silent.

Maryann tried to make her face look sad, but it just looked wicked. "Everybody knows about your mother, about how she—"

Behind Hazel, Samuel began to cry. She heard the deep

suck in of breath and the sound of the sobs that he tried to muffle. Hazel didn't know why she did what she did next. She didn't plan it. She just heard the sound that Samuel was making and it reminded her of the time she saw some older boys tying up a puppy and throwing stones at it. Her mom had taken her by the hand and pulled her along as if she hadn't seen anything, as if the whimpers of the puppy were nothing. So Hazel lifted up her hands and shoved Maryann in the chest. Hard.

Maryann's voice choked midword and she tumbled backward. Her arms pinwheeled and she landed with a thump on the floor. A hush fell over the cafeteria, and all the adults in the room descended upon the scene.

Maryann was crying and so was Hazel. Samuel wiped at his eyes and sank down into the bench. Connie began speaking a mile a minute. "We just came over here to say hello to Samuel and to introduce ourselves so that he could make some *other* friends and I guess Hazel got jealous or something because out of nowhere she just pushed Maryann. Oh my goodness, Maryann, are you okay?" Connie fell to her knees and wrapped her arms around Maryann. It was like something straight out of one of the soap operas Hazel's grandmother watched.

"That's not true. They came over and were making fun of us, and they were saying mean things about Samuel. Right, Samuel?"

It was her word against Connie and Maryann's, but once Samuel told them what had really happened, it would be okay.

The teachers' heads turned and they all looked at Samuel.

He had his father's lunch box gripped to his chest like a shield. He looked at Mrs. Sinclair and Mr. Hiccolm and then back to Maryann, but never at Hazel. "It was nothing," he said.

So then, for the first time in her life, Hazel Kaplansky was marched down to the principal's office.

Hazel was impressed by the inside of Mrs. Rushby's office. The walls were all painted a muted yellow, and student artwork hung in plain black frames as if it were a museum. Her desk was big and metal with a glass top that let you see right down to her feet. Mrs. Rushby always wore heels, and today they were green with a snakeskin print. Hazel wondered if they were real snakes, and if so, what kind. They might be wild, venomous snakes, from someplace like Argentina. Or perhaps, she imagined, there were snake farms, where simple garden snakes lived short, miserable lives before becoming shoes.

While Hazel pondered the origin of snakeskin shoes, a teacher explained what had happened in the cafeteria, or Connie's version, anyway. Then Mrs. Rushby said, "Thank you. I can take it from here.

"Hazel Kaplansky, Hazel Kaplansky," Mrs. Rushby said. Her red-framed glasses were on the tip of her nose and she seemed to be looking not at Hazel but at a spot on the wall behind her head.

Hazel sat on her hands and sucked in her lip so she wouldn't explode out of her hard wooden chair to exclaim that the whole situation was misrepresented and it wasn't fair that the victims were always blamed.

Mrs. Rushby shifted her gaze so she stared directly at Hazel. "You know that your mother and I went to school together?"

This was not something that Hazel had known, but it didn't surprise her. Most of the town had grown up in Maple Hill and then just stayed. Hazel herself, of course, had other plans.

"She and I were actually good friends. She was a spitfire, that one."

Hazel had a hard time associating either spit or fire with her mother.

Mrs. Rushby chuckled to herself. "When we were in sixth grade she took on a whole group of eighth-grade girls because they were writing these lists and circulating them around: ugliest girl/boy you'd most like to kiss, nastiest teacher, that sort of thing. Your mom thought it was mean and she told them so."

Hazel looked down at her lap. "If you say so," she mumbled.

"I do," Mrs. Rushby replied. "Now then, why don't you explain what happened?"

Hazel's hands flew out from under her legs and began waving around. The words came out of her like water from a fire hydrant: "It wasn't like they said at all. Samuel and I were just sitting there minding our own business when Maryann and Connie came up. And they started saying how we were hopeless triangle people and how I lived in the cemetery and Samuel, well, they didn't get that far, but he was crying and I pushed her.

I don't know why he didn't stick up for me. Some friend. But they started it. And I know they have everyone fooled, but Maryann and Connie are *not nice*, and I know that violence is never the answer, but some people just deserve to be shoved."

Mrs. Rushby folded her hands together and regarded Hazel, nodding. She picked up her pen and wrote something on a piece of paper. "They don't have me fooled," she said.

Hazel, who had been fairly shaking with righteous indignation, stilled.

"The truth of the matter is that there have always been girls like Maryann and Connie and there always will be. Which is not to say that I condone it. I'm just letting you know that this is something you will have to deal with, even as an adult. While it may seem that some people deserve to be shoved, you simply cannot go around shoving people. Do you understand?"

"Yes, but—"

Mrs. Rushby shook her head. "I might not be able to make those girls nice, but I can help you to have an easier life, so let me reiterate: you cannot go around shoving people, no matter how angry or hurt they make you."

"I understand, but—" Hazel needed to make Mrs. Rushby see how they were going after Samuel for no reason. That they had made him cry *on purpose*. When everyone was telling *her* to be so nice to him, they just waltzed up and made him cry.

"You will be going home for the rest of the day, and tomorrow, too, which is the most lenient sentence I can give for fighting."

"It wasn't fighting," Hazel said.

Mrs. Rushby pushed her red glasses up into her thick brown hair. "You are making it increasingly difficult to help you. Why don't you try sitting on your hands again?"

Hazel blushed, but did as she was told.

"Rest assured that Maryann and Connie will also be punished for antagonizing you."

"They'll say they didn't do it. And since Samuel won't stick up for me, it's just my word against theirs. Two against one."

"But I believe the one," Mrs. Rushby said. "And I am the principal." She picked up a stack of papers, read them over, and then tapped them against the desk. "Sometimes our friends disappoint us, Hazel."

"Maryann and Connie are not my friends."

"I'm speaking about Samuel."

Hazel scowled.

"I imagine that he wanted to stick up for you. I imagine he's feeling terribly guilty right now that he did not. If he felt he could have, he would have. There's more to the story than you know."

"What else is there?" she demanded. People kept making reference to Samuel's story, but no one would tell her, least of all Samuel. She couldn't imagine anything that would justify his betrayal of her. Not even his dead father.

Mrs. Rushby looked at the spot on the wall above her head again. "It's not my place to say. The point is that when we have friends, we take them as they are, faults and all, because sometimes their faults are out of their control. Do you understand?"

Hazel said she did, but she wasn't buying Mrs. Rushby's story. Samuel had let her down, simple as that.

"Good. I'll have Mrs. Dunbarton call your parents. You can wait in the office."

Hazel took a seat on the wooden bench of the main office and contemplated what evil fate awaited her.

Suspended

Hazel had never been grounded nor suspended, and she wasn't quite sure how she was supposed to act. She got dressed in her drabbest clothes and went downstairs making the saddest face she could.

Her parents seemed to have warmed up slightly. The day before, the car ride home had been silent as a tomb. It even had the cold, still-air feeling of the granite mausoleum Hazel was using for the fallout shelter. Her mother had driven with her eyes straight ahead all the way back to Memory's Garden. She had pulled into the driveway of the cottage and stopped the car. With her hands still on the wheel she'd said, "It seems to me that a girl your age and of your intelligence should know a better way to deal with conflict than with violence."

"Mom, she—"

"It seems to me that a girl who likes to talk so much might

have the proper words to tell another child that she's out of line."

"I was too angry—"

"It seems to me that anyone from Maple Hill would know that this is a small town and everything we do reflects back on our families. *And*," she said before Hazel could try again to interject, "it seems to me that someone raised in this house would have a little more respect and think about her family, her actions, and the repercussions before acting impulsively."

Then she'd been grounded indefinitely, which she had tried to argue was cruel and unusual since even the worst criminals got to know the length of their sentences, but her parents had not been swayed.

Hazel tried to make her face even sadder as she put her cereal bowl in the sink, the last bit of milk sloshing out of it onto the plates below.

She picked up her school library's copy of *Charlotte's Web* that Mrs. Sinclair had more or less forced on her the week before, saying she needed to move beyond mysteries. She hadn't been interested then, but suddenly this story of a pig with its head on the chopping block seemed relevant. Book in hand, she headed into the living room. Though she knew little about being grounded, she felt certain that television, even educational television, was forbidden.

Her mom looked up at her, shook her head, and said, "Uh-uh."

"Should I go to my room to read?" Hazel asked.

"No reading," her dad said. "Weeding."

She groaned inwardly, but didn't complain. Weeding was her absolute least favorite thing to do, and her parents knew it.

"Mrs. Vorschat is being buried today. Stay away from the funeral."

Hazel nodded and started to go outside, but as she went by the front door, she saw the *Maple Hill Banner* on a small table, and Mr. Short's face looked right back at her. Above him was the headline:

First Red Spies Identified at Switzer Factory

The article said that Mr. Short and a young man in his twenties that Hazel didn't know were going to be questioned by the committee on suspicion of having Communist ties. Hazel couldn't believe it. Not Connie's handsome, friendly father. He couldn't be a spy! But Hazel remembered when she had mentioned to her father how gregarious Mr. Short was, her dad hadn't bothered to be impressed by Hazel's use of a four-syllable word. Instead he had said, "You don't get to head the union by being unfriendly."

They did say that a lot of the Communist ringleaders were in the union.

Mr. Short and Mr. Jones! Hazel dropped the newspaper with a dull thud. Of course: it made sense now why Mr. Short had been giving something to Mr. Jones. It was top-level confidential secrets he'd gathered at the plant. It was awfully bold of them to do it right out in the open like that, but maybe that was part of their plan: if it didn't look like they were hiding anything, then no one would suspect them. No one but Hazel. Now that the investigators were onto Mr. Short, it was only a matter of time before they made the Mr. Jones connection. Maybe she ought to go to them with everything she knew. But no, Samuel was right. They still had no concrete evidence. Nancy Drew always waited until she had all her evidence in place before going to the police. Hazel needed to do the same thing.

"Hazel Kaplansky!" her mother called from back in the kitchen.

"Mom, I—"

Hazel's mom pointed outside without saying another word.

Hazel knew when she was beat. She left the paper where it was and went outside.

She decided to work by the statue of the Three Graces. As she walked, she could see Mr. Jones across the way. The one good thing about being suspended was that it gave her more time to observe him. He had finished digging the grave the day before and now was standing above it with his shovel, ready to smooth things out. Her gaze traveled over to the garden shed. That's where he stored all the secrets. She needed to get in there.

As she set to work devising her plan, she got down on her knees and began plucking out crabgrass, dandelions, and stray bits of ground cover. After a moment, she looked up at the sculptures. "Yes, Abitha, it is a school day. I've been suspended." She gathered the weeds she had pulled into a pile. "It means I can't go to school for the day, but it's a bum rap. It was self-defense."

She moved closer to the base of the statue. "I was sticking up for a friend." There was a big weed with roots that went deep and wide and she had to lean way back to pull it. "Then he left me out to dry, swinging in the breeze, you know. So I don't know if we're friends anymore."

She kept moving around the base of the statue. "Oh, Tabitha, I'm glad you asked. You see, Maryann and Connie, I've told you about them. They were being their same old rotten selves and they started to say something awful about Samuel and it was like something just swelled up inside of me and I pushed Maryann as hard as I could and she fell down right on her butt."

She laughed, and the hollow sound echoed around the stones.

"Yes, she did deserve it."

Her weed pile was pretty big, so she went and got the wheel-barrow and filled it. She tugged up a few more around the edge of the pond. All the while she was stealing glances at the garden shed. She'd been out there most of an hour already and Mr. Jones hadn't gone anywhere near it. She said good-bye to the Three Graces. "Nice talking to you girls."

In the time she'd been weeding, the funeral had begun. Mourners were around the grave in their black clothes. There were few things sadder than a funeral on a gray fall day, the trees barely holding on to their leaves. Hazel made a big circle around to get to the compost pile, where she dumped her weeds on top of the husks of acorn squash they'd had for dinner the night before.

Living right next to a cemetery, she'd had many occasions to think about her own funeral. When she was little, she had wanted a white casket with silver satin inside. She'd wanted the casket to have her initials carved in curlicue letters on the outside. Now, though, she wanted something much more simple. She'd seen a man buried in a casket that was a perfect rectangle, made out of a dark wood. She thought that seemed rather dignified. She'd have a big headstone listing all her accomplishments.

HAZEL KAPLANSKY
STAR STUDENT
HOLDER OF KNOWLEDGE
SOLVER OF MYSTERIES

She thought that was far more important than the Bible quotes that most people put on their headstones. It would certainly help people like Samuel with their research.

She'd want her funeral to be somber and sad, with lots of wailing to show how much people missed her. Maybe someone could throw themselves on her coffin and beat the wood with their fists. Mrs. Vorschat's funeral was far more subdued. It was pedestrian, which, Hazel had learned, did not mean walking, but ordinary, and Hazel was not ordinary.

She started back into the cemetery, thinking about the night before when she'd overheard her parents talking about her and Samuel.

"I don't know what's going on. Hazel has never been in trouble before. Clara Rushby said she was sticking up for the Butler boy. It's hard to fault her for that."

"That's it precisely. She never had any trouble before that Butler boy came back."

"George, try to have a little sympathy. Lacey Switzer might have made a mistake, but that boy didn't do anything wrong."

"Of course. And it's nice for her to have a friend, but—"

"It's not his fault. His situation, it's, well, just not his fault." Her mother's voice had sounded sad and weary.

"I know, I know. Of course." He'd sighed. "But I don't think it's a coincidence that she's gotten in trouble since he's come around."

"True."

"I know he needs a friend, but if it's going to be at the expense of Hazel . . ."

"I know," her mom agreed. "So what do you want to do? Tell her they can't be friends?"

A breeze kicked up some leaves and they danced around her legs like her flitting thoughts about what her parents had said. *His situation. He needs a friend. Not his fault.* Maryann and Connie said that everyone knew why he'd come back to town. What was his situation and why did everyone seem to know about it except Hazel? What had his mother done that was so awful?

She bit her lip hard. Maybe *she* was a Communist, too! That made a lot more sense than blaming the Lis. If Samuel's mother was Red, it would be the perfect opportunity to get spies into the Switzer plant. Maybe that's why she wasn't around. Maybe the FBI had her. And that was probably why Samuel kept questioning whether Mr. Jones was a spy. Maybe Samuel had even been thwarting her all along.

She rounded a curve and there, as if by magic, was Mr. Jones in Pauper's Field. She dropped to her knees as if she were weeding and observed him. He wasn't doing anything but standing, his back to her. After a moment, he left, the gate creaking closed behind him. She waited, filling the wheelbarrow with more weeds in a part of the graveyard that wasn't used yet. Once she was sure he was gone, she crept down to the paupers' graveyard. At Alice's headstone she saw something glinting. She dropped to her knees and brushed aside some of the fresh dirt. It could be any number of things. Gold coins. Jewels. A gun.

Her hand closed around something small and cool. When she lifted it up, she found it was a tiny wooden doll, no bigger than her pinkie, shaped like a bowling pin. Her eyes grew wide. She knew what this was. It was one of those nesting dolls. *Russian* nesting dolls. Her grandmother had a set, and Hazel liked to play with them. Each wooden doll could be twisted apart and inside was a smaller one. The doll The Comrade had left behind was the smallest one, solid wood that didn't come apart. The doll was painted wearing a black jumper with a red shirt underneath. Her hair was black and the eyes were green. A small daisy was painted on the black jumper.

A Russian doll left at Alice's grave: her first piece of tangible proof!

Invitations and Gifts

Hazel wasn't sure how she was going to avoid Samuel back at school, but it was Connie of all people who made it easier. On Hazel's way into the building, Connie stepped out of a side hallway. Hazel stopped short. This had to be some sort of a setup. She looked over her shoulder, sure there would be a mob of angry fifth graders, but there was only a group of third-grade boys. Still, Hazel kept her mouth shut.

Connie extended her hand. In it was a bright yellow envelope. "It's for my birthday. My mother says I need to invite the whole class because, well, just because." She shook the envelope in Hazel's direction.

Hazel hesitated. If she took the invitation, then Connie would assume she actually wanted to attend the party, and Hazel would rather be locked in a room with the alien plant-monster in *The Thing from Another World*. What she really wanted to do was take the invitation and throw it on the ground and maybe even stomp on it for good measure. She was about to do just that when she had a startling realization: this could be the break in the case she'd been looking for. Nancy Drew had faced a similar situation in *The Secret of the Old Clock*. She needed to get inside the Tophams' house to try to find the old clock that had a will hidden inside it, so she used the ruse of selling tickets to a charity ball to get into their house. Well, Hazel could use the party as an excuse to get into the Shorts' house to find more evidence to tie Mr. Jones to Mr. Short.

Hazel reached out her hand to take the invitation. Connie didn't release it. She looked at the envelope, then back up at Hazel as if she couldn't quite believe this was happening. "It's awfully nice of you to invite everyone."

"My mom said I had to."

"So you said." Hazel tugged and the invitation came loose in her hand. "Of course I will have to check my social calendar. This is a busy time of year."

Connie took a step back. "You do that," she said. "My phone number is on there so your mom can call my mom and let her know if you're coming."

"Marvelous!"

Connie rolled her eyes, and turned to go, not realizing that Otis Logan had come in the door behind her. She nearly pigeon-toe-walked right into him. He jumped back with his hands held in the air like he'd just been caught in a robbery. "That was close," he said.

"Sorry," Connie said breezily, and Hazel knew she didn't mean it.

"I sure wouldn't want to catch the Commie germs off of you." It was a typically stupid thing for Otis to say. Communism wasn't a disease, not really. They called it the Red Menace, but it wasn't like the Blob that swallowed you up. It was something you chose. Just because Mr. Short chose to be a Red spy didn't mean Connie was a Communist, too. Otis, though, thought he was clever as could be and started guffawing as he limped down the hall.

Connie stood straight as a board. Then without even looking at Hazel or saying anything, she marched away toward the classroom, leaving Hazel in the hall holding the sunshine-yellow envelope. Hazel hurried to class and took her seat just in time; she didn't even have to give a glance to Samuel.

Samuel, Hazel quickly realized, was nearly as relentless as she was. All morning he looked at her with sad eyes, but she didn't care. Or she told herself she didn't care, and concentrated so hard on making it look like she didn't care that she almost believed it.

Music class was the hardest.

"Announcement!" Mrs. Ferrigno sang once they were all settled. "The school will be putting on a recital to celebrate the fall harvest season, and we shall be performing a percussive piece." She shook a piece of paper. "'Simple Gifts,'" she declared, and began warbling: "'Tis a gift to be simple, 'tis a gift to be free."

She dispensed with the usual pageantry of handing out instruments and gave the students what they always got. "We have so much work to do. Rehearse, rehearse, rehearse!" Hazel was stuck with her crooked triangle sitting right next to Samuel.

The piece called for them to ding their triangles each time the chorus came up. It was all percussive instruments, with no one singing, but if they had been singing, it would have been like this:

'Tis a gift to be simple, 'tis a gift to be free,
'Tis a gift to come down where we ought to be.
And when we find ourselves in the place just right,
Ding!
'Twill be in the valley of love and delight.

Mrs. Ferrigno was nervous about this added responsibility for her triangle players.

"Triangle people," Maryann muttered, and rubbed her arm. She'd been feigning injuries all day: back, arm, leg, even her head, which she hadn't come close to hitting. Hazel bared her teeth at her.

"You understand, you two, right? You understand when you need to play?" Mrs. Ferrigno asked.

Hazel nodded, but all she could think about was that she was sitting right next to a traitor. She shifted away a little.

Mrs. Ferrigno began by teaching the parts to the other players, so Hazel sat back and thought about what it would take to get her to turn tail on a friend like that. She was narrowing it down to the threat of death to her puppy—if she had a puppy, which her parents said could not happen, given where they lived and a dog's propensity for digging—or the kidnapping of her parents. Certainly not the mere intimidation by a couple of girls.

Of course, this gave more credence to the theory that he was protecting his Red mother. He knew she was on the trail of the Communists and he was trying to throw obstacles in her path.

"Hazel," he whispered.

She untied and retied the skinny laces of her brown-and-white saddle shoes. She wanted penny loafers with a bright copper penny in each one, but her mother said saddle shoes were more practical.

"Hazel," he whispered.

"Vibraslaps!" Mrs. Ferrigno called out.

"I'm ignoring you," she whispered back.

He looked down in his lap.

Mrs. Ferrigno started working with the xylophones and the glockenspiels. Maryann and Connie wore looks of intense concentration. "You'll get it, you'll get it. Good!"

"I need to tell you something," he whispered.

Mrs. Ferrigno glanced over at them and wiggled her eyebrows like little worms slithering above her eyes.

"You've already gotten me in enough trouble." She moved even farther away from him.

"Now let's add the ratchets and rattles."

The period was nearly over by the time she got to Hazel and Samuel. "Now, Hazel and Samuel, Maryann and Connie will play their part of the chorus, and then you will chime in."

Hazel laughed, but Mrs. Ferrigno just drew her worm-eyebrows closer together. "Is something funny?"

"Chime in," Hazel said. "I thought you were making a joke."

"This is serious work, Hazel. Can you handle it?"

"Yes," she said with a sigh.

They practiced a few more times and then Mrs. Ferrigno said, "From the top!"

The first time, Hazel hit the note perfectly, which elicited a small, surprised smile from Mrs. Ferrigno. Then they did it again and Hazel was looking at the vibraslaps with envy. As their part came up, Samuel elbowed her. She'd been ready, but just to get him back, she didn't play her note.

Mrs. Ferrigno sighed and threw her hands up into the air. "Hazel Kaplansky, what am I going to do with you?"

"Sorry, Mrs. Ferrigno. It won't happen again."

Mrs. Ferrigno turned to the class. "I'm sorry to end on such a low note, but that's our time for the day. Please put your instruments away." The class began to shuffle and rise. "Carefully, carefully," Mrs. Ferrigno sang.

On the way out the door, Samuel tried to catch up to her, but she sidestepped some classmates and tucked into the girls' room, even though they were supposed to return directly to class. She stood with her back against the chipped sink and wondered how long she could keep avoiding Samuel.

In the Turret You See the Whole World

After school Hazel hadn't gone more than a few steps toward the bike rack when Samuel jumped into her path. "I'm sorry," he said.

"A little late for that," she replied.

"I need to show you something. About Alice."

The story of the Russian doll burbled on her lips, but she clamped down. "I'm afraid your assistance on that project is no longer needed. *Someone* was being made fun of, and *someone else* stuck up for him, and that someone else, who was me, got in trouble, and that first someone, who is you, didn't do anything, and now that second someone is grounded and needs to go directly home with no stops and no talking and no nothing."

"I'm sorry," he said again. "I froze."

"Yes. You did," she said, and started walking.

He fell into step beside her. "I have some information that I want to run by you."

"Just tell me, then."

"It'll be easier to show you."

"As I've already explained, I'm grounded."

"Can't you just tell your parents you're working on a school project?"

"Lie to them? Sure, and if I get caught I'll just be grounded for another indefinite period. I'll be grounded indefinitely to infinity."

"Could you just ask to go to my house? My grandmother says you're a nice family."

Hazel thought of the conversation she'd overheard between her parents. Going to Samuel's house was definitely not going to be approved.

"Hazel, please," he said. His eyes were wide and gray as clouds. He looked like he might cry. She didn't think she could stand to hear that gulping sobbing sound again.

"Oh, all right." Hazel figured her parents would be outside working since the clouds had blown through and now it was a warm, bright October day, perfect for planting bulbs.

"I want to stop at the library first," he said.

"Samuel! Do you not understand that I am grounded and I am taking my life into my hands just by agreeing to talk to you?"

"I want to ask Miss Angus something about the case."

Hazel slapped her forehead. She always liked when people in the movies slapped their foreheads and had been looking for an excuse to do it herself. "What is wrong with you?"

"What do you mean?"

"You can't go asking Miss Angus about this."

"Why not?"

"Adults don't think we should talk about death. They think you should put it in a box and bury it in the ground."

"They talk about it. My grandmother—"

"They don't think it's normal to talk about it, especially not for kids. Trust me on this. If we ask questions, they'll shut us down faster than you can say 'Who the heck was Alice?'"

"So we're back on the case?" he asked, extending his hand.

Hazel hesitated, but the truth was that Samuel was the second-smartest person in town, and she still needed his help. She reached out and took Samuel's small, warm hand. "We're back on the case."

Samuel and Hazel walked up Brattle Hill past all the brick houses to an old Victorian at its peak. The house was painted a deep purple, with blue trim, and it loomed over the town like a castle in a storybook. Samuel, though, opened the door like it was nothing. They hung their coats in a closet and started up a narrow set of stairs. Up and up and up and then he pushed open a door and they went into a large circular room. There was a bed, a desk, and a bookshelf overflowing with books, but Hazel noticed none of these things. She crossed the room to a picture window that offered a view like none she had ever seen. "You can see the whole town from here." Indeed it looked like a train set laid out in front of them. All the familiar things were there: Main Street with its handful of stores, Wall's Garage and the barber shop across the street, the school, the factory, even Memory's Garden on the north side of town.

"When I was little I used to think I could control it all. I'd point my finger and pretend I was moving cars. It would make me cry if a car turned right when I'd told it to turn left."

"When you were little?"

"I used to come here with my mom sometimes. This was her room."

Hazel stared down at her town bustling and moving about like she was watching a movie. She looked back over her shoulder at Samuel and her eyes caught on a huge stack of Batman comic books. She had never seen so many comics all in one place. "Wow! You really like Batman!"

Samuel nodded.

"I'm more of a Superman girl myself."

"Not me. Superman's an alien. He was born with his special powers. Batman, though, he's just Bruce Wayne, just a regular guy, or so it seems. He uses his brains to fight crime."

"I never thought of it that way." She kind of liked the idea. Maybe secret crime fighter could be added to her list of future occupations. She decided she would need to spend some time thinking of possible superhero names.

Samuel sat down on the edge of his bed. "I'm sorry I got you grounded."

"It's okay," she said with a shrug. "It got my parents to take their heads out of the plants and actually look at me."

"At least they're there."

Hazel reddened. "I'm sorry. I didn't mean that. I forgot about your father, how he's—" Hazel could talk and talk and talk, but it seemed like when it really mattered, her words got garbled.

Samuel, though, just shook his head. "Not him. My mother."

"Oh, I know all about your mother," Hazel said, meaning to reassure him.

Samuel's face darkened. "What do you know?"

Hazel opened and shut her mouth. She hadn't intended to tell him she knew his mom was as Red as Mr. Jones. A good detective would never blow a lead like that. She wanted to trust him, but he had left her high and dry in the cafeteria. Given what he said about Batman, though, about using his brains to do good, she thought maybe she could trust him after all. "Well, I figured out that she's a Communist. That's the secret everyone's been talking about when they talk about your secret past. She helped them to infiltrate the plant, and now she's in hiding. And at first I thought you were trying to sabotage my case against The Comrade in order to protect her, but now I think you're on my side because you value truth above everything."

Samuel didn't say anything for a while. He stared out the window at the town below, and so Hazel stared, too, stealing glances at him. He blinked a few times in rapid succession, but other than that, his face didn't seem to move at all. Out in the town, the cars crisscrossed the streets with no idea that someone was watching them from way up on the hill.

"Hazel, you have a one-track mind, you know that?"

"Mr. Wall says I'm relentless."

"My mother is not a Communist."

"Are you sure?" Hazel asked. "Sometimes the family is the last to know. Those Red spies dupe their parents and their kids right along with everyone else. I'm sure it's a hard thing to hear, but maybe just think about it for a minute."

Samuel shook his head. "It's not that. It's something that no one will say, but everyone is talking about."

Hazel sat on her hands to let Samuel tell her what he needed to say.

"I don't even know where she is right now."

Hazel wanted to ask how that was possible, but she bit down on her tongue because she knew it would come out all wrong.

Samuel filled the quiet place. "She was . . ." He paused. "Empty."

"Like crazy?" she asked, and then slapped her hand over her mouth to stop herself from making it worse.

"Just empty. She tried to fill herself up." He picked up a comic and began flipping through it with his thumb. The pages made a soft fluttering sound. "Do your parents drink at all? Alcohol, I mean?"

"Not really," she said. "Becky Cornflower's dad had a bar cart and when he came home every night he'd pour himself a glass of whiskey. And I know that Connie Short's mom likes to drink brandy Alexanders."

"My mom likes to drink a lot. Whatever she gets her hands on. She drinks until she sleeps for days. That's why I can't live with her anymore. She was drinking and she went out to get more and drove herself into a snowbank. She didn't even notice. She was sleeping."

Hazel didn't know what to say. Once on a trip to Boston she'd seen a man slumped over on the sidewalk with red eyes and a nose like a city map. He'd asked in a slurred voice for some change. Her mother had pulled her close and they'd side-stepped him. When Hazel asked what was wrong, her father had told her that the man was a drunk. Her mother said it was a disease and those who suffered from it needed help, just like someone with polio or tuberculosis. In her mind that's how she'd always pictured drunks: men with sad eyes, thinning hair, and sagging bellies, not someone's mom.

"My grandmother won't talk about it. She says I'm safe now." He put down the comic book and looked out the window toward the school. "I'm not sure what safe is."

As he spoke, she'd been moving closer and closer to him. Sometimes she and Becky used to sit right next to each other, their legs crisscrossed over each other's. They'd be reading or talking or whatever. She didn't know if you could sit with a boy like that, if it made a difference. So, to compromise, she slid right next to him on the bed, and took his hand in hers.

Whatever Samuel had wanted to show her, he didn't get a

chance to because his grandmother came into the room, saw them sitting on the bed together, and misinterpreted the situation. She flew across the room, grabbed them each by the hand, and dragged them down the stairs. She was awfully strong for an old lady.

They sat at the kitchen table looking at the lace tablecloth while Mrs. Switzer called Hazel's parents. Hazel wanted to take the wooden doll out of her pocket and slide it over the table to Samuel, but she was too scared of Mrs. Switzer.

Both of her parents came to get her this time. They talked to Mrs. Switzer in the parlor, and there was no laughter to make Hazel believe that she might be getting off with a light sentence. They spoke in hushed tones and only stray words filtered into the kitchen: *given the past . . . never been like this before . . . the times we live in . . . monitor the situation . . . keep them apart.*

Hazel and Samuel exchanged a glance, but it only lasted a second, and Hazel wasn't quite sure what she saw in his eyes. Sadness, maybe, or regret, and something that looked a lot like resignation.

Hazel sat in the backseat of the car and didn't even try to plead her case. She went inside, put on her work clothes, and went back outside to do more weeding. She set to work in the high-rent district, picking out the tiny weeds that popped up between the graves—clover, mostly, but also a few white-and-purple forget-me-nots.

The List

Even without being able to see Samuel, Hazel had plenty to do with the investigation. It was like she had all the pieces of a jigsaw puzzle except for one right in the middle: the one that would make the whole picture clear. She needed undeniable proof. Her best bet, she figured, would be to watch Mr. Jones and Alice's grave as much as possible in the hopes of catching a drop-off.

When she came home from school, she hurried inside and changed into her play clothes. Before she could make it back outside, her mother stopped her. "Hazel, I need you to run to the market for me."

"The market? Now?"

"If you want to have dinner tonight, yes."

"Can I get TV dinners?"

Her mother hesitated, and Hazel thought she might relent.

"No," she said. "We're having tuna noodle casserole and we're out of tuna. I thought for sure we had some, but there's none in the pantry."

"Really? That's strange," Hazel said, though of course she knew that there was one can in her mausoleum fallout shelter, and two more in her closet.

"I just need you to run to the A&P and pick up two cans."

There was no getting out of this. "Okay," she said.

"And bread. A loaf of bread." Her mother dug through her purse and pulled out her wallet. She removed one dollar and handed it to Hazel. "Be quick. I want to get dinner started."

"Aye, aye, Captain!" Hazel said.

Her mother rolled her eyes.

Hazel rode as fast as she could to the store. The shift changed at the factory at four o'clock, and if she hurried, she could get back in time to catch someone coming off the day shift to do a drop.

Leaving her bike outside she rushed into the store, which was lit up as brightly as fireworks, nearly smacking right into Mrs. Wood and Mrs. Logan, who were standing in front of the door chitchatting. "Sorry, Mrs. Wood. Sorry, Mrs. Logan," Hazel said, even though they were the ones blocking the way. All she needed was word getting back to her mother that she'd been rude at the A&P.

She sidestepped around them, and didn't mean to eavesdrop, but they were right there. "The investigators have a whole list. They're just figuring out the best way to release the names," Mrs. Logan said, her lips twisted into a slim smile.

"I've heard that when they release the list, this whole town will be topsy-turvy," Mrs. Wood said, her eyes evaluating the other women in the store. The waist of her dress was so tight, Hazel wondered how she could even breathe, let alone gossip.

"Me, too," Mrs. Logan agreed. She patted her hair. She had short tight curls and shorter bangs, just like Mrs. Eisenhower. It made her face look round and shiny as a bowling ball. "I heard it goes right up to the top."

"I heard everyone will be shocked!" Mrs. Wood laughed and it sounded just like Maryann's wicked cackle.

They were talking about the list of suspected spies! Oh, how she wanted to tell them she had it all figured out, how the biggest problem wasn't in the factory, it was outside it.

"Of course, Pastor Logan has nothing to do with it. At least *I* can feel safe in that. So many other women in this town must be right on the edge of their seats."

Hazel pretended to be intensely interested in a display of pickled onions. The jars were stacked up like a pyramid and she wondered if it worked the way it did in the cartoons. If she picked out a jar from the bottom corner, would they all come tumbling down?

"Not me," Mrs. Wood said. "I'm sure that Mr. Wood is innocent. Not a drop of Red in his body."

"Oh, of course, I didn't mean to *imply* anything," Mrs. Logan said, her voice like syrup. "I meant some *other* women in town."

Anthony's mother pushed her cart over and reached out for a jar of onions. "I couldn't help but overhear. Such a tragedy!" she exclaimed, but her eyes were bright. "Why, just last night I was saying to my Sal that if Will Short is on that list, anyone could be. I don't know why he's not talking. He must have something to hide, that's what I told my Sal."

"I think they ought to make them all take a loyalty pledge," Mrs. Wood declared. "Then we'll see where we stand."

"Clean house!" Mrs. Logan agreed. "Just like Eisenhower's doing with the administration."

Anthony's mother put the jar back on the display, and twisted it so the label was facing just the right way. "Your Maryann is friends with that Short girl, isn't she?"

Mrs. Wood smoothed her dress. "They have been friendly, yes."

Hazel had to bite her lip to keep from guffawing at that. Friendly as fleas, those two were.

"I don't know that I would let my Otis go around with a girl like that," Mrs. Logan said. "Anthony isn't friendly with her, is he?"

"Oh my, no!" Anthony's mother said.

Mrs. Wood picked up one of the jars of pickled onions and made a big show of reading the label.

"I'm sure Connie is lovely," Mrs. Logan went on. "But the influence, you see. I just don't think it would be safe for a young girl to be in that household."

Hazel leaned in so close she brushed against the display.

"Hazel Kaplansky, do you need some help?" Mrs. Logan asked.

Hazel jumped. "Excuse me, ma'am?"

"Do you need some help?" She said each word slowly as if Hazel were hard of hearing,

"I was just contemplating these pickled onions. Have you had them? Are they tasty?"

"Did your mother send you to fetch something, Hazel?" Mrs. Logan asked.

"You know, actually she did. Tuna. Do you know what aisle that's in?"

"Aisle three," Mrs. Wood said with a sigh.

The three women looked at her with something like pity and something like scorn in their eyes. Hazel wanted to tell them not to bother because she was never going to grow up and be stuck gossiping next to a stack of pickled onions. She was the one who should pity them.

"Thank you," Hazel said.

She hurried on her way, but not before she heard Mrs. Wood say, "No wonder that girl's so odd, with a mother like Lydia."

"Hardly keeps an eye on her, letting her run wild around the cemetery all day. What kind of a mother does that?"

"Did you hear what she did to my sweet Maryann?"

Hazel wanted to turn back and knock the whole display of pickled onions right down on top of them. They'd be covered in a gooey pickly mess and it would serve them right. But she wasn't going to give them any more reason to gossip about her or her mother.

On the way to the tuna she passed the bakery and grabbed a loaf of bread. It was nineteen cents, which left her enough money for three cans of tuna, so she'd be able to add one more to her stash. She brought the bread and tuna to the counter, paid the cashier, and was on her way, still with plenty of time to witness any suspicious behavior.

While she waited for dinner to be ready, Hazel set herself up in the crook of her favorite maple tree. She watched, and watched, and watched. Nothing. The only creature who paid any mind to Alice's grave at all was a gray squirrel. What a bust.

Bad Influences

Hazel's parents and Samuel's grandmother may have decided that they should spend a little time apart, but they couldn't keep Hazel and Samuel from talking at school. At recess, they sat on the wall near the building—the one typically reserved for delinquents—and Hazel told Samuel about the fruitless stakeout. Then he told her that something about the gravestone was nagging at him.

He pulled out a magnifying glass and peered closely at his rubbing.

"Where'd you get that?" she demanded, not even trying to keep the jealousy out of her voice.

"My grandmother gave it to me."

A group of boys ran by tossing a baseball back and forth.

"Did you hear about Mr. Short?" Hazel asked.

"Connie's dad?" he asked, turning his book to look at the rubbing from a different direction.

"Right. He's one of the spies at the factory."

"One of the alleged spies."

"Here's the thing: He comes by the cemetery sometimes and drops things off for The Comrade. Then The Comrade goes and locks them in the garden shed."

Samuel stopped and looked up at her. "Well, I suppose that is suspicious."

"Oh!" she cried out, digging in the pocket of her dress. She wouldn't let her mother buy her any dresses without pockets. "I almost forgot. I found this the other day." She held out the small wooden doll she'd found on the grave.

He took the doll from her. "A *matryoshka*. Nice."

"I found it in with the chrysanthemums. What do you think it means?"

Samuel rolled it around in his fingers, then handed it back to her. "It could have sentimental value. Or it could mean nothing at all."

"It's a clue. It's *Russian*."

"You are gathering an ample amount of evidence that *could* be used to support your claim. Still nothing definite."

"Exactly, and so I figure we need to get into that—"

"It's been cleaned!" he exclaimed. "Someone's taking good care of it."

"We knew that already. It's Mr. Jones." Their peers raced around the playground, up and down the slides, jumping over tires, flying from swings.

"Yes, but why?" Samuel asked.

"So the other spies know where to leave the secrets."

Samuel rubbed his fingers roughly against the cement of the wall. "I still want to know who she is."

"Ding! Ding!"

Hazel looked up and there were Maryann and Connie. They were holding imaginary triangles and saying, "Ding! Ding! Triangle people go Ding! Ding!" Then Maryann said, "Ding dong is more like it."

Hazel made her most menacing face. "I'll have you know that I've taken out restraining orders on both of you. You can't come within twenty feet of me. Or Samuel."

"Oh, sure," Maryann said, and threw her hair over her shoulder.

"It's true. Check with Mrs. Rushby."

"I should have a restraining order against *you*," Maryann said. "You pushed me."

"It was self-defense," Hazel said. "And the judge agreed. So scat." She waved her hand at them dismissively.

They hesitated and then Maryann said, "Fine. We'll leave you two alone, but not because you said so."

"Right," Connie agreed, crinkling her freckled nose. "We don't want to be near enough to catch the weird off of you."

"It was pathetic enough when she was hanging around Becky Cornflower."

"Ugh. I don't blame Becky for moving away. I wish I could move far, far away, too," Connie taunted. "Arizona wouldn't be far enough for me if you were my only friend, Hazel. I'd move all the way to Alaska. If it ever becomes a state, it'll be so good Americans will have a place to get away from weirdos like you."

"Actually, it would likely have more to do with Alaska's strategic location," Samuel said. "With its closeness to Russia, it would be militarily advantageous for Alaska to be a state rather than a territory."

Maryann sneered, and no one looks pretty when they sneer, not even girls with perfect blond hair. "You two are just perfect for each other. Triangle people. You're practically adorable."

"So adorable it makes me sick," Connie added. They both made retching and dinging noises as they walked away.

When Hazel looked back at Samuel, he was bright red and wouldn't catch her eye. Now it was her turn to look away. She tucked her knees up to her chest and tried to stop herself from blushing as madly as he was.

Samuel cleared his throat. "The one thing we know about Alice is that she's connected to Mr. Jones." He held up his hand to stop her from interrupting him. "Maybe you're right and we do need to investigate him."

"Really?" Hazel didn't even care that he still wasn't buying her theory about Alice being just a name. "You know what this means, don't you? Stakeout!"

Samuel frowned. "That's not the appropriate form of investigation for this situation."

"How can you say that? It's the perfect form."

"We can't see each other out of school, so how could we even get together to do it?"

"Can't you just say you're going over to do a grave rubbing? We don't even have to talk. I bet we'd get better information if we were spying from different viewpoints."

He shook his head. "I don't think my grandmother wants me to leave the neighborhood."

Then a brilliant thought came to her. "Halloween! You, me, stakeout in the cemetery, then trick-or-treating. It will be fantastic!"

"There's the small matter that we aren't supposed to be talking to each other."

"It's all in how you present it, Samuel. Trust me." She explained her plan to him, and even told him just what to say to his grandmother.

"You think this will work?" Samuel asked.

"Oh, sure," she said, though really all she had was hope.

Later that night, Hazel laid out the argument before her parents:

"Insomuch as I have only been able to trick-or-treat once in my life," she began. Her parents had taken her trick-or-treating when she was three, but the town teenagers, sensing the lack of authority, took the opportunity to vandalize the graveyard. Hazel had been allowed to dress up after that, but they never left the house: her mom handed out candy while her dad patrolled the graveyard with a flashlight. "And insomuch as this was meant to be my first time trick-or-treating by myself. And insomuch as Samuel is not allowed to go trick-or-treating alone, and so won't be allowed to go if I don't go with him, and we all know what a sad, sad childhood he's had, I hereby propose that you allow me a one-night reprieve from indefinite groundation—which, by the way, I'm pretty sure violates the Geneva convention—to go trick-or-treating. Samuel will even help with weeding beforehand."

Her mother looked up from her *Horticultural Digest* and swallowed her soup. "What was that, dear?"

"She wants to go trick-or-treating."

"But she's grounded."

"It's for Samuel," Hazel reiterated. "His grandmother won't let him go alone and he doesn't have any other friends."

Her parents exchanged a look. Playing the Samuel card was risky. She knew her parents felt sympathy for him, but they also were convinced that he was somehow responsible for all her recent bad behavior.

"Did you hear the part where Samuel was going to help me weed?"

Her parents exchanged a look. More like several looks, as if they were trying to come to an agreement using only their eyes.

"Will Mrs. Switzer allow Samuel to go trick-or-treating with you?"

"Oh, I'm sure she will if you say it's okay. Don't you see that Samuel's joy and happiness is in your hands?"

"That's a little much, Hazel," her father said.

"Quite a bit much," her mother concurred.

"Sorry," Hazel mumbled. She tried to make her eyes as wide as she could so they could see how sad and pathetic her plight was.

Her dad shook his magazine. "You know, when I was your age, we didn't do any of this trick-or-treating."

Hazel tried not to look exasperated.

"It's a form of extortion," her mom said. "Kids going from house to house and begging for candy. My mother never would have let me do something like that."

Hazel wiggled in her seat. She wished they would just tell her one way or the other.

"I suppose it wouldn't hurt to give them another chance," her father said.

"Oh, all right," her mother said. "But the grounding isn't over."

"What are you going to be?" her dad asked.

"I was thinking maybe a historical figure like Eleanor Roosevelt or Amelia Earhart. Do you think I could make a plane out of cardboard boxes before Saturday?"

"I don't know about a plane, but I think I have an aviator cap up in the attic," her mom said. "Your great-grandfather used to fly, you know."

Hazel imagined herself with her cap and goggles, a scarf blowing back in the breeze. This was shaping up to be the best Halloween yet. Of course, as she herself should have known, life didn't always live up to expectations.

Parade of Ghouls

"Gum?" Hazel demanded. "Gum? Who brings gum to a Halloween party?"

Her mother pushed a long strand of her hair back from her face. "Girls who don't tell their mothers about the Halloween party and the need for snacks until the night before, that's who." She plunged her hands into a sink full of soapy dishes.

"You could have made chocolate chip cookies. Those take no time at all."

"Everybody loves gum," her father said. "After World War II, American soldiers used to give it to German kids. They'd come running for blocks."

"We don't live in Germany."

"Hazel," her mother said, but her tone said the rest: *zip it*. She wiped at her hair again, leaving a trail of soap bubbles across her forehead.

It's true that the night before Hazel had been so excited about going trick-or-treating and making her costume that she'd forgotten until bedtime to tell her mother that she needed to bring something to share for the classroom Halloween party. "Now?" her mother had demanded. "You tell me now?" But then she had said she would take care of it, and Hazel had gone to bed. Four packs of Wrigley's gum was not what she had expected when she woke up, but it was too late: she had to go to school. And she wasn't going to let the gum ruin her excitement for the day.

She tucked the packages into her knapsack, and headed out to her bike.

She pulled her goggles down over her eyes. They were darkened and a little cracked, which made seeing and thus bike riding a bit difficult, but she wasn't going to take them off. She had woven wire through her white scarf so it would look like it was blowing behind her. Her father had an old bomber jacket. "From my rebel days." He had laughed, and Hazel wondered what on earth that could mean. She wore khaki pants and canvas sneakers. As she sped down the hill to school, she felt like she really was Amelia Earhart, flying over the ocean, nothing but blue sky and blue water in front of her, no place to go but around the world.

"I don't think Amelia Earhart wore sneakers," Samuel said when he saw her.

"Well, Amelia Earhart got to fly her plane. We have to walk in the Halloween parade. What are you supposed to be, anyway?"

Samuel was wearing the same clothes he always wore. He bent over and took something out of his satchel. "I'm a ghost," he said, and threw a sheet over his head. He adjusted it so that he was looking through two cut-out eyes.

"No one ever actually dresses as a ghost," she said.

"Exactly," he replied.

They walked together through the school toward the front door, where the annual Halloween parade was getting set to begin. Students of all ages were dressed in their costumes: skeletons laughed with clowns, Howdy Doody chatted with a Rocket Ranger, a pack of hobos drifted down the hall. The Halloween parade was one of Hazel's absolute favorite times of the year. She'd been Raggedy Ann, a gypsy, a flower (at her parents' insistence in first grade), and a wizard, but Amelia Earhart was certainly her best costume yet.

When Hazel and Samuel stepped into the bright sun, they saw Maryann and Connie dressed as identical bunnies. They wore pink jumpsuits made out of some soft material, pink ears on headbands—each with the right ear folded down—and had pink noses and black whiskers drawn on their faces.

"A rabbit's ears would never look like that in real life," Hazel whispered. "One up and one down? That's ridiculous."

"Almost as ridiculous as a pink rabbit," Samuel replied.

Hazel grinned. It was nice to have someone else who valued truth and integrity and sticking up for the facts.

Mrs. Sinclair came hurrying out dressed as Annie Oakley

and begun ushering her students into a line. She was one of the only teachers who dressed up, which made Hazel like her even more. "Ready, children, let's get ready!"

They lined up as best they could, each jostling to see the parents along the street below. It was all mothers, except for one man, who— Hazel squinted. She couldn't believe it. What was her father doing at the Halloween parade?

Behind her, Otis Logan was shifting from foot to foot. He had on a gray jumpsuit. "What are you supposed to be, anyway?" she asked.

Normally Otis would have made a snide remark, but instead he wrinkled up his freckled nose and said, "I'm one of the spies at the factory."

"That is scary!" Anthony said, laughing. "My father says the whole place is crawling with them."

Otis replied, "My mother says when they catch the spies, they ought to put them out in those things they used in the old times, where the guy was all propped up in the town square and folks threw garbage at them."

"The stocks?" Hazel prompted. She didn't think that sounded very Christian of Otis's mother, but she didn't say anything. She noticed that Maryann took Connie's hand and gave it a squeeze.

Timmy cleared his throat. "My father works at the factory, and he says there's no way any of them are spies." He spoke to the ground, and the skin under his freckles turned as pink as Maryann's and Connie's bunny ears.

"Then why won't they say anything?" Otis asked. "Why won't any of those union guys sign the loyalty pledge to prove they're all American?"

"They've got nothing to prove. The committee has it all wrong," Timmy said.

"Are you calling Senator McCarthy a liar?" Otis asked. "'Cause I'm pretty sure that's treason."

"I'm saying you should watch your fat mouth," Timmy said.

To which Otis responded the only way he knew how: he shoved Timmy. Otis was a lot bigger than Timmy, but Timmy barely tumbled back. Maryann and Connie emitted simultaneous squeals with their hands over their mouths.

Mr. Hiccolm was on them in a moment, pulling apart the boys before they could start something. He dragged Otis back to the end of the line, where he wouldn't bother anyone.

Connie and Maryann were in front of Hazel and Samuel. Their bunny ears flopped as they spoke. "What a brute," Maryann said.

"Sure is," Connie agreed, without her usual enthusiasm for echoing Maryann.

"Hey, don't worry about them," Maryann said. "What's that your mom has?"

Connie squinted. "Oh, that's a movie camera that my dad got the last time he was down in New York."

Timmy let out a low whistle. "That's pretty nifty," he said. "My dad wants to get one, but he says he's going to wait until they come down in price a bit, which means he will get it in 1967." He shook his head.

A movie camera? Hazel elbowed Samuel and mouthed the words "Spy gear."

"What?" Samuel asked. He was going to have to get better at lip reading if he was going to be any good as a spy.

Hazel leaned in closer. "Spy gear. He got that camera because he's a spy."

Connie tugged at her bent rabbit ear. "Where's your mom, Maryann?"

Maryann pointed. "She's down the street with Mrs. O'Malley and Mrs. Logan."

"I wonder why my mother isn't with them," Connie said, chewing her lip, and for a second Hazel, who was eavesdropping as a matter of course—detectives don't get to take a break in the middle of a case—wondered why Connie sounded so concerned.

"My mom's probably jealous of that new camera. She likes to have everything new first and can't stand when someone else has something nicer than her."

Hazel thought that seemed a lot like Maryann herself.

"Sure, I guess," Connie said.

"Don't sweat it, Connie," Maryann told her. "Jeez, I've never met anyone who worries as much as you do."

Just then Hazel heard someone calling her name. "Hazel! Over here! Hazel!" Her dad was standing on the sidelines, in between Mrs. Short and the clump of other mothers. He was waving like crazy, and of course dressed in his short-sleeved button-down shirt, even though it was cold and all the mothers had on winter coats. Hazel gave a small wave and her father responded with a thumbs-up.

"Is that your *dad*, Hazel?" Maryann asked. She and Connie laughed.

Now, Hazel knew that her father was a little odd, with his goofy grin and the dirt stains on his knees, but she didn't know what was so funny about it. "Sure is!" she replied, and plastered on a manufactured smile.

Mrs. Sinclair took her place at the front of the line and the parade began. Connie had her waddling walk and Samuel had trouble with his cut-out eyes, so they moved in sort of a jerking, lurching fashion, which Hazel thought was rather undignified. Still, the mothers—and Hazel's dad—clapped and waved and the kids all waved back. Except for the little first graders, who were terrified by the whole thing.

Samuel leaned a little closer to her. "My grandmother finally gave in," he said. "We can go trick-or-treating tomorrow. And, you know, the other thing."

Maryann looked over her shoulder and seemed ready to say something mean, but then Samuel stumbled on the edge of his sheet and nearly crashed into her. She screamed, then snickered and muttered, "Triangle people."

Hazel patted Samuel on the back and said, "Maybe we should hem that sheet before we go trick-or-treating."

They did a loop around the parking lot and then it was time to go inside for the Halloween party, after which they'd be let out early for the day, which was another reason why Halloween was one of Hazel's favorite days of the year. Before she went inside, she rushed over to her father. "Look at you, Amelia Earhart!" he said. "Looks like a great day for a fly-around. Not a cloud in the sky!"

"What are you doing here?" Hazel demanded.

The smile on her father's face faltered. "I came to see the parade."

"You've never come before."

"Well, the truth is, Mom felt a little bad about the gum, so we decided I should just head on down to the parade. And I'm glad I did. What a sight!"

"Why didn't Mom come if she felt so bad?"

"The bulbs finally arrived, the right ones, and she's getting them in the ground. What's the big deal? Aren't you glad to see me?"

Hazel couldn't believe her dad didn't notice that he was the only father there. This wasn't a Dad Event, this was a Mom Event, not that her mom ever came to these sorts of things. She was always working. But even the moms who worked in the Switzer factory managed to switch shifts and come to at least some of the things at school. "Sure I am, Dad. I've got to go inside now."

He ruffled her hair and sent her on her way.

As she walked to her classroom, she could hear Maryann's voice echoing all the way down the hall. "Gum? What kind of a square brought gum to the party?"

The Stakeout

Samuel walked over to Hazel's house on Halloween, his costume in his satchel. She found him a pair of work gloves and they went out into the graveyard. She had her Mysteries Notebook tucked into the pocket of her overalls. She still hadn't been able to find a magnifying glass, and decided that binoculars would make her too obvious.

"We're going out to weed!" Hazel called to her father, who was pecking with his index fingers at the typewriter in the office. Hazel's mother usually did the typing.

"Make sure you get around all the sculptures," he replied without looking up.

Hazel turned to Samuel and whispered, "Our cover story is set." She looked at her watch. "Time is currently . . ." She paused to do some quick computations. "Fifteen hundred hours. Dusk is at approximately seventeen hundred hours, giving us nearly two hours to complete our mission."

"I'm still not so sure about this," Samuel said.

"You're the one who said we could find out about Alice by learning about The Comrade."

"Mr. Jones," he corrected. She decided not to argue, and together they went outside in search of their subject. There were no funerals scheduled, so Mr. Jones didn't have any graves to dig, but usually her parents found some odd jobs for him to do. She pushed the wheelbarrow and they stopped occasionally to pick weeds. They did a few loops around the cemetery, but didn't see him. Hazel glanced at the garden shed. Locked up tight.

"I guess this means no stakeout," Samuel said, not sounding sufficiently disappointed as far as Hazel was concerned.

"Well, actually, I need to show you something. Then we can do another search for him," Hazel said. She walked with him over to the mausoleum.

"Is this part of the case?"

"No." She pushed open the door. "I'm making a fallout shelter here. See."

With her head, she gestured for him to peek in so he could see her stash of canned goods.

"It's not airtight," he told her.

"I know," she replied. "But here's what I'm thinking: If it's airtight, that's no good. We'd run out of oxygen. The stone and cracks allow for just enough air to go in and out. Sure, we might be exposed to a bit of radiation, but not enough to kill us."

Samuel scratched his elbow while he considered this. "Not a bad thought, actually," he said.

"My parents don't know about it yet, but if the Russians *do* send us a warning—which I doubt they will—I'll say, 'Don't worry, Mom and Dad. Just follow me. I have it all under control.' And if we don't have a warning and it's just the flash of light, I'll grab them both by the hands and say, 'Forget Bert the Turtle, come this way!' and we'll run right to safety." Hazel tugged the door closed.

"You've thought it all through."

"Of course. This is serious business. I know it would be too far for you to come last minute, but if there is warning, you'd be welcome. There will be enough food. You just need to bring your own sleeping bag."

"What about my grandmother?" Samuel pushed his glasses back up the bridge of his nose.

"Does she snore?"

"I don't know."

Hazel had a hard time picturing Mrs. Switzer sleeping on the cold floor of the mausoleum, but in the event of an atomic attack, she supposed anything was possible. "Okay. But then you guys should probably bring some extra food if you can."

Samuel nodded. "Thank you."

"No problem." She picked up the handles of the wheelbarrow. "We should get back to the matter at hand."

Eventually they found Mr. Jones fixing some slats in the wooden fence at the rear of the cemetery. They chose a place where they could see him but were somewhat protected by a large statue of an angel that Hazel had always called Rufus.

"So what exactly are we hoping to see?" Samuel asked.

Hazel pulled a dandelion. "Ideally we'd see someone from the plant do a drop-off at the grave, or a direct exchange with The Comrade. Admittedly, that's not likely, especially now that the heat is on. So we should focus on building up a profile of him, so when we do go to the FBI and Senator McCarthy, we can give them a full report. We need to get an understanding of the subject, his patterns and habits, you know."

"I see," Samuel said. He pulled out a few weeds and put them in the wheelbarrow. "Don't you already know about his daily habits?"

"We *think* we know, but we don't. You never really know about someone."

"I know about you," he said. "I mean, I know you aren't a murderer or anything."

"As far as you know," she said. "That's the thing about spies. They live among us and only the truly wise can spot them." She arched her eyebrows so he would know that she was among the truly wise, in case there was any doubt.

"I see," he said again. He made steady progress weeding his patch of the graveyard, approaching the task in his typical orderly manner. Hazel would have been faster than him, but spent more time peeking at Mr. Jones.

With his bare hands, The Comrade was prying off the old, broken pieces of wood. Hazel took out her notebook and wrote: Very strong.

He worked without rest, and so Hazel wrote: Focused.

She put the notebook by her knees and began pulling weeds as she watched him keep working. It seemed a little strange that a spy would take a job that required so much physical labor. If she were a spy, especially one at the top level with a whole cell of other spies that she was in charge of, she certainly wouldn't take this kind of a job. She'd be a nightclub singer, maybe. Though perhaps that would draw too much attention to herself. She would be a librarian, then. She could hide the secrets in books, ones that weren't popular, and then the other spies could find them. She giggled at the thought of Miss Angus being a spy: her tall, lanky frame wrapped in a trench coat as she snuck down the one slightly darkish alleyway in Maple Hill, a book filled with secrets under her arm.

"What?" Samuel asked.

"Nothing. My mind just wandered. Won't happen again."

Mr. Jones lifted up a new board and began hammering it in.

Able to wield a blunt object with force and precision.

"What are you writing down?" Samuel asked.

"No cheating. Take your own notes."

"It's not cheating if we're partners."

Hazel sniffed. She didn't want to share what she had written down, because it wasn't terribly exciting. The Comrade hadn't met anyone, and he hadn't gone anywhere near the grave or the garden shed. Stakeouts, she was starting to think, were actually kind of boring.

Mr. Jones worked at a steady pace, moving on to carefully putting new boards in the empty slots. There was a rhythmic thunking to his hammer that Hazel found soothing, and she thought she heard, however faintly, that he was humming.

"My grandmother wasn't sure about letting me go trick-or-treating with you. She said she wasn't so sure about a boy and a girl being friends."

Hazel picked up a trowel and stabbed into the earth, then wedged out a deep-rooted weed. "Connie thinks we like each other, you know, like girl-boy stuff."

"Connie reads too many romance stories," Samuel said.

"That's what I thought, too," Hazel said.

"It's a completely ridiculous idea."

"Not completely, completely ridiculous," Hazel said. "I think I would be considered quite the catch. I'm smart and clever and I make good jokes. I've built a fallout shelter. My mom says that eventually I'll grow out of this baby fat, not that it really matters. So I don't think it's completely ridiculous that you would have a crush on me."

"You forgot modest."

"What's the point of modesty? I'll be modest when other folks start to realize how remarkable I am."

Samuel shook his head and began gathering up the small pile of weeds that he had amassed. Then he dumped them into the wheelbarrow. "He's leaving."

"What? We hardly have any notes."

"You can write that he's careful about picking up his work site."

They both watched him walk the length of the graveyard back toward the garden shed.

"I guess that's it for today," Samuel said.

"Wait! He's going into the shed. That's where he stashes his deliveries from Mr. Short. Come on!"

"Come on where?"

"We need to get a closer look!"

Before she could stand up, Mr. Jones emerged from the shed holding an ax. He strode right toward them. "Oh, no," Hazel whispered. Samuel said nothing. They couldn't run; they'd blow their cover. So she just kept weeding as fast as she could. She was digging her hands into the dirt like a groundhog, so fast and hard that her fingertips began to hurt.

With a few long, quick strides, he was in front of her. He looked at her, the wheelbarrow, and then at her notebook.

"What are you doing?"

"Weeding," she said. "And a school project on plant identification. Killing two birds with one stone, you know. Ha-ha." She winced at her use of the word "killing."

He looked down at the ground. "I think you've done enough," he said. His voice stayed the same: flat and low.

"What?" She began recoiling.

Mr. Jones swung the ax up onto his shoulder. The sun glinted off the clean blade. His gaze flicked from Hazel to Samuel, then back to Hazel, as if deciding which of them to chop first.

This was where it all ended, she thought, her heart beating fast. It didn't matter that it was broad daylight, that her parents were in the house. This would be the exact moment that she ceased to exist. It was too soon. Everyone said that, of course.

Everyone thinks their time is too short, probably, Hazel thought, even old people who can't even get around or think straight. Probably even Mrs. Buttersbee, who Hazel sometimes saw in the grocery store walking around with just a head of cabbage in her hands, probably even she would say "It's too soon! I'm not ready!" when the time came. But with Hazel, it really was. She had great things in her future. Great, spectacular, impressive things, like traveling to space, or maybe she would discover a cure for the common cold *and* cancer, or she would write a comic strip that was in every newspaper in the United States and Canada. Maybe she would do all these things. But not if it ended now. Not if Mr. Jones captured them and sent them to Siberia.

"You've pulled that spot clean down to the dirt."

She looked: he was right. There was a round patch of dirt about a foot across in front of her. When she looked up, there was only blue sky dotted with cotton-ball clouds. He was gone, and her future, for now, was still possible.

"Having a foot race?"

Hazel and Samuel both jumped and turned to see Hazel's father standing in the kitchen. He was making a cup of tea, dipping the tea bag up and down in the hot water.

Hazel and Samuel breathed heavily. They had sprinted from the graveyard to the house after Mr. Jones left.

"I've never seen two kids run so fast," he said. He took the tea bag and tossed it into the compost, then picked up his book *New Strategies for Cemetery Horticulture.*

Teacup in one hand, book in the other and held up in front of his face, he started for the kitchen door.

"Dad?" she called after him.

"Yes?" he replied, not lowering his book.

"Is there some reason that Mr. Jones would have an ax?" Her voice cracked on the word "ax."

Hazel's dad put his book down on the table. He looked first at Hazel and then at Samuel. "You two aren't bothering Mr. Jones, are you?"

"No, of course not," Hazel said.

Hazel's dad looked at Samuel. "You sure?"

"Yes, sir," he replied.

"Because Mr. Jones has had a tough life and he works hard for us. The last thing he needs is for a couple of kids to be harassing him. And the last thing I need is to have to hire another gravedigger."

"We weren't harassing him. He just came out of the middle of nowhere with an ax, and I was curious as to what task needed an ax."

"You've got a curiosity about axes?" her dad asked, eyebrows lifted.

"Well, an ax does raise some suspicions."

Her dad picked up his book again. "Just leave him alone, okay?"

"Okay," Hazel said.

"Good," he replied. He walked through the doorway and down the hall toward the front room.

"Maybe he's right," Samuel said.

"What? Are you kidding me?"

"I just mean maybe we're in over our heads."

"We're not even near our necks. We just need to investigate a little more. You'll notice, by the way, that my dad never answered the question. Which means he probably doesn't know why The Comrade had the ax. Which is suspicious, don't you think?"

"Your dad trusts Mr. Jones."

"My dad's a trusting guy. After all, I told him all we wanted to do tonight was trick-or-treat. Speaking of which, we should get into our costumes!"

"I never thought I'd see the day," Samuel said.

"What?"

"That something would pull the relentless Hazel Kaplansky off a lead in the case."

"This isn't just something, Samuel. This is Halloween!"

Trick-or-Treat

It was true that the mission of the day was to spy on The Comrade and that mission had ended in failure and a near-death experience. Still, Hazel could not contain her excitement as she straightened out her scarf. She was about to go trick-or-treating for the first time in seven years.

As they set off, the sun was still up, but starting to edge out of the sky. She hazarded a glance back to the graveyard. Getting into her costume had dissipated some of the fear she'd felt when The Comrade came striding toward them, but now she was worried that he'd be waiting for them, and Samuel, in his stupid ghost costume, would not be able to move well enough to run away.

Her parents had given them strict instructions to stay in neighborhoods with sidewalks and to come back before it got truly dark. She led Samuel into a street with a cul-de-sac. It was a new neighborhood and all the houses looked the same.

There were a number of other kids, mostly younger with their parents. They walked up the front walk and rang the doorbell of the first house. "Trick-or-treat!" Hazel yelled before the door was all the way open.

"My, my," said the young mother, baby on her hip. The mother was part of Pastor Logan's family, though Hazel couldn't recall exactly how. Second cousins, maybe. "A ghost. Scary! Do you see the scary ghost, honey? Do you?" The baby could not muster much interest. "And what are you, sweetie?"

"I'm Amelia Earhart," Hazel said.

"Why, how creative of you."

She extended the bowl of candy and they each took one candy. "Go on, take two," she prompted, and so they did.

The next house played out almost the exact same, only this was Mrs. Redstone, who worked down at the post office and couldn't hear very well. Hazel had to yell "Amelia Earhart!" three times before Mrs. Redstone understood her.

"I can't believe people don't know who I am," Hazel said as they moved on to the next house.

"That's why you should go with something simple and classic."

"Amelia Earhart is classic," she said, adjusting her scarf, which was starting to droop.

They finished the loop of the first neighborhood. The night had the faintest hint of cool, and a gentle wind rustled the remaining leaves in the trees. It was just about a storybook-perfect Halloween night. As they walked on to the next neighborhood, Hazel said, "You know what's wrong with music class?"

"We're destroying a beautiful song?"

"No. Mrs. Ferrigno undervalues the triangle. I think the triangle is a noble instrument."

"Noble?" Samuel asked.

"Quiet yet firm. I mean, the glockenspiel, sure it's pretty, but anyone can sound good on a glockenspiel. Working the triangle takes skill."

"Hazel, I have to elbow you to make sure you don't miss our cue."

"That's because I'm not being challenged enough."

They rang the doorbell on a large house. Almost before Samuel's hand was down from the buzzer, Mrs. Logan threw open the door. She was dressed like the good witch in *The Wizard of Oz*. "Happy Halloween!" she called out. "Why, it's a ghost and a, um, a— What are you, Hazel?"

"Amelia Earhart," Hazel said.

"Oh, isn't that, um, different?" She dropped a box of raisins into each of their bags. Raisins. That was even worse than bringing gum to a Halloween party.

Hazel rang the next doorbell. Waited. No one came. This was Mr. Hood's house, and she knew he was home because Mr. Hood only left the house on Tuesday mornings for grocery shopping. Otherwise the farthest he came was to his front door so he could yell at kids to scram off his front lawn. She pressed again. The door opened and an old man peered out. "Who's there?"

"Trick-or-treat!" Hazel called out.

"Blast it!" Mr. Hood replied. "Is it time for those shenanigans again?" He dug around in his pocket. "Here's a dime for the ghost and"—he looked down at his hand—"a nickel for the bandit."

"I'm not a bandit, I'm Amelia Earhart!"

"You're off my front porch is what you are!"

"Yes, sir," Samuel said, and dragged her off the steps.

"That was Mr. Hood. He's cantankerous."

"Let's just keep going."

A group of younger kids raced by Mr. Hood's driveway, their fathers following along behind them.

The next stop was Ellen Abbott's house. Ellen's mother, who was as mousy as Ellen herself, opened the door. "A ghost and a motorcycle racer!"

"I'm Amelia Earhart."

"Amelia who?"

"Earhart. Woman pilot."

"Oh. Well, here's your candy."

Hazel shook her head as they were walking down the front steps. "As I was saying, I just think that if Mrs. Ferrigno gave me a chance, she could see that I could shine on that triangle, and I bet she'd even give me a solo."

"A triangle solo?"

"Sure. Why not?"

"I don't think a triangle has enough notes."

"It's not the instrument that's the problem. It's a lack of imagination. In the proper hands a triangle could be as impressive as a piano."

"A piano?"

"Well, at least as impressive as a vibraslap."

The next house was Mrs. Buttersbee's. Hazel rang the doorbell. Hazel loved Mrs. Buttersbee's name. It made her think of the honey butter her grandmother made to spread over toast: so sweet it burned the back of her throat. She was a talker, though. "Hazel Kaplansky!" she cried out when she opened the door. "It's been a few years."

"Seven," Hazel said.

Mrs. Buttersbee ushered them into the house. In the front hallway, there was a sideboard with a Crock-Pot full of hot apple cider. She began ladling out two paper cups' worth. Year after year, Hazel had heard the other kids complain about Mrs. Buttersbee. Stopping at her house always took forever, they said, since she talked to you for ages while you drank her cider. "You were a, wait, don't tell me. You were a pumpkin the last time you knocked on my door."

"That's right," Hazel said. She took her cider and sipped it.

"And who's this ghost?" Mrs. Buttersbee asked.

"Samuel," he replied.

"Not Samuel Switzer?" she asked.

"Samuel Butler," he corrected. He took the cup of cider, but he hadn't cut himself a mouth hole, so he couldn't actually drink it.

"Well, now, isn't that a hoot," she said. "All right, you two, come stand here and I'll take your picture."

They stood side by side while she struggled to get her camera out of its leather case. She had to keep adjusting the lens with her trembling hands. No wonder the other kids avoided this place. No amount of candy was worth all this.

Behind Mrs. Buttersbee was a cuckoo clock shaped like a Bavarian cottage. Just as Mrs. Buttersbee finally got her camera set, the hour changed and seven windows on the house opened. Out of each window emerged a gnome dressed in lederhosen and contorted into a dance pose. They spun on spindles for a minute, then stopped and counted off: *one, two, three, four, five, six, seven*. Then each gnome went back into the cottage with a soft slamming of the window.

Seven o'clock! Her parents would be expecting her home soon, and they still had the other side of the street to do.

"Oh, dear!" Mrs. Buttersbee said, lowering her camera. "That clock was my husband's and it startles me every time." She lifted the camera. "Let's try this again."

Hazel tried to strike her most Amelia Earhart–like pose. "Okay," Mrs. Buttersbee said. "One, two, three." It was another couple of seconds before her finger actually pressed the button. The flash went off and Hazel saw the light for minutes after as purple dots.

"We ought to go," she said.

"So soon? It's been a quiet night."

"We've got to get back home. It's getting late."

Mrs. Buttersbee nodded. "Well, then, I suppose you two ought to take the bulk of this." Her candy bowl was still nearly full, and she shoveled heap upon heap into each of their bags. Lemon drops, Turkish taffy, and Mary Janes. Hazel's eyes grew wide at the thought of it all. There were some anise bears, too, but Hazel figured she could trade those with Samuel for some of his root beer barrels, because he probably didn't know any better.

"Thank you!" she said, and Samuel echoed it.

Mrs. Buttersbee held the door open, and as they made their way down the walk, she called, "Good night, Caspar! Good night, Amelia!" Hazel couldn't help but smile. Maybe the only person who got her was a lonely old lady, but at least somebody did.

Hazel glanced longingly at the jack-o'-lanterns on the other side of the street, but she didn't want to push it with her parents. "Ready to go home?"

Samuel glanced down at his bag full of loot. Neither had ever seen so much candy. "I suppose we must," he agreed.

To get back to Hazel's house they wound around the graveyard.

"What's that?" Samuel asked.

She followed his finger and saw in the center of the cemetery a light glimmering like a flame.

Spirits from Beyond

"I knew it!" Hazel said. "It's a drop-off. We've got them now!" She started marching forward.

Samuel grabbed her by the arm. "Hazel, wait! They have candles."

"So?" she asked, but she stopped walking.

"If it really was a drop-off, they'd use flashlights, or no lights at all."

Hazel contemplated this. As much as it disappointed her to believe it, he was probably right. Then a new idea came to her, quick as crickets. "The Comrade is performing satanic rituals in our graveyard."

"Now you think that Mr. Jones is a devil worshipper?"

"All Commies worship the devil," Hazel replied.

"Try not to jump to conclusions."

Hazel ignored him. She was like Trixie Belden: sure, she

jumped to a lot of conclusions, but nine times out of ten she was right. "If he burns even a blade of grass my parents are going to flip their lids!" She squinted, trying to get a better view. She was ready to set off and to catch The Comrade in the act, but then she hesitated. If he was lighting candles and doing rituals in the graveyard, then that was illegal. But it wouldn't prove that he was a spy. It would be like when Eliot Ness got Al Capone for tax evasion. "Let's take this slow," she said. "Let's just go get a closer look."

Hazel walked down the sidewalk toward a small side gate. She peered out into the graveyard. Normally her father patrolled Memory's Garden on Halloween, but she couldn't see the light from his flashlight. *Oh, no!* she thought. *What if The Comrade has him and is torturing him for information?* They had to move quickly. "Let's go," she said.

Samuel hung behind, his sheet waving in the breeze like a flag dangling from a flagpole. "You know, maybe we should get your parents. It could be some greasers drinking beers."

Hazel stopped and looked back at him. "We won't let him see us. Come on. Give me your flashlight."

"What? No. It could be a weapon if I need to defend myself." He tucked the flashlight under his sheet.

"Now who's jumping to conclusions? Just turn it off so we can creep closer without him seeing us. There's plenty of light from the moon."

They both clicked off their flashlights and began walking

across the grass. Samuel tripped over a headstone and cried out. Hazel slapped her hand over his mouth. "Shh!"

"Your hand is clammy," he told her.

"Well, it's a little chilly."

"You're nervous."

"I'm not even going to dignify that with a response." But Hazel could not deny the way her heart beat like the little drum that Arthur Gayle got to play in music class. It was not nerves, she told herself; she wasn't scared. It was anticipation at finally catching The Comrade doing something, and that was enough for Hazel.

When they got closer, Hazel instructed Samuel to crawl and they scooted their bodies along the ground like soldiers on the Korean battlefield. Hazel's brown outfit blended right in, but Samuel's white sheet seemed to pull the moonlight to them like a spotlight, and she almost wished she could leave him behind.

They began to hear voices, low and humming. "That's a lot of people," Samuel whispered.

"Maybe it's not a ritual," she said, her heart beating faster. "Maybe it's a spy meeting after all, and they disguised it as a ritual."

"That seems like a bad disguise."

"He's probably grown so confident here he doesn't think that anyone can catch him. But we'll show him, won't we?"

"We should go get help," Samuel said. His voice trembled a little bit. Maybe she shouldn't put him in this situation, especially if he was as fragile as everyone said. She looked up ahead at the flickering light. Still, Samuel was someone who wanted to know the truth of things, and they were close to the truth of Mr. Jones.

"We're just going to look," she told him. "We won't confront him."

They crept along, trying to avoid sticks and other potential noisemakers. The smell of the candle smoke drifted over to them. A few more steps and they could make out four people crouched around a candle.

"They look pretty small," Samuel said.

One of the bodies swung a lantern around and Hazel and Samuel were bathed in light. They both jumped up, screaming. They screamed so loud and so high that Hazel wasn't sure what sound was her and what sound was him.

The lantern fell to the ground, and Hazel dashed over to pick it up. She shined it on the figures running away, the handle still warm in her hand. She would have recognized them anywhere: two sets of bunny ears with one ear pointing up and the other down. One sprinted, while the other waddle-ran like a duck trying to take flight. A witch's hat and Raggedy Ann hair followed after them. "Maryann Wood, I know that's you! And Connie Short, too!" The girls didn't stop and didn't look back.

Hazel and Samuel kept going to where the girls had been. There was a circle of rocks with wax of different colors drizzled over them. The candle in the center had been knocked over and a thin line of smoke trailed up from it. One large rock had a star drawn on it.

"What is all this?" Samuel asked.

"Séance," Hazel replied. "Stupid girls." She kicked at the rock, then bent over to pick up the candle. It was warm and soft in her hand and she squeezed it hard. "I wonder what they were trying to find out?" And then she grinned: another riddle to solve. First The Comrade, then Samuel's story, and now Maryann and Connie's séance. It was like all these mysteries kept falling into her lap, one after another. That, she decided, had to be the sign of a true detective.

Tree of Too Much Knowledge

When Hazel arrived at school on Monday, she marched right over to Maryann and Connie. After a dramatic pause to get their attention, she dropped the candle on Maryann's desk. "Okay, ladies," she said. "Spill."

Maryann looked at Connie and rolled her eyes.

"What I'm saying is, I know you were at the graveyard Saturday night. What gives?" She tried to sound matter-of-fact, like they all knew what was going on and all that was left was for the culprit to confess.

"What gives?" Connie mimicked.

"What gives you the right to talk to us?" Maryann asked.

Hazel tapped her finger on the candle. This was not going the way she had planned. In her version the girls started weeping and then told her everything. Still, she kept her cool just like Nancy Drew would. "Hey now, you were the ones who were at the graveyard, even though it's closed after dark. You can be arrested for trespassing. Plus you violated my restraining order. And I haven't ratted you out to anyone, so I think you ought to tell me everything."

"You never had a restraining order," Maryann said. "I asked my mom."

"Maybe, maybe not," Hazel said. She slid onto her desk facing the girls and channeled every detective in every book she had ever read. "Here's how I see it. You came to the graveyard. You held your little séance. You got caught, and you ran. Maybe you were running because you were caught, or because you scared yourself with the whole stupid séance thing. Or maybe, you're hiding a different secret entirely."

Maryann and Connie exchanged smirks. "If we had a secret, we wouldn't tell you."

"All right, then," Hazel said, leaning back. "You want to play hardball. I'll just put the screws to you. I'll tell my parents that it was you who moved the rocks and lit the candles. That it was you who drew the pentagram. They'll call the police and you can take it up with them."

Connie bit her lip, but Maryann remained strong. "What do you care what our secrets are?"

"I just want to know if it's worth desecrating a grave for."

"What does desecrating mean?" Connie asked.

"It means time in the slammer," Hazel told her.

Connie looked at Maryann with wide eyes. Maryann, though, smirked her smirkiest smirk. "It doesn't mean anything.

She's lying. She's always talk-talk-talking without saying any-thing."

"Have it your way," Hazel said. "Keep the candle."

She went back to the cubbies and willed herself not to look over her shoulder to see what her effect had been.

Connie stood at the pencil sharpener, spinning the handle round and round and round.

"You're not going to have any pencil left," Hazel said, hold-ing her own dull pencil in her hand.

Connie jumped. Then she leaned in close. "Meet me at the apple tree by the library after school. I have information for you."

"What kind of information?" Hazel asked.

"The information you want."

"Interesting," Hazel said.

"So you'll meet me?"

"I'll consider it."

"Don't tell your parents anything until you talk to me. I promise it will be good." Connie took her pencil, blew the dust off the sharp tip, and headed back to her seat next to Maryann, who demanded what she was doing talking to Hazel.

Hazel rushed over to Samuel. "We have an insider con-tact," she said.

"Something about Alice?" Samuel asked, looking down at his paper, where he was writing a list of ancient Greek heroes. He was getting much better at the subterfuge required for being a detective.

"No. The séance case."

Samuel glanced up at her for a second, then back to his paper. "I wasn't aware we had taken on a second case," he said.

"Side job," Hazel said, grinning. "You catch the jobs when you can, right?"

Samuel stopped writing and looked at her. "It's not all a game, you know."

"I know." She shifted her gaze to his list: Achilles, Heracles, Odysseus.

"I mean, Alice was a real person. Mr. Jones is a real person." His fingers gripped the pencil like a vise.

"I know," she said again, then blew her hair out of her face.

"It just seems like you're playing make-believe and—"

"I'm not playing make-believe," she said. "This was my idea in the first place, you know. And something else happened in the cemetery. That's where I *live*. It's my job to find out what's going on."

"Okay. Forget I said anything."

"I will," she replied, and huffed away.

She went back to her seat and took out her own workbook, but all she could think about was how much Samuel's words had stung her. They weren't true, of course. She wasn't playing any games. But she didn't like that he would think she was, even for a minute.

The apple tree by the library was overgrown and untamed. No one plucked its apples, which were more bitter than sweet. Her dad said it was the Tree of Too Much Knowledge, and her mom would laugh and say "No such thing."

As Hazel stood under it, kicking at rotted chunks, she thought about what Samuel had said. She had been thinking about it all day. It churned in her brain and her stomach and made her so upset that in gym class she had thrown the ball hard enough that Mrs. Warsaw told her she ought to consider taking up softball.

Samuel was angry at her, she knew. Maybe it was because he was afraid she'd become friends with Connie instead of him. Hardly. Hazel knew that in books it always turned out that the mean girls were actually nice, they were just afraid, or had mean parents, or were trying to fit in, but once you got to know them, they were fine. Hazel knew that those stories were lies. Some people were just mean, and Connie was one of them.

In fact, Hazel was growing certain that Connie had ditched her, that this was all part of some scheme Maryann and Connie had cooked up to embarrass her. Maybe they even knew that she was grounded and could get in trouble for coming home late. She was picturing the two girls snickering together when she heard someone whisper "Meet me in the listening booth."

She stood up and looked over her shoulder, but no one was there. On her way into the library, she stepped on one of the apples. She felt it squish under her saddle shoe. She tried to wipe it off, but some was still stuck in the treads and around the toe. She frowned, but she had an appointment to keep, so she went into the library, nodded to Miss Angus, and made her way to the listening booth and sat in the chair. She was still not convinced that this wasn't some sort of a trick, but then Connie, wearing sunglasses that did nothing to disguise her, waddled into the booth.

"What's that smell?" she asked.

Hazel glanced down at her shoe. "Secret. None of your business," she replied.

Connie shrugged as if she didn't care. "This goes no farther than this room."

"I may need to tell my associate," Hazel replied. She took out her notebook and flipped it open to a new page.

"Samuel?"

Hazel nodded.

"Oh, all right. It's not like he has any other friends that he could tell." She lifted up her sunglasses. "Maryann will kill me if she knows I told you, but I'm not willing to go to jail for desi—what was that word you said?"

"Desecrating a grave," Hazel said. She grabbed one of the

little yellow library pencils from the table, licked the tip, and was ready to write.

"You're taking notes?"

"A detective always takes notes," Hazel said.

Connie rolled her eyes, and then smiled to try to cover it up. Hazel, of course, was not fooled.

"Right," Connie said. "We were doing a séance. We read about how to do it in a book."

"You can do it in your house," Hazel said. "I mean, not that they're real, but that's where people normally do them. In the parlor."

"We don't have a parlor," Connie said.

No one did, as far as Hazel knew. No one except Samuel's grandmother.

"Anyway, we didn't want our parents to know what we were up to. Plus the book said to try to get close to the spirit world, and that was as close as we could think of."

"It's not their spirits in the ground. It's just their bodies."

"Well, that's what we were doing there. And I'm sorry if we made a mess, but we had planned on picking it up. It's just that you and Samuel surprised us. So, that's it. That's what happened."

"That's not it."

Connie chewed on the edge of her thumb. "You mean you're still going to tell your parents?"

"No, I mean I want to know what you were doing a séance about. Who were you trying to contact?"

Connie put her sunglasses back down over her eyes. "You have to swear not to tell."

"Of course."

"Pinkie swear." Connie held out her pinkie, and Hazel hooked hers into it. She and Becky used to pinkie swear about things—never wearing makeup except in dramatic productions, always being best friends—and it was strange to feel someone else's pinkie hooked into hers.

Connie grimaced, but then confessed, her words running together in a rushed stream. "Okay, so, Maryann wanted to find out if Timmy likes her."

Hazel unhooked her pinkie. "You did all that to find out if a boy likes Maryann?"

"Well, we thought it would be a fun thing to do, and we had other questions, too. I had a question that we didn't get to because you and Samuel came barging in on us."

"Why didn't you just ask Timmy?"

Connie widened her eyes. "You can't just ask a boy that."

"Why not?"

"Well," Connie began, then started chewing on the edge of her thumb again. "Well, that's just not how you do it. Because then he would know that she liked him. And she doesn't want him to know that she likes him unless he likes her back."

Hazel closed her notebook without ever having written anything down. "That's the stupidest thing I've ever heard. And I've heard a lot of stupid things."

Connie pursed her lips. "Think of it this way. It's not like you'd just go and ask Samuel if he liked you, would you?"

And then she let herself out and, looking both ways, scurried out of the library.

A moment later, Hazel left the booth. She went downstairs to the children's room, where Miss Lerner was finishing up a story time. She wished she were still little enough for story time. The way Miss Lerner's voice rose and fell with the story was soothing, like a hot water bottle under your covers in the winter.

Out the window, which was at street level, Hazel could see Connie's penny loafers waddling away. She wondered what Connie's question had been. Was she wondering about a boy, too?

Story time finished and the kids all spread out around the library looking for books to take home. Hazel walked over to Miss Lerner and listened as she described *Mike Mulligan and His Steam Shovel* to a little boy who looked suspicious that a book could be as exciting as a real steam shovel.

Once Miss Lerner had convinced the boy to take the book home—and come back with a full report on any inaccuracies—she turned to Hazel. "You're looking a little glum, Hazel."

"I suppose I feel a little glum," she replied.

"The whole town is these days," Miss Lerner said. "Even the kids. I read *Goodnight Moon*, and half the kids couldn't be bothered to find the mouse."

"What do you think it's all about?"

Miss Lerner raised her eyebrows. "It's about the factory, Hazel. What else? No one trusts each other anymore."

"Someone threw a brick through the Lis' window."

Miss Lerner nodded. "I saw it. Some of us collected money for them to get it fixed."

"Mr. Li wanted to leave it. So people would know, I guess."

Miss Lerner stacked up the books from her story time, and carried them to her desk. Hazel trotted along behind.

Hazel looked at her shoe. "I'm sorry about what I said about Mr. Bowen."

Miss Lerner gave her a soft smile. "I know you didn't believe it. But that's the problem with all this: a whisper becomes a rumor becomes a fact."

"That's why we need to figure out who the real spies are. We need to smoke 'em out, and fast."

Miss Lerner put the books down and looked at Hazel with eyes as sad as the puppies in the Richmonds' pet shop. "What if there aren't any spies?"

"Of course there are spies. Why else would there be an investigation?"

Miss Lerner sighed. "When you're a little bit older, Hazel, maybe you'll understand."

Hazel frowned. "That's what adults say when they don't know the answer, either."

Miss Lerner looked up, surprised, but her expression softened. "You're probably right about that. I don't know why good folks turn against one another. Maybe it's fear that if they don't accuse someone else, they'll get accused themselves. Maybe it's a way of working out an old vendetta. Or maybe they just get caught up in the moment, and they start to believe things that couldn't possibly be believed. Like Mr. Short heading up some sort of spy ring—"

"Oh, Mr. Short isn't the head of the spy ring!" Hazel exclaimed, but then stopped herself.

"I'm glad to hear that from you, Hazel. Not everyone has such an open mind."

Of course Hazel couldn't tell Miss Lerner that she did think Mr. Short was involved, she just didn't think he was in charge. She knew for certain that was Mr. Jones. So she said, and considered it a truth, "I like to keep my mind open to all possibilities."

Holes

As Hazel rode her bike home, she chewed on her lip. All that rigmarole to find out that Maryann liked Timmy. Big whoop. She had much bigger things to worry about, like spies and the people of her town doubting one another when she knew the whole story but just couldn't prove it. If she had cared about something as little as boy-girl stuff, which she didn't, she could have just made some observations at school. Now she was going to get in trouble with her parents for not coming directly home after school. Plus she had rotten apple on her shoe. Plus Samuel was mad at her. Again.

Maybe it wasn't worth it being friends with someone so touchy.

Maybe it wasn't worth it having friends at all. Because all they did in the end was leave. They moved to Tucson and never wrote letters. Or they got mad every other day. She hadn't realized how good she'd had it in those weeks after Becky left and before Samuel arrived. She had just gone about her business, playing her games in the graveyard and reading her books. Now she worried Samuel would tire of her, and she would have a Samuel-shaped hole, and she didn't like it.

She was afraid she was starting to get a town-shaped hole, too. It's true she planned to leave Maple Hill as soon as she could, but she still wanted it to be there, just the way she liked it. With Mr. Wall and the library and her school—all of it quiet and the same. She didn't like people throwing bricks in one another's windows. She didn't even like Otis shoving Timmy. Maybe that's how you know you really love something—how you feel when other folks start to tear it apart.

She didn't want to go home, so she rode her bike in and out of cul-de-sacs. If she was going to get in trouble (again), she might as well enjoy her last moments of freedom. Mrs. Buttersbee was outside tending to her chrysanthemums, which she kept in big pots on her front step. She seemed to be having some trouble. Hazel slowed her bike, hopped off, and walked up the path.

"Why, if it isn't Amelia Earhart!" Mrs. Buttersbee exclaimed.

"Just Hazel today," she replied. "Do you need some help?"

Mrs. Buttersbee smiled and lowered herself down onto the front step. "I most certainly do. The wind came by and knocked them all over."

"No problem," Hazel said. She began straightening the

pots back up. Some of the dirt had fallen out of the pots, and she brushed it from the cement steps into her cupped hand, being careful not to get it onto her school skirt. If she ruined any more of her nice clothes, her mother would have a conniption fit.

"I used to have the most beautiful gardens in the whole neighborhood," she said. "Hostas and peonies, and you should have seen my holly bush in the winter. People used to offer to buy boughs from me."

"That's nice, Mrs. Buttersbee," Hazel said. She didn't know why old people always spent so much time reminiscing about the past. Even when she was old, she'd be looking forward.

"I have blackberry bushes out back. The neighbor boy, Randall, used to come and pick them for me." She wiped her wrist across her brow. "You could come pick them in the summer if you'd like. You can take as many as you want, and I'll make jam with the rest. I haven't made jam in ages." Her eyes lit up as she spoke.

"That sounds nice," Hazel said. She really didn't like picking berries; it was always hot and there were too many bees and prickers. Plus poison ivy always seemed to grow among the blackberry brambles. It was like weeding, with obstacles. But she did enjoy fresh jam. "I would love to do that." Hazel patted the dirt in around the plants. "I need to be going. I'm grounded, and I'm already late getting home."

"Grounded? Whatever for?"

"It's a long story," Hazel said.

"Then we'll have to save it for another day. In the meantime, help an old lady up?" She reached out her arm, and Hazel took it in both hands, and pulled her to her feet.

When Hazel let go, she saw two dirty smudges on Mrs. Buttersbee's sleeve where her hands had been. "Oh, no!" Hazel cried.

Mrs. Buttersbee just smiled, though. "It's no bother. Reminds me of when I was out here doing it myself. You run along now. I don't want you getting into any more trouble on account of me."

Hazel said good-bye and hopped on her bike. She rode to the hill and pedaled hard, standing up and shifting the bike from side to side. It was a big, steep hill, and a lot of people got off their bikes and just walked up. But Hazel was not a lot of people. By the end of the hill she was barely moving, but she made it to the top. She raised her fist in the air.

This hill was not as high as the one on the other side of town, where Samuel lived, but it still gave a good view. She could see the graveyard and her house, and, behind her, she could see Samuel's house, his peaked turret. She wondered if he was in that room looking out in this direction, trying to make the cars and the people do what he saw in his head.

She coasted along for a bit, in no hurry to get home. She was only going to face certain punishment. Then again, what could they do? It's not like they could ground her for any longer than they already had.

She pulled up alongside her house and tucked her bike

into the garage. She opened the door and peered around. Her parents weren't in the kitchen. She went down the hall and saw the office door was open. With a deep breath, she went to the door to face her fate.

Her dad looked up from a stack of books. "Hello, Hazel," he said. "How's things?"

Did he not realize what time it was? That she was late? "I was just visiting with Mrs. Buttersbee," Hazel told him.

"Mrs. Buttersbee!" her father said. "She's a nice lady."

"I went there after school," Hazel said. "Instead of coming right home."

"Is that so?" he asked. He took a pencil from behind his ear and noted something on a piece of paper.

"Where's Mom?" she asked.

"At some meeting," he said through the pencil, which he now gripped in his teeth. "Concerned Mothers of Maple Hill or something."

"What are they concerned about?"

"The spies, I suppose. The alleged spies, as your mom says." He made a check on his piece of paper. "And when Mom's away, the cats can go to Li's! Grab your coat and we'll head out."

"I'm in my coat."

Her dad looked up from the book. "So you are. Well, then grab my coat and meet me by the door. I can practically taste the pork dumplings."

Hazel went and opened the closet door. It smelled like

mothballs and the pipe that her grandfather had smoked back when this was his house. When she was little she'd liked to crouch down on the floor of the closet, close her eyes, and just smell. She tugged her father's coat off the hook, making the hanger swing back and forth.

Her dad caught her there, staring at the swinging hanger and thinking about her mom at a concerned mothers meeting. Her dad grabbed his coat from her and said, "Sometimes I just wonder what goes on in that head of yours."

"You don't even know the half of it," she replied. But soon she would have the proof and she'd be able to tell him everything she had figured out, and boy, wouldn't he be surprised.

Banished

Connie's punishment for talking with Hazel was swift and severe: banishment. At least that's how it appeared to Hazel when she arrived the next day to find Connie sitting at her desk, her pretty lips pushed out and her eyes red-rimmed. Maryann had her arm around Patricia O'Malley. They were giggling and glaring at Connie, and Hazel almost felt bad for Connie. Then Connie demanded, "What are you looking at?" and Hazel knew that she'd been right about Connie after all.

Hazel sat down in her seat baffled that this huge blowup had started with a boy. With *Timmy*, of all the boys. Sure, he looked a bit like Ricky Nelson from *The Adventures of Ozzie and Harriet*, with his poof of light brown hair, wide eyes, and smirk of a smile. But he smelled like baloney and wasn't very smart, either.

When Ellen Abbott came out of the cubby area, Maryann called, "Come over here, but don't get too close to Connie. She might be contagious."

Ellen looked from Connie to Maryann, and back to Connie. "What has she got?" Ellen asked. "It's not polio, is it? It's okay if it's chicken pox, because I already had that, but I don't want polio."

Maryann rolled her eyes, but getting Ellen Abbott over to her was key to her plan, Hazel could see that. Choosing Ellen over Connie was just about the meanest thing Maryann could do. The absolute worst would be if Maryann chose Hazel as her new best friend. "Communism," Maryann whispered. "It's got her whole family."

Hazel blinked. "That's not how it works," she said. "You don't catch Communism. It's a choice."

Next to her, Samuel winced.

Maryann snickered. "You would know all about it, wouldn't you?"

"Well, I do know about most things, but yes, actually, Samuel and I have been investi—"

"Your whole family is a bunch of Red sympathizers. Maybe your family and Connie's family ought to have a commune together. Isn't that what Commies do? You could all go live in her stupid fallout shelter."

"Oh!" Patricia exclaimed. "I bet that's why they have the fallout shelter in the first place!"

"What are you talking about?" Hazel demanded.

"You're so smart, you figure it out," Maryann said.

But Patricia was too proud of herself. "Since Mr. Short is a Red spy, he *knows* the Commies plan to bomb us, so he had the fallout shelter built. I bet he has a special telephone, and they'll call him on it, and he'll take the whole family down underground. At least that was the plan before Senator McCarthy caught him." She tossed her red hair over her shoulder and grinned at Maryann.

"I guess your mom is smart being nice to the family," Maryann mused while spinning her long, flat blond hair around her index finger. "Maybe she thinks it will keep her safe. Me, I'll put my faith in Uncle Sam."

"Why are you talking about my mother?" Hazel asked.

Maryann and Patricia laughed and Ellen gave her a look of sympathy. "What?" Hazel demanded of Ellen. *Rumor. Whisper. Lie.* The words echoed in her brain.

"At the meeting last night—" Ellen began, but again Patricia was too excited. Her bright green eyes flashed.

"At the meeting last night your mother told the other mothers to lay off the Commies."

But that was impossible, Hazel thought. Why would her mother have said something like that?

"She said that we all should be ashamed of ourselves turning against one another like this." Maryann licked her thin lips. "She said it wasn't the Communists tearing the town apart. It's us."

Hazel dropped her head into her hands. Now the whole town probably thought her mother was a Communist sympathizer, and soon they would find out that The Comrade, the head of the whole spy ring, was working for her. No one would ever believe it was a coincidence.

Mrs. Sinclair bustled into the room. "To your seats

children, to your seats!" As soon as they were all seated, she
had them stand again for the Pledge of Allegiance. Hazel spoke
with deep fervor. No one could doubt her loyalty to her country. Still, when they sat back down, Hazel made the mistake
of looking over her shoulder to see Maryann smirking at her.

At recess Connie sat alone on the wall. The bright sun shone
on her curls, and she looked like one of those paintings of a
chubby angel. Folks liked to think about those pink-cheeked
angels watching over their loved ones when they were dead,
and Hazel often found cards with their pictures in the flowers
left on the graves.

The difference, though, was that Connie did not look
peaceful or helpful. She looked as sad as an under-watered plant.
"Connie the Commie," that's what they were calling her.

"It doesn't work that way," Hazel complained to Samuel.
"Connie isn't a Communist just because her dad is. At least, I
don't think so."

Samuel picked up a rough piece of granite and tossed it in
his hand. "I think your mom was doing the right thing."

Hazel narrowed her eyes. "Sure. Making everyone think
our family supports the Communists, that was a great decision. Just swell."

"She's trying to keep this town together. Isn't that what
you want?"

Hazel shook her head. Of course that was what she wanted, but there were good ways to go about it, and not so good ways. Her mom's way was putting a big target right on the family. She couldn't think about it anymore, so she turned her attention back to Connie. "I suppose Connie will want to be friends with us now."

"Why?"

"Because she doesn't have any other friends."

"Maybe," Samuel said. He bent over and picked up a smooth, white pebble and placed it next to the rough one in his hand.

"Of course we'll tell her to get lost," Hazel said. "But it won't be because of her dad. It will be because of her."

Samuel spoke without looking up. "That would make us no better than her."

Hazel was glad that Samuel wasn't looking, so he couldn't see the emotions on her face: surprised, angry, then, finally, agreement. She was a better person than Connie and that meant she had to act better. This was a bitter pill to swallow.

After school Hazel hopped on her bike and pedaled hard to catch up with Connie, who was walking home alone. Connie waddled with her head down, kicking a stone and sending it skittering along in front of her.

Hazel was feeling pretty good about her choice. She'd thought about it all afternoon. She *was* a good person, and most certainly a better person than Maryann Wood, who had dumped Connie at the drop of a hat. It was especially generous of Hazel to be nice to Connie after she had been so wicked. Hazel liked this feeling of generosity. She was sure that Connie would be so surprised and grateful she might even faint to the ground. After which she would hop up and tell Hazel that she was the kindest person ever to have lived, and surely she didn't deserve Hazel's friendship, but she was happy for it.

Hazel coasted on her bike up alongside Connie and jumped off in her patented, graceful move. Connie did not say anything. In fact, Connie did not even look up. Hazel thought that maybe Connie was just embarrassed. So the two walked side by side in silence for a while. Maple seeds fell from the trees and spun down like little kamikaze helicopters. The girls' feet crunched over fallen leaves.

Finally Hazel could stand it no longer. "I'm sorry about what happened in school today," she said.

Connie looked up, but didn't say anything.

"I wasn't ignoring you with everyone else. We just never talk, you know. But I noticed how everyone was being mean to you, and I thought that was pretty low."

A maple seed fell right down on Hazel's shoulder and she brushed it off. They were going uphill now. For a waddler, Connie could move pretty quickly, and Hazel had to huff along after her with her bicycle.

"What I'm trying to say is that I know how it feels not to have any friends, and I don't think it's your fault your dad is a spy, so if you want to be friends with me and Samuel, we decided that would be okay."

Connie stopped walking. She turned and faced Hazel, her cheeks red and tear stained. "I know you were trying to help today, but don't you know, Hazel, when someone like you tries to help, it only makes things worse?"

"I was only pointing out that just because your father is a spy doesn't mean you're a Red, too."

"Don't ever talk about my father," she said, her voice tight. "In fact, don't ever talk to me again."

With a sharp turn, she went waddling off on her way home, leaving Hazel standing dumbfounded on the sidewalk. A maple seed fell, twirling faster and faster in front of her eyes before spinning to a stop on the ground. Even though she should have known what to expect from Connie, she couldn't help but be disappointed.

The Light in the Graveyard

Hazel opened the door to the mailbox hoping for a letter from Becky. There was nothing. She closed it. Then she opened it again, just in case she had missed something. Sometimes the letters got pushed way into the back. She squinted, but still saw nothing. Every once in a while spiders built their webs back there, and once a paper wasp had constructed a small nest. Still, Hazel steeled her jaw and reached her hand in to feel around.

Nothing. Nada. Zilch.

It wasn't like Becky to not write. She prided herself on her conscientiousness. Maybe some terrible fate had befallen her. Maybe she had been kidnapped or had gone for a walk in the desert and been ripped apart by coyotes. Before Becky had left, Hazel had provided her with carefully researched information on all the poisonous snakes of the region, including illustrations. Maybe Becky hadn't had a chance to read it and a Western diamond rattlesnake had sunk its fangs into her ankle. Hazel couldn't help but think it would serve her right.

She had written Becky several letters detailing the investigation, but so far had only received one reply that had barely mentioned the mystery: a cheery *Good luck!* Instead the letter had been full of tales of the kids she had met in Tucson, the parties she was going to, and she even hinted at liking a boy, Ronnie O'Ryan. Becky and Hazel were not party people. They were not the type to get crushes on boys. Why, it was called a crush. Who would want a boy to smush her down so small there wasn't even a bit of her real self left? She wondered what could have possibly gotten into Becky to make her change so much. It was like she'd been taken over by some sort of alien being.

She clomped inside the house and dropped her knapsack with a dull thud on the floor. Her mother happened to be coming out of the office into the hallway and said, "My, aren't you in a sour mood. What's troubling you?"

Hazel couldn't believe her mother was standing there smiling like nothing in the world was amiss. "What did you say at that meeting?" she demanded.

The smile faltered on her mother's lips. "That's a grown-up matter, Hazel. You don't need to worry about that."

"Did you say we needed to lay off the Communists? Is that what you said?"

Her mother sighed and rearranged her scarf on her head.

"Not exactly, Hazel. I said that we were making things worse by getting all riled up. That if we really were concerned mothers, we wouldn't dwell on what was going on at the factory, because that's scary for you kids, but instead we should try to come together as a town."

Hazel looked at her mother agog. "Do you realize what you've done? Now everyone thinks we're in on it!"

"Hazel, I'm sorry if it came back to you like that, but—"

"Why did you choose this moment to be a concerned mother?" Hazel yelled, her voice echoing up the stairs.

"Hazel—"

"You should have just stayed out of it like you always do!"

"Sometimes you have to step up and say the difficult thing, Hazel, even if it's unpopular."

"That's easy for you to say. You don't have to go to school and have every kid think your mom loves the Reds. Did you ever even think of me?"

She didn't wait for an answer. She flew up the stairs, and her mother didn't follow.

It was time for Hazel to take matters into her own hands. She changed into her play clothes, found a set of pliers, a hammer, and a screwdriver in her father's toolbox, and headed out to the garden shed. Hazel couldn't recall if Nancy Drew had ever needed to pick a lock. In the comics, the detectives would hold their ears up to the locks and listen for clicks, but this wasn't a combination lock, it was a padlock, and anyway Hazel didn't know how to do that, so she would need to use brute force. She jammed the screwdriver into the keyhole, then hit it with the hammer. It made a huge clanging noise, but nothing else happened. She looked over her shoulder. She had made sure that Mr. Jones's truck was gone, but the noise seemed loud enough to alert her parents. When the back door of her house didn't open, she hit the screwdriver again and again and again. She hit it—*bang!*—because she was angry with Becky for not writing back, and—*slam!*—frustrated with Samuel, and—*crash!*—disappointed in her whole town. *Bang! Slam! Crash!* But most of all she was mad at her mother, who didn't seem to understand the way the world worked. *Bang!* Who didn't understand that now the whole town was looking at them. *Slam!* And if Hazel didn't find the proof she needed soon—*crash!*—then the next people being investigated by Senator McCarthy might be the Kaplanskys. *Bang! Slam! Crash!* Until the whole lock smashed apart.

She pulled open the door.

Hedge trimmers. Push lawn mower. Four shovels. Three rakes. Grass seed.

Hazel's heart sank.

But then in the back she saw something stacked in a corner under a tarp. Hiding things under a tarp was more or less a confession. She crept over and pulled the tarp back to reveal six Switzer safes.

She tried to open one, but of course it was locked. She tried the rest, with the same outcome. This was it, though. She knew it. There were secrets in those safes. Secrets she needed to get out. She just needed a plan. Or a trustworthy locksmith.

She was still thinking about it that night in her bedroom, trying to come up with a way to open the safes, when she was supposed to be doing her homework. She wondered how long it took to learn how to crack a safe, and if they had books on it in the library. She was filling a paper bag with cans so she could bring it out to the mausoleum the next day.

She was working on beans. She had baked beans aplenty, but she wanted to make sure she had kidney beans, too. Finding none in her stash, she decided to go downstairs to get a can or two, depending on how many her mother had in the pantry.

When she got down to the kitchen she glanced out the window toward the cemetery. Off in the distance she saw a faint, glimmering light. She threw her hands up in the air. "Unbelievable," she muttered. Maryann and her new crowd were out in the cemetery trying another séance. On a school night, no less!

Hazel pumped her arms as she strode into the cemetery. She was going to put an end to this once and for all. It was bad enough that she had to deal with those girls at school, but for them to come to her house—her *home*—at night and disturb her there, it was all too much. Striding across the grass, she composed in her mind what she would say to them.

Just who do you think you are to come to this place and disturb it? It's their final resting place. As in resting. As in do not disturb. All for your silly little crushes on boys who can barely hold the cymbals properly!

There were two of them leaning together, crouched over a grave in Pauper's Field. They were so close they seemed to move and shift as one.

Do you even know where you are? she went on in her head. *These people have been dead for decades and you're lighting candles and saying spooky words and I can't believe you would even think that would work in the first place. Just how few brain cells do you have?*

Her fists were clenched and her jaw squeezed tight. She felt as angry as she had the day she pushed Maryann, but instead of a sudden eruption of rage, this was a simmering pot of spaghetti sauce about to boil over and splatter the walls. She ought to have called the police. That would have shown them. But there was another part of her that needed to take care of this herself, to tell them once and for all what she really thought. She threw open the gate, spread her legs wide into an Old West gunfight stance, and called out, "Hey!"

When they stood up, she realized it was not a "they" at all, but a "he." Mr. Jones. The Comrade. He looked at her with icy eyes. He held a lantern that flickered on his skin. Her knees shook, but she stood her ground.

"It's awfully late for you to be out here all by yourself," he said, his voice calm and steady.

She swallowed hard.

"Your parents know you're out here?"

She shook her head, but then said, "Yes," her voice cracking.

"Well, which is it?" There was a hint of a smile at the edge of his lips.

"Yes," she said again, more firmly this time. "Yes, they know I'm here. As a matter of fact, they're on the phone with the FBI right now, so don't you try anything, Mr. Jones. Or whatever your name really is."

"The FBI?" He was a good actor. He honestly looked confused. But of course he was a good actor: he was a spy.

She took a few steps back. "Don't act all innocent with me. I had you figured from day one."

"I'm afraid I don't know what you're talking about."

"I know what you are. I know about Alice. I figured it all out. Me!"

He took a step toward her, lifting his hand again. Something metallic flashed in the moonlight. A knife! She was sure of it. She turned to run but tangled her feet together and fell with an *oof*. She heard him moving toward her, and so she did the only thing she could think of, though it wasn't dignified or heroic. She screamed. "Mom! Dad! Help!"

The lights flashed on in the house. Mr. Jones looked at the house and then back at her with the most curious expression on his face, as if he were already imagining her as a brainwashed automaton back in Russia. He leaned toward her, the knife hand extended. She scrambled back away from him, nearly crashing into her father's legs.

"What's going on out here?" her mom demanded.

"Call the police," Hazel gasped. "Call the FBI."

Mr. Kaplansky looked from Hazel to Mr. Jones, then back to Hazel again. He crouched down and put his arm around her. "Hazel, what happened?"

"He's not who you think he is. He has a knife. He's not—"

"I think you should go," Mrs. Kaplansky said. She placed herself between Hazel and Mr. Jones.

Mr. Jones hesitated for a moment, but he didn't protest. "Yes, ma'am."

He backed away from them slowly, then turned and walked away. Mrs. Kaplansky collapsed down beside Hazel and gathered her daughter into her arms. "What did he do to you, Hazel? What happened?"

"He's been coming out here, and Samuel and I were watching him and—"

"Did he hurt you?"

"He's a spy," she said. "He's the Russian spy, the one all the spies at the Switzer plant are reporting to. Connie's father and all the rest of them."

Hazel felt her mother stiffen and then she let Hazel go. The night air was still and cold between them. When her mother finally spoke, her voice sounded as if it were coming from far away. "You march yourself right inside and straight to your room."

"Are you going to call the FBI?"

Her father coughed. "Hazel, I suggest you get inside and make yourself invisible."

Hazel stared at her parents. They didn't believe her. She

stood up and dusted herself off. "It's true. I found this Russian doll he left behind and he stole an American flag and the garden shed is full of Switzer safes and—"

"Hazel!" her mom barked.

Hazel knew this fight could not be won. She slunk back into her house and then collapsed onto her bed, staring at the ceiling. If her parents weren't going to help, then she would have to call the FBI herself.

Canned

"Hazel Elizabeth Kaplansky!"

Hazel had not yet finished brushing her teeth when her mother's voice yelled from her bedroom. She spit out the toothpaste and rinsed her mouth with water.

"Hazel!" her mother yelled again.

"Coming," Hazel replied, trying to sound cheery, like the good girls on TV. She had never seen her parents so angry and now it seemed her mom was even angrier. They would change their tune, though, when the truth came out.

Hazel walked lightly down the hall and into her room. When she saw her mother holding the brown shopping bag full of canned beans, her stomach dropped. "Explain this," her mom ordered.

Hazel knew she was doing the right thing setting up the mausoleum as a bomb shelter, just like she was sure about

Mr. Jones. In both cases, though, she knew her parents would not see it her way. "I plead the Fifth," she said.

"You what?" her mother demanded.

"I plead the Fifth. I choose not to incriminate myself." Hazel had always considered this a silly strategy—if you were afraid of incriminating yourself, surely it meant you had something to hide. Now, though, faced with the ire of her mother, and lacking a suitable explanation, this seemed her best option.

"This is not a court of law. You have no rights. Tell me why there are canned goods in your closet."

Hazel sighed and sat down on her bed. "You're not going to like it," she said.

"I already suspected as much."

"You know we live under constant threat of atomic annihilation, right? Mrs. Cornflower told me that if the Russians ever came they would put us in a sausage grinder feet first unless we declared allegiance to the Communist Party."

Hazel's mom shook her head. "Becky's mother was being overwrought."

"I know," Hazel said. Or at least she thought she did. She wasn't entirely sure what "overwrought" meant. She would have to look it up in the dictionary later, if her mom ever stopped yelling at her. "The real threat is the atomic bomb. If they drop one of those we need a place to hide. Why, the Shorts have a fallout shelter, and if anyone knows the plans of the Commies, it's Mr. Short."

"Hazel, you're talking in circles."

"I was making us a fallout shelter, Mom. I'm gathering canned goods for us to live on. Flashlights, too. I've been trying to get some sleeping bags, but that's harder."

"In your closet? You're building a bomb shelter in your closet?"

"Of course not," Hazel said. "That wouldn't protect us at all. It will be in one of the mausoleums."

Hazel's mom pinched her lips together and puffed out her cheeks so she looked like a balloon ready to pop. Then she let the air out, slow as could be. She took another deep breath before she spoke. "Hazel, do you realize what you've done?"

Hazel knew exactly what she'd done. She'd set them on the path to safety. But she also knew that her mother did not want to hear that. So she kept quiet.

"The mausoleums, those aren't places for you to play."

"I wasn't playing, I was—"

"What do you think would happen if the family of a person interred in the mausoleum knew you were hiding canned goods there?"

Hazel supposed it depended on the person. Some people would probably be upset, but others would admire her practicality, she felt sure of it. "I had to protect our family. No one else was."

"If someone had found that—" Hazel's mother shook her head. "Hazel, you could have put us out of business."

Hazel bit her lip.

"Tomorrow, first thing after school, you will come home, and you will remove anything you put in that mausoleum."

"But, Mom—"

"You will clean it out so that no one, and I mean no one, will be able to tell that anyone has been inside."

"Mom, if there's a—"

"All the cans will be back in the pantry."

Hazel wanted to stay silent and strong, calm like Sherlock Holmes. But she didn't. "You don't understand anything, do you? This is all because of you!"

"Me?"

"*You* weren't keeping us safe, so I was. You're so busy trying to prove there are no spies that you can't even see one under your nose—"

"Hazel, Mr. Jones is not a spy. You need to stop telling that story. And if you see Mr. Jones, you'd better not say anything to him other than 'sorry.' That is, if we can get him to come back to work after the stunt you pulled. What were you even doing out in the graveyard?"

"I saw a light. The better question is what was *he* doing there? Have you asked yourself that?"

"I do not like your tone," her mother said, her own tone cold as a winter morning.

Hazel opened her mouth.

"Good night, Hazel." Her mom spoke before she could. Then she left the room, turning out the light as she went.

Hazel flopped back on the bed. Why couldn't her parents

understand what kind of danger they were in? A bomb could come any day. There were Russian spies living right in their town. Worse was that: now Mr. Jones knew that she knew his secret, and they were doing nothing to protect her. She imagined him coming back to the house. She'd be in that sausage grinder by morning, and buried all around the graveyard so no one would ever find her. And while that would prove she had been right all along, she wouldn't be around to experience the satisfaction. She slipped out of bed and locked her door. She knew it wouldn't stop The Comrade if he came to get her, but at least it would slow him down.

Inside the Mausoleum

The mausoleum Hazel had chosen was stone, with columns flanking the door. Her plan had been to come back and organize the cans, maybe even get some shelving, but of course that plan had been ruined by her mother, who was so angry she'd sent Hazel to clean up the fallout shelter without changing out of her school clothes. If another skirt was ruined, this time it would be her mother's fault. Somehow Hazel was sure her mother wouldn't see it that way.

She glanced over her shoulder. Her mother stood on the back steps watching her and made a sweeping motion toward the door. Hazel sighed and pushed as hard as she could. Having been opened and closed a few times, the heavy stone moved a little easier now, but it still took all her weight.

With a deep breath, she stepped inside. The air was ten degrees cooler and still as glass. She shivered. The walls were lined with neat drawers like a filing cabinet. Inside each of the drawers was a body and somehow that bothered her much more than the bodies buried in the ground. Each body had a story, a family, a life. And now here they were stacked up like her canned goods.

How had everything gone so wrong so quickly? Her cover was blown and Mr. Jones knew she was onto him. Her mother had found her stockpile, so now when the bombs were dropped they would have nowhere to go—if The Comrade let her live that long.

She grabbed a bag in each hand and carried them outside. As she set one down, the bottom of the other ripped, sending cans spilling out all over the cemetery. Her mother threw her hands in the air and started back into the house. Hazel couldn't help herself. She stuck out her tongue. Her mother hesitated, then held up a warning finger. Then she continued on her way inside, leaving Hazel gaping and wondering how her mother always seemed to know exactly what she was up to—or figured it out. Her mother should have been a detective.

Hazel scanned the graveyard for Mr. Jones. She was conflicted—a feeling she wasn't used to, and didn't like. On the one hand, she was more certain than ever that Mr. Jones was a spy. On the other hand, her parents had made it clear to her in no uncertain terms that she was to have nothing more to do with him—beyond writing him an apology note for her deplorable behavior. They just couldn't see what kind of danger lurked right in their cemetery.

Hazel started picking up the cans, stacking them three or four high. Lima beans, carrots, Spam, tuna fish. They would have eaten well in the bomb shelter. Hazel could just picture it, all of them sitting around a kerosene lamp, eating out of tin cans. Her parents would have no choice but to talk to her, what with all their horticulture magazines and catalogs still in the house, which was full of toxic air—if it hadn't been blown to smithereens by the blast. *Hazel, we just can't thank you enough. Why, Hazel, without you, we would be dead and glowing. We're so sorry, Hazel, so sorry we doubted you. So sorry that everyone doubted you, Hazel.*

"Hazel!"

Hazel looked up and there was Samuel. "I figured it out," he declared.

"Figured what out?" Hazel asked, picking up a loose can of pitted olives. She detested olives, but her mother loved them.

"The headstone. What was bothering me. There was no moss."

"Yeah, so? You already noticed that."

"That was the red herring. I noted that, and we assumed Mr. Jones had cleaned it."

"We *know* Mr. Jones cleaned it."

"Sure," Samuel said, waving his hand in the air. He looked around then, and noticed all the cans. "What are you doing, anyway?"

"I'm cleaning up cans."

"What about your fallout shelter?"

"My mom has ordered it shut down," she said. She stepped to the side and held out her arm like a conductor ushering a passenger onto a train. "If you go in, bring out a bag."

Samuel walked in, and Hazel followed him. "It's eerie-quiet in here," he said. His voice echoed softly. "Like even the sounds from outside are hushed."

"Way too quiet for my taste," Hazel said.

"It's peaceful," Samuel said, his voice as wistful as a summer rain.

"That's the point," Hazel said. "Anyway, I think it's a little sad all these bodies stacked up like they're in an apartment building or something."

"You wouldn't want to be buried here?"

"Oh, no," she said. "This isn't even really buried, is it? No, I want a shady plot so people are comfortable when they come to see me, and a simple, sturdy casket, and a nice stone with all my accomplishments on it and maybe a statue."

"I think I'd like to be cremated," Samuel said.

"Cremated? Why? Who will have your ashes?"

Samuel shrugged, then bent over and picked up a bag of canned goods. Hazel picked up the other and they went outside.

Cremated. That was just like Samuel, she thought. Even in death he'd try to take up less space. Not her. She decided then and there that she definitely wanted a sculpture. It would be her, but done classically, like the Greeks. She would be dressed as Athena, the goddess of war, with a spear and a shield, and an owl on her shoulder to represent her wisdom. She would have to write it all down when she got inside.

"The stone," Samuel said as they began walking toward the house. "That's what I came to tell you about."

"What about it?" Hazel asked.

"I was so distracted by how clean the stone was that I didn't look closely at the letters." He put down his bag of cans and dug his graveyard book out of his satchel. He flipped through to a page with barely legible words. "Think of an old stone. Think of the way the letters are. They're fuzzy around the edges, right?"

"Sure. Wind and rain and everything wear them down."

He flipped through the book to the Alice headstone. "Look at this," he said.

Hazel studied the letters. "Sharp as can be. So?"

"So we were wrong about the dates. We were looking back in the Civil War era, but this is newer."

"But no one has been buried there for decades."

Samuel shook the book at her. "Someone has, Hazel. We need to get back to the library."

Hazel looked at the cans, then at her house. "I'm grounded." She wasn't sure if she wanted to be involved in the mystery anymore. Samuel was right. It wasn't a game. So far she'd been chased with an ax, been grounded, been threatened, and thoroughly angered her parents. Not to mention that she had a Communist spy on her tail. Maybe solving mysteries wasn't all it was cracked up to be.

"You're giving up? I thought you were relentless."

Hazel looked around at the bags of cans. She looked at her stupid saddle shoes. Her parents didn't trust her to make even the most basic of decisions. *No one* trusted her. No one ever let her do anything. Mrs. Ferrigno wouldn't let her play anything but the triangle. Mrs. Sinclair made her sit in the second row. Miss Angus didn't want her on the second or third floor of the library. They all treated her like a baby. Her parents had told her that she needed to grow up, that she had made up the whole thing about Mr. Jones being a spy, that it was all her overactive imagination. She had no proof, they had told her, and was just harassing a nice, quiet man. It's not like she could fall any lower, so she might as well do what she wanted.

"Okay," she said. "But help me with these first."

The Story of Mr. Jones

Hazel kicked one of the rotten apples that had fallen onto the sidewalk outside the library, and it skittled away down the cement, leaving a brown trail behind it. She and Samuel hadn't spoken much on their way to the library, walking side by side with Hazel's bike between them. She still hadn't told him about her confrontation with Mr. Jones the night before. She wanted to, but she worried that he might react the same way her parents had: like she was the one who had done something wrong.

She sighed. And then she sighed again. Then she coughed.

"Are you okay?" he asked.

"What? Yeah, I'm fine. Why?"

"You're making a lot of funny noises."

They reached the apple and she kicked it again. "I made contact with the subject last night."

Samuel stopped walking right at the base of the stairs. "You what?"

Then it all spilled out of her and she didn't even care who might have heard her. "He was in the graveyard last night, only I didn't know it was him. I thought it was Maryann and when I got there he was creepy and I screamed and my parents came but they didn't believe me."

"Wow," Samuel said.

"Exactly." She bit her lip. "There's something else you need to know."

"What's that?"

"I told him that we know his secret. I told him that I knew about Alice, about everything. It just slipped out. I didn't mention you by name, of course, but he is a spy, and it wouldn't be too hard for him to figure out who my associates are."

"Associate," Samuel said. "Singular."

"Associate," Hazel agreed glumly.

He shook his head. "I really hope that you are wrong about this man."

"Why?"

"I wouldn't want a spy coming after us. Come on, let's go do this in a safe manner. For once."

They went up the stairs and Hazel pulled open the heavy wooden door. Together they walked to the third floor. On the way inside, Hazel had picked up the Burlington papers, plus the *Maple Hill Banner* to find out if there was any new information about the investigation at the plant.

When she spread out the paper, there was Connie's handsome father looking back at her. He still wasn't talking, and the investigators were getting angry. She thought that maybe she ought to try to find the phone number for Senator Joe McCarthy and his Senate Permanent Subcommittee on Investigations and hand the whole big mess over to them. Samuel was right. Now that Mr. Jones knew she was onto him, she wasn't safe. Her whole family wasn't safe. As a matter of fact, he could be at the house right now with her parents tied up, waiting for her to come home so he could send them all to Siberia. She bet her parents would be regretting that they hadn't believed her.

The only problem was, she didn't know how to find the phone number for Senator McCarthy or the FBI, and the only person she could think to ask was Miss Angus. She tried to come up with a good cover story. Maybe she could tell Miss Angus that they were doing career exploration and she wanted to be an FBI agent. She didn't know if women were allowed to be agents, though. If not, she would fix that. She could be the first woman FBI agent. That would certainly be exciting and noteworthy. She was imagining herself being sworn in when Samuel said, "Huh."

"What?" she asked.

"Once I realized that it was a new grave, I decided to search from that angle. I used the indices to find information about Memory's Garden, and look what I found."

He pushed back his chair, and Hazel leaned over to look at

his screen. She saw the photograph first. In it, the man was blurry, as if he were trying to step out of the photographer's frame. His head was tilted down, but his eyes were lifted, so she could see his sorrow. Her parents stood beside him, looking younger, with somber expressions on their faces. The article was dated July 19, 1941, about a year before she was born.

She read:

MAN RETURNS TO HONOR SISTER

Paul Jones returned this week to place a headstone on the grave of his sister. Alice Jones died in 1932 at the age of ten from influenza. At the time, the family could not afford a headstone or a plot. Alice was buried in Pauper's Field.

"When Mr. Jones came and spoke to us about it, I must admit I didn't believe him at first," says Lydia Kaplansky, co-proprietor of Memory's Garden. "Pauper's Field hasn't been used in almost seventy-five years. There were many buried there during the early nineteenth century, but none since the Civil War. Or so we thought."

Mrs. Kaplansky's husband and co-owner, George Kaplansky, chimed in, "When he came and asked about putting in a headstone, we did some research and sure enough there was a notation in

the records. It seems influenza swept through
Maple Hill that year. It being the Depression, many
folks couldn't afford a burial. The town paid for
them to be buried in a little knoll on the edge of
Pauper's Field. None of them have a headstone."

None of them, that is, until now.

Mr. Jones, who now lives in Texas, said he was
just glad that his sister's grave was finally
marked. "It's been weighing on me ever since she
died."

Hazel read the article again. Her body felt heavy. "Well,
that's a disappointment," she said.

"I think it's nice," he said.

"I wasn't looking for nice," she replied. "Of course, this
doesn't actually prove anything."

"Hazel," said Samuel, exasperation edging into his voice.

"Well, sure it explains the headstone, but there's still the
matter of the safes."

"I am sure there's some other sort of explanation. An honest one."

"Maybe." But even as she said it, a sinking feeling came
over her. The sinking feeling of having done something really,
really wrong. Like when she told Becky she didn't know why
she wasted so much time watching the popular girls when
they were never going to let her be one. She was just as bad as
whoever had thrown a brick through the Lis' window. It

was like Miss Lerner had said: she'd gotten all caught up in the rumors, and she hadn't been able to see the truth.

"I told you he wasn't a spy. He's just sad. He came back so he could be near her and watch over her."

"But she's gone," Hazel said. She had gathered all that evidence, and in the end it had amounted to nothing. Maybe she wasn't such a super-sleuth after all. Nancy Drew would never have made this kind of mistake. Mr. Jones was an honorable man. He'd come all the way from Texas, first to get Alice a headstone and then he had returned to be by her grave.

"Not to him she's not." Samuel's voice was hard and Hazel knew she had made him angry again, though this time she had no clue as to why. "I wonder if she even had a real funeral," Samuel added.

"What do you mean?" As far as Hazel was concerned, a real funeral was one in which the body went into the ground.

"Like with an official presiding and folks saying nice things about her."

"I'm not sure," Hazel said.

"Not just her, but all those people. They didn't even mark their graves, Hazel."

Samuel looked near tears again and Hazel was baffled as to why he was so upset; it wasn't like he knew those people. "Headstones are expensive."

Samuel shook his head. Hastily, he rose to his feet. "I've got to go. I'll see you at school tomorrow."

"Okay," Hazel said. "Bye."

She watched Samuel walk away and wanted to call out to say she was sorry, but she didn't know how to apologize when she wasn't even sure what she had done. Instead she took out a piece of paper and a pencil and started working on her apology note to Mr. Jones. It was going to have to be a good one.

Birthday Un-Party

If there was one good thing about being in deep trouble, it was that Hazel would not need to go to Connie's birthday party. Or so she thought. Her mother had a different idea.

Saturday morning Hazel was about to head into the cemetery for more of her forced labor, but her mother stopped her. "Where do you think you're going?"

"Weeding."

"Not this morning you're not."

For a moment Hazel let herself believe that her parents had realized that even though she had made a terrible mistake about Mr. Jones, she had done it with the best intentions. Not to mention that the fallout shelter in the mausoleum had been an expression of love. So, she hoped, her mother was going to tell her that the grounding was over.

"You have a birthday party to attend."

Hazel opened her mouth, but what could she say?

"I've put a dress on your bed. Wear your Mary Janes."

"But they rub my toes funny," Hazel protested.

Hazel's mom raised her eyebrows, and Hazel knew not to argue.

The dress her mother had picked out was plain awful. It had been her Christmas dress the year before. She hated it then, and she hated it now. The white top was made of some sort of stiff, satin-like fabric. There was lace around the collar that itched like red ants were biting her. The skirt had crinoline under it that bunched up every time she sat down. She had grown since the previous year, so now the dress was tight around her chest and belly. She wasn't sure how she was going to be able to breathe. In fact, she just might pass out in the Shorts' living room from lack of oxygen. That would serve her mother right.

When Hazel got downstairs, her mother was looking at the sheet of paper that Hazel had torn out of the notebook—the one labeled "Doctoral Dissertation Ideas."

"What is a dissertation anyway?" Hazel asked.

Her mom jumped a little as if she hadn't been expecting Hazel to be there. "After you finish college, you can keep studying for something called a PhD. It's an advanced degree."

"Oh, Samuel wants to do that."

"He'll make a good candidate, whatever he decides to study. So would you."

"Why do you have a list? Are you going to get one?"

"I thought I was," Hazel's mom said. She put the sheet back down on a stack of papers.

"Did you fail out?" Hazel tugged at the neck of her dress.

Hazel's mom sighed. "No, Hazel, I didn't fail out. I got married."

Hazel wasn't sure how to respond to this. "Because you got married, they wouldn't let you get a PhD?"

"It's not that simple, Hazel."

"But I don't understand what you mean. It's not fair that they didn't let you stay in school."

"It was my choice, Hazel. A PhD takes a long time, and your father and I wanted to start a family."

Hazel looked down at her shiny shoes.

"Oh, Hazel," her mom said. "Sometimes the world isn't set up to give us everything we want. It's changing, and I hope it will be better for you. I just couldn't see a way to be a wife and a mother and an academic. But working here, it gives me a chance to do what I love. Not a lot of women get to do that. Do you understand?" Hazel's mom tousled her short hair the way she had when Hazel was still toddling around spouting nonsense words. "Come on. You're going to be late for the party."

Hazel's mom drove her in the old Ford, but she didn't say anything. She seemed to be looking at some faraway place instead of at the road.

When they pulled into the driveway, her mother reminded

her, "Be sure to say hello to Connie's parents. Don't just eat the junk food. Say thank you. Sing the right words to 'Happy Birthday.'"

"I know, Mom," Hazel said.

"I know you do. But reminding you is my job."

Hazel's mom waited in the car until Hazel was inside. It was the fanciest-looking party Hazel had ever seen. Not that she'd seen all that many parties. There were balloons everywhere, and pink and white streamers twisted and hung around the living room. Dance music played on the record player, but no one was dancing.

No one was dancing because the only other guest there was Ellen Abbott, who sat in an overstuffed armchair with her feet dangling off the edge. Her long hair was pulled into tight braids. Connie herself stood next to a table with chips, vegetables, and dips. She wore a sparkling pink dress, her hair neatly curled, and she was sucking on her lower lip.

"Where is everybody?" Hazel asked.

Connie sniffed, but didn't say anything.

"That's a nice dress, Hazel," Ellen said.

Hazel sighed. "It's not a nice dress. It's a baby dress and it barely fits me. Anyone can see that."

At that, Connie ran out of the room, and a moment later a huge wail came echoing down the hall to them.

Ellen said, "Why do you always have to be such a pill, Hazel Kaplansky?"

Hazel couldn't believe that horsey Ellen Abbott was

calling *her* a pill. Everyone knew the reason they couldn't go on any field trips that year was on account of Ellen Abbott and how she always threw up on the bus.

A moment later, Mr. Short came into the room. His Hawaiian print shirt didn't match the glum expression on his face. "Girls, it seems Connie isn't feeling so well, and I think we're going to cut this party a little short. I'll drive you home."

"I need to use the restroom first," Ellen said.

That was the other thing about Ellen: she had a tiny bladder. She probably went to the bathroom six times a day.

"Right down the hall on the left," Mr. Short said, pointing.

With Ellen gone, Hazel was alone with Mr. Short. She still had one big, nagging question, and she figured it was now or never. "Mr. Short, why'd you bring all those safes over to Mr. Jones?"

Mr. Short didn't look surprised or guilty. "He was unlocking them. When folks lose their keys, they can send the safes back to us. We're supposed to keep duplicates and master keys on hand for all the different kinds of safes, but sometimes something's gone wrong with the lock, or we're missing the key. Mr. Jones can pick the lock."

Maybe she hadn't been 100 percent wrong about Mr. Jones after all. "Because he's a thief?" she asked.

For the first time, Mr. Short lifted his sad eyes to look at her. "No, Hazel. He's not a thief. He has locksmith training."

"It seems like you ought to have a locksmith on hand in the factory."

"We do. But Chuck's getting older, and his hands don't work so well."

"So fire him and hire Mr. Jones."

Mr. Short took a sip from his caramel-colored drink. "I don't suppose your parents would like that much. Anyway, Chuck's been there forever, and he's in the union. You can't get rid of a union man just because someone better comes along."

Hazel nodded. She didn't know a lot about unions, only that the folks who worked at a place banded together to make sure the owners treated them right. "Aren't you the head of the union?"

"I am."

"And that's why they're investigating you, right, because of union ties with the Communists?"

Mr. Short sputtered on his drink. "Well, now—"

"It's okay, you can tell me. I'm good at keeping secrets."

Mr. Short put his drink down and ran his fingers through his hair. "It's no secret. All this talk about Communists in our plants—it's not about finding threats to the United States, it's about busting up the unions. Why, at the GE plant they've all jumped ship already. I haven't done anything wrong, and neither has anyone else at the factory."

"You ought to just tell the investigators that."

Mr. Short sighed. "If I talk, then other guys who plead the Fifth, they look guilty for *not* talking."

"Why can't you all just tell the truth?"

"Times like this, the truth has a way of getting twisted." He looked out at the empty living room. The balloons and streamers seemed a lot less festive. Hazel and Mr. Short were both so quiet, thinking their own thoughts, that Hazel could hear the ice in his drink cracking.

Rumor, whisper, lie, Hazel thought. And she'd been just as bad as everyone else in town.

The Story of Samuel

After Mr. Short steered his blue Packard into her driveway, Hazel waved good-bye and waited for him to pull out. Then she jumped on her bike. Her parents thought she was at the party, and she was going to use that time as best she could. She needed to find Samuel, to let him know about the safes. She couldn't go to his house, though; they still weren't supposed to spend too much time together. She hoped he might be at the library.

Inside the library, she cruised by Miss Angus, who was putting *The Catcher in the Rye* on a display shelf. "Walking feet, Hazel!" Miss Angus called out. Hazel slowed down until she reached the stairs, which she took two at a time. There were a few families downstairs, and Timmy was sitting in a corner reading a book, which was strange because she had never, ever seen him read a book before.

Breathless, she found Miss Lerner. "Have you seen Samuel?" she asked.

"Good afternoon to you, too."

"I'm sorry. I just need to find Samuel. It's about, it's about a project we've been working on."

"I haven't seen him all day. But I'm glad you stopped in. Do you have a minute?"

"Sure," Hazel replied.

"Come with me."

Miss Lerner put her hand on Hazel's back and led her around behind her desk to a little office. Hazel's heart began to flutter. This was it. Her lowest moment was about to become her highest. Her exceptional intelligence was finally being recognized and she was going to be honored with a position on the library staff. Miss Lerner shut the door. "Would you like some tea?" she asked.

Hazel considered it. She thought it would be quite librarianish to drink a cup of tea in the afternoon, but she was far too excited. "No, thank you," Hazel replied. She scanned the room. The office looked fairly normal: a desk, a chair, an electric teakettle, and stacks of magazines with pictures of book covers on them.

"Sorry about the mess," Miss Lerner said.

"Oh, it doesn't bother me," Hazel told her. "In fact, I believe that a cluttered desk is the sign of a busy mind. My desk is quite cluttered, too. It drives my mom crazy, and it probably didn't help when I told her this quote I read once: 'Dull women keep immaculate houses.'"

"Interesting."

"Thank you."

"So. How are you these days?" she asked.

"Fine," Hazel replied. "How are you?" She was truly perplexed now. Maybe this wasn't the job offer she had expected. Had Miss Lerner called her back for some sort of social visit? Maybe she was being invited to a special reading club for the truly brilliant. Oh, Samuel would be jealous! Unless of course Samuel was already a part of the reading club. In which case, well, she would still want to join, but it did make it a little less special. She wondered what kind of books they read. The thick ones, she decided, the ones with the worn brown covers and the funny smell that were always in the stacks.

"You haven't been around the library much lately."

"I've been busy," Hazel said. "Samuel and I *have* been to the library, actually. We've been up to the third floor. I'm quite adept on the microfilm machine."

"I'm glad you brought up Samuel," Miss Lerner said. "He's actually who I wanted to talk with you about today."

Hazel slumped a little. So he was in the secret club already, and she was just an afterthought. Perhaps he had even suggested that she be invited since he knew she was feeling bad about the whole Mr. Jones thing. Oh, that would be the worst—to be included out of sympathy!

"It's a hard thing to talk about. To explain. To begin." She cleared her throat. "I went to school with Samuel's mother, Lacey Switzer. We were good friends." She played with the locket that hung around her neck; Hazel wondered if it had a picture of Mr. Bowen in it. "Back then, people sometimes judged other people by where they were from, what jobs their parents had, how much money. It wasn't right, but that's the way it was."

Hazel didn't know why Miss Lerner was talking like that attitude was all in the past. It was still like that. She and Samuel were living proof.

"Lacey was, well, she's a Switzer. Samuel's father was Randy Butler."

Hazel wondered if that was the same Randall who had picked Mrs. Buttersbee's blackberries.

"Randy's dad sometimes worked shifts at the factory, but mostly he sat around the house or the VFW. He'd been injured in World War I, folks said, and never recovered. So Randy never had much direction from home, you know. He was always getting into little scrapes. No one in the high school— no one in all of Maple Hill—understood what Lacey saw in him. She never talked about it, just got this kind of dewy glow in her eyes. Maybe she thought she could save him. Personally, I always thought she was doing it to make her parents mad."

Hazel looked down at the patterned carpet. Miss Lerner was talking the same way she'd just said was wrong: judging Randy for his family situation.

"It all happened so fast. One thing after another. There's no easy way to say this. This is an adult conversation. Do you think you're ready?"

All her life she'd been longing for adult conversation, but now that she was on the brink, she didn't know if she wanted to hear what Miss Lerner had to say. But she couldn't *not* hear it. Not after all the whispers and innuendos. It was her nature, the very core of it, to need to know everything that anyone else knew. She was still wearing her party dress, and it seemed to be constricting around her torso, making it hard to breathe. Hazel nodded.

"Lacey made a mistake. She did something nice girls don't normally do. Don't *ever* do."

"She cursed?" Hazel asked.

Miss Lerner gave a quick smile, but then she shook her head. "Lacey was, well, she was with child. Samuel." She hesitated. "Lacey and Randy weren't married, you see."

Hazel rocked back. "Oh," she said. It all made sense now. The secret. The way people talked about Samuel. How they looked at him. His mother had been unmarried when she had him. Unmarried and still in high school. She could practically hear the cackles and whispers of women like Mrs. Wood and Mrs. Logan.

"It was winter when she told me, right before Valentine's Day. By that point, Randy was already gone."

"Gone?" Hazel asked. "Gone where?"

"Like a lot of boys, he enlisted after Pearl Harbor. School didn't hold much for him, so he dropped out and joined up. He figured it was the best way he could give a good life to Lacey. They planned to get married when he came back. Only he didn't come back."

"He was killed?"

Miss Lerner nodded. "He never even knew she was pregnant."

Hazel could picture a man-sized Samuel away in Europe or Japan, lonely in his bunker, missing Samuel's mother. And then he was gone. How different Samuel's life would have been had he come back. Hazel didn't have any words for the saddest story she had ever heard.

"The Switzers sent Lacey away. They said she was off to a finishing school down South, but everyone knew the truth. She came back with the baby. The Switzers didn't even bother to try to hide it. She didn't stick around for long. It's hard to say she was ever even here. I went over a few times to try to talk with her, to play with the baby. She was there, but she was—"

"Empty," Hazel finished for her, thinking of how Samuel had described his mother.

"Yes. That's a good way to put it. Then she and the baby disappeared. People said she came back to Maple Hill from time to time. You'd sometimes see the light in her turret. But no one ever saw her in person. And now Samuel is here. You understand, don't you, how much he's been through?"

"Yes. He needs a friend." Hazel felt low about how she'd been treating him. What happened with his parents, it was a tragedy—and it wasn't his fault. But everyone at school—everyone in town—was talking about him and making assumptions about what kind of boy he must be, just because of one mistake his parents made.

"Yes, definitely, but I can also tell you what he doesn't

need. He doesn't need to be going around graveyards digging up old stories. He doesn't need to be caught up in any silliness."

Hazel felt her cheeks flush: Miss Lerner thought she was silly, that she and Samuel had just been playing a game. But there was more to it than that, and more to Hazel. She stood up. "Thank you, Miss Lerner," she said. It was no use to try to explain that Samuel hadn't gotten the idea from her; poking around in graveyards was what he did. She heard what Miss Lerner was saying: Samuel needed a friend, but he didn't need her.

Hazel rolled her bike off the sidewalk and onto the street and hopped on. She had all these stories churning around in her head. There was Mr. Jones with his lost sister and Samuel with his lost father. She had never lost anyone and yet just thinking about it made her sad. Soon her stomach was roiling as much as her head and she wished she were back home under her covers never having learned the truth of any of this. The truth was just too heavy sometimes.

She'd only gone a block when she realized her tire was flat. Again. She got off the bike and started pushing it in the direction of Wall's Garage. As she walked, her shin hit the pedal and she said one of the words her mother told her never to say, and she got angrier and angrier at her dad and his promises to fix the tire. He would fix it, she thought, if it had flowers growing out of it. He would fix it if it had a Latin name.

Then, as if someone had come from behind and shoved her, she thought: *Samuel doesn't have anyone to get angry at.*

Instead of making her feel better, the thought made her feel small, and even angrier, though now the anger was directed at herself, which was an entirely uncomfortable emotion.

She staggered into Wall's Garage feeling as heavy as cement.

"Hello there!" Mr. Wall said. "Don't you look nice today!" He was sitting on a folding lawn chair just outside his office, toothpick jutting out from between his lips.

"Hey, Mr. Wall," she replied, unable to keep the glum out of her voice. She was sure he was going to ask what was wrong. She would tell him that everything was fine, and he would say good, because adults often asked if things were all right, but really they just wanted to hear that you were okay.

Instead, though, he looked at her and looked at her bike. "You know, Hazel, not that I mind seeing you so often, but I could fix your tire if you'd like."

"My dad's going to do it. Someday."

Mr. Wall hesitated. "Of course. Then again, it's awfully quiet here today. I haven't practiced my tire-fixing skills in a while. You'd be doing me a favor."

Hazel knew that Mr. Wall wasn't being entirely honest. But he also wasn't lying. "Okay," she replied.

"Bring her on in."

She pushed her bike into the place where the cars normally went. Mr. Wall came out with a toolbox and a small piece of black rubber. After removing the wheel, he used a screwdriver to wedge her tire off the wheel frame. Hazel sat down on the little cart that Mr. Wall used to slide under cars to work on them.

"It's a slow leak," she told him. This much her dad had explained to her.

"When I'm done, it will be a no-leak." He grinned at her and she wanted to grin back, but she couldn't, what with all the churning and the roiling.

Hazel used her heels to roll herself back and forth, back and forth. She held her skirt up so it didn't brush against the grease- and oil-stained floor. "Mr. Wall, have you ever known someone and then found out something about them that made you think about them in a whole different way?"

Mr. Wall measured out a patch and cut it. "I guess we've all had that happen at some point in time."

Hazel nodded. "I guess so."

He put some sticky stuff on the tire, then laid the patch over it.

He held the screwdriver in his mouth, so when he spoke, his words sounded like they were bent at odd angles. "I guess the important thing to remember, though, is that you have to think about who they are to you, and who they might be, not who they were."

Hazel thought on that for a little while. She spun the trolley in little circles. "And if you'd been mean to them because you didn't know the whole story? Like what if their past actually did matter and what you found out made you realize that you had them wrong all along?"

He held his hand on the patch so that it would set. "That is a trickier thing."

"It is."

He looked down at his patch, nodded, then started to put the tire back on the wheel. As he maneuvered it onto the frame he said, "It can never hurt to come clean." He put the wheel back on the bike, making sure to tighten all the bolts. "There you go. Good as new. Just fill it up with air and away you'll go."

"Thanks, Mr. Wall."

"Thank you," he replied.

She rolled the bike out to the air pump, filled up the tire, and was on her way.

Hazel got home before the party would have ended, so she looked for her parents in the office. Her mom was sitting in the desk chair eating an apple with one of her old textbooks on her knees. "Mr. Short drove me home," Hazel announced.

"That was nice of him. Did you thank him?"

Hazel couldn't remember if she had or not, but she said yes, and then she went upstairs and changed out of her dress, making sure to hang it up in the closet, and put on dungarees and a T-shirt. She walked out through the graveyard past the Three Graces. "Not today, Abitha. I'm not in the mood."

She kept going until she got to her favorite tree, and climbed up it, then nestled herself in the crook. The bark felt hard against her back and she kept shifting to try to get comfortable. She looked down at her house. There was a light on in the office. Maybe her parents were meeting with a family and there would be another grave soon, another life tucked away into Memory's Garden.

She let her legs hang down and leaned forward so she was lying across the branch. She put her cheek down on the bark and let it press in. *What is wrong with me*, she wondered, *that Miss Lerner thinks I might damage Samuel? Is he so fragile, or am I so rough?*

Out of the corner of her eye, she caught some movement. Lifting her head, she saw Mr. Jones in Pauper's Field. He stood by Alice's headstone holding a small stuffed animal. He looked up to the sky before bending over and placing it next to the grave.

When he was gone, Hazel dropped out of the tree, her canvas sneakers crunching the leaves. With a glance toward the house, she rushed over to the headstone. The stuffed animal was a mouse with pink ears, white whiskers, and shiny green eyes. Hazel knew that mice didn't have green eyes, no more than a rabbit would have one ear flopping down, but it didn't matter.

That's when Hazel knew what she had to do.

The First Apology

Hazel came right home from school on Monday and waited on the back stoop for Mr. Jones. When she saw him come over the rise with a shovel on his shoulder, she jumped to her feet. She began with confidence, but with every step her intensity waned. Just as she was about to turn back, Mr. Jones spotted her. His eyes narrowed as he regripped the shovel in his hand.

"I was wrong," she said.

"You certainly were," he replied.

"You must admit that Paul Jones is an entirely dubious name," she told him.

"You'll have to take that up with my parents."

This was not going as she had planned. She had expected him to be so grateful, so relieved that it was all a big misunderstanding, that he would clap her on the back and they would laugh, and he would admire her for being so keenly aware of potential threats, even if she had been wrong about this particular one. "Plus you did arrive right before the investigations started."

"Seems they caught on rather quick if that was the case," Mr. Jones said. "You mustn't have thought I was much of a spy."

Hazel reddened. "I'm sorry. I didn't mean any offense."

Mr. Jones raised his eyebrows, but he let her comment drop. "I bet you dollars to doughnuts there ain't any spies working in a graveyard."

Hazel was torn between wanting to ask what "dollars to doughnuts" meant, and telling him that "ain't" wasn't a proper way to speak.

"The point is, my conclusion flowed from available evidence."

"Such as?" he demanded. He placed the tip of the shovel in the ground and leaned on the handle.

"Such as your name."

"You mentioned that. Though I suppose it's only fair to tell you that it's actually Paul Jankowski."

Hazel's eyebrows shot up. That sure sounded like a Russian name.

"It's Polish," he said, as if he'd read her mind. "Like Kaplansky, correct?"

Hazel nodded.

"My parents changed it when we came over. Wanted to blend in."

"So you're not actually an American?"

"Naturalized," he said. "Go on. What else have you got on me?"

"Well, it was suspicious that you were receiving property from Mr. Short and storing it in our garden shed, but I found out it was safes and Mr. Short told me why you had them."

"So you were the imp who broke my lock."

"A good detective does what she has to do."

"As far as I can tell, you had nothing but circumstantial evidence. Nothing that would hold up in a court of law."

"I didn't need it to hold up in a court of law. I just needed to have enough evidence to call in the FBI." Hazel frowned. "For example, I saw you steal an American flag from Soldier's Field."

"It was tattered. I replaced it. You can go check if you want."

"My other piece of evidence is that you've been rather suspect in your behavior around Alice's grave. You even put that doll, the whatchamacallit, the Russian nesting doll, on her grave."

"Well, there you might have a slight something, but the truth is, that was hers. I stole it years ago, just to be a pest, and figured it was about time I gave it back." His shoulders drooped, and he said, "All right. That's enough of this game. Just leave us be."

Hazel dug her toe into the dirt. "I need your help," she said.

"My help? You thought I was a Russian spy, and you nearly lost me my job, and you're coming to me for my help?"

"I read the story in the paper. I found out what really happened. I'm sorry about your sister. My parents say I'm not supposed to talk to you anymore. Not to bother you."

"So what's this?"

"I'm saying I wouldn't ask if I didn't need it. It's for a friend."

"Ah," he said, his face still not giving anything away.

The story spilled out of Hazel. She told Mr. Jones what Miss Lerner had told her about Samuel's parents, how he had lost his father and his mother. She told Mr. Jones that Samuel had never believed that Mr. Jones was a spy, and that he felt bad about what they'd done. So did she. Then she told him about her idea.

He let it all settle for a moment. The story had taken a long time to tell, and the sky was turning golden orange. Hazel shivered in the evening air.

"Okay," Mr. Jones said. "I'll help you."

36

Interviews & Stakeouts

Samuel had taught her his way of research, but Hazel still preferred hers: interviews and stakeouts. She took her Mysteries Notebook and rode her bike around town asking questions. She noted everything in the book, and she kept a list of all her witnesses. She started at the library. She'd heard Miss Lerner's story, but now she talked to Miss Angus. She pulled open the wooden doors and walked straight to the reference desk. "Miss Angus, I have a question," she announced.

Miss Angus pushed aside a stack of books she had been examining. "Reference services for children are provided in the lower level, as you are well aware, Hazel Kaplansky."

Hazel stood her ground. "I already spoke to Miss Lerner. I need a second opinion."

"I don't trade in opinions. I trade in facts."

"Then I need more facts to complete the picture." She

tugged on the straps of her knapsack and explained what she wanted to know.

Miss Angus tucked her pencil into her bun. "Let's sit a spell." They sat at a table with a green reading lamp that made her notebook paper look almost yellow.

Miss Angus looked at her expectantly.

"So, Miss Angus, I just want to know what you remember."

"I suppose the best thing is to tell the story from beginning to end." Hazel had to write quickly to keep up with Miss Angus's quick pace.

"Thanks, Miss Angus," Hazel said as she closed her notebook.

"It's Mrs. Angus, Hazel."

Hazel had never known there was a Mr. Angus, and she immediately wondered who he was, where he was, and what he was like. She imagined him as tall and as slim as Mrs. Angus, and the two of them walking around the house raising single eyebrows and shushing each other. Before she could ask about him, though, Mrs. Angus added, "You ought to go see Mr. Wall. He'd be a terrific primary source for this project." So Hazel got on her bike and rode to his garage.

"Hello there, Hazel," he said.

She hopped off her bike while it was still rolling. "Hi, Mr. Wall."

"Don't tell me your tire is flat again."

"No, sir, you fixed it up right," she said, shaking her head. "Actually, there's something I wanted to talk to you about."

"I always love a conversation with you, Hazel." He brought

out another lawn chair, and they sat side by side. He got her a soda out of the icebox, but she hardly had time to drink it from writing down all that he was saying. The sun was way up in the sky and she had to squint against the brightness of the white paper of her notebook. She'd filled two pages with Mrs. Angus, and now she was going to fill three or four more. She'd been right all along that interviews were the way to go.

"That everything?" she asked when he stopped talking. She took two big swigs of the soda.

"It's never everything, Hazel, but that's a good start. You should go see Mrs. Buttersbee."

With a giant gulp, she finished the bottle. "Thanks for the soda."

"Anytime."

She rode past the houses in her town, houses she had seen hundreds of times, every day for her whole life, and had never thought of all the stories that were contained inside of them. Each one had several people, each person had countless memories. All the memories laced together to make the story.

She turned down the cul-de-sac where Mrs. Buttersbee lived, then left her bike leaning against the porch.

When Mrs. Buttersbee answered, she looked confused. "It's not Halloween again, is it?"

Hazel shook her head. "I came to ask you about the past. Do you have time?"

"Time and the past are all I have these days," Mrs. Buttersbee said, laughing to herself.

She led Hazel into her house and told her to sit on an

overstuffed couch with a pink-and-green floral pattern. "Let me get you a drink," she said. "Some tea?"

The soda was still sloshing in her stomach, so she said, "No, thank you." But Mrs. Buttersbee toddled out all the same, and came back with a glass full of cider. "Left over from Halloween," she explained.

Hazel took it and said thank you. Then she put the glass on a coaster on the wicker coffee table. She opened up her notebook. Before she could ask a question, though, Mrs. Buttersbee pulled out a thick scrapbook and began paging through it. "I keep track of everything. All the comings and goings."

"That's real nice," Hazel said. "But actually there's a specific part of the past that I wanted to ask you about."

"Of course," Mrs. Buttersbee said, still flipping through the book. Hazel saw page after page of yellowed newspaper articles and white bordered photographs.

"Mr. Wall said—"

"Little Charlie Wall?"

"I guess so."

Mrs. Buttersbee smiled. "Little devil, that one."

"He told me—"

"There," Mrs. Buttersbee said. She put her finger down on a newspaper clipping that showed a picture of a young woman in a graduation gown. The headline read: "Local Scholar Off to Smith. Full Scholarship." Hazel looked at the picture, forehead furrowed, then read the name under the picture: "Lydia Tenley."

Hazel's eyes grew wide. "That's my mom?"

The girl—her mother—held her diploma tightly in her hand. She had a grin that stretched so far across her face it seemed to touch her ears. She'd been top in her graduating class and was off to Smith College in Massachusetts. She wanted to study science, biology, probably, and maybe become a doctor. That's what she told the reporter, anyway.

"This can't be right," Hazel said. "If she was going to be a doctor, how'd she end up back here?"

"What's wrong with here?" Mrs. Buttersbee asked.

Hazel shook her head. It would take her days, weeks, to explain why she was going to get out of Maple Hill as soon as she could and see the world. It seemed like her mom could have done that, but instead came back to work in the graveyard. And she seemed happy. It didn't make any sense. "Can I take this?" Hazel asked. "I'll bring it back."

"Oh, keep it," Mrs. Buttersbee said, patting her hand. "I'm sure you'll value it more than I do."

"There's someone else I want you to tell me about."

Mrs. Buttersbee smiled when Hazel said the name. She flipped through the book to show a picture of a young man in uniform. He had a serious expression and yet there was some twinkling in his eyes and a slight upturn of his smile that made Hazel think he was a happy man. "What do you want to know?" Mrs. Buttersbee asked.

When Hazel got home, she found her mother in the office with a pencil tucked behind her ear and a pile of bills in front of her as she tapped information into the adding machine. Hazel stood in the doorway for a moment before her mother said, "What is it, Hazel?"

"Mrs. Buttersbee gave me this newspaper article." Hazel extended the yellowing paper to her mother. It wavered a moment in the space between them.

Hazel's mom looked at the picture for a full minute, maybe more. It was like her emotions were a movie playing across her face, one right after the other.

"I never knew you were so smart," Hazel said.

Hazel's mom lifted her gaze and looked right at Hazel, and Hazel thought, *This is it, I'm really going to get it this time.* But instead her mom just started laughing. "Oh, Hazel," she said once she finally had control of herself. "Where do you think you get it from?"

Hazel took a few steps so she was standing right next to her mother's desk. "I don't understand it. You had all these dreams, and you wound up back here."

Her mom looked down. "I fell in love with your father. He had this job. It was steady and secure. It made sense for us to start a family."

"You didn't become a doctor because of me?"

"It was nothing like that. By that time, I didn't even want to be a doctor, not a medical one. I wanted to be a professor of horticulture."

"I still don't understand."

"It's complicated, Hazel."

"Why do grown-ups always say that?"

"Sometimes in life you have to make choices. I wanted marriage and a family and a career. And I got all of that. In spades. It might not be my dream career, but it's something."

Hazel pursed her lips. She still didn't understand why her mother had made the choice she had. "Well, I think I'm going to choose differently."

"I know you will, Hazel," her mom said. "The world is open to you; you just have to take it. It wasn't always like that. Anyway, why were you at Mrs. Buttersbee's? You're still grounded, you know."

Hazel was tired of lies and subterfuge, so she told her mother her plan. At the end, her mom said, "Hazel, this may be the first of your big schemes that isn't hare-brained. I'm proud of you."

"Does that mean I'm not grounded anymore?"

"Temporary reprieve through Thursday. Now go tell your father it's going to be another night at Li's."

"Sure! Of course!" Hazel started for the door. She stopped and glanced over her shoulder. "It's not too late, Mom. You can go back to school and get that doctorate degree."

Her mother smiled, looked down at the mess in front of her, and said, "What? And leave all this behind?" She laughed.

Sometimes her mother's jokes made no sense at all.

The Second Apology

Thursday after school, Hazel rushed home. She had a lot of work to do. After she got into her dungarees, she went outside and found Mr. Jones, who was just finishing putting a small headstone into the ground on the edge of Soldier's Field. He patted the dirt down hard around it. "It's perfect," Hazel told him.

"Told Mr. Winthrop down at the monument yard that you'd come by and help him sort granite stones."

"Sure, of course," Hazel said. She crouched down and began weeding the area while Mr. Jones loosed a chrysanthemum plant from its pot and placed it in the ground. They had decided upon chrysanthemums because Hazel thought they were strong and steady.

As they worked, Hazel kept stealing glances at him.

"If you have something to ask me, go ahead and do so," he finally said.

And so, the first question that popped into her mind she let fall out of her mouth. "Why did you have an ax that day?"

Mr. Jones squinted and pointed to the fence he'd been mending. "It was a tree on the other side. A branch kept growing crooked and so I cut it off to keep the fence whole. What did you think it was for?"

Hazel blushed. "Oh, that was about what I'd expected."

Mr. Jones raised his eyebrows. "Was it, now?"

"Yes," she said, nodding as if that would make it more true. "Where'd you get the limp?" she asked.

"I joined the army. I went abroad—back to Poland of all places—and got hurt."

"Were you shot? Did you find yourself behind enemy lines, alone and afraid?"

He shook his head. "Nothing like that. I'm no war hero. We were trying to repair a broken bridge and some materials fell on my leg. About near crushed it."

"Oh," Hazel said, unable to hide the disappointment in her voice.

"Now I have a question for you," he said. "Fair is fair, after all."

"Okay," she said.

"Why do you spend all your time here in this graveyard?"

"I've got nowhere else to be. No one else to see."

"You've got that boy," he said. "Why else would we be doing all this work?"

She let that settle in a little. "Some people think that Samuel is about to break. And I guess I don't have a history of being too careful with things."

"What do you think?" he asked.

"I think he's stronger than people give him credit for. But I think maybe they're right about me."

"Well, then, it seems to me that you ought to let Samuel decide for himself what he wants to do. And as for you, there's no rule that you have to stay the same way forever."

Hazel patted the dirt down around the base of the flowers. "I don't know how else to be."

"It's not a how else," he said. He dug the edge of the shovel into the ground. "It seems to me like you're a smart girl, but maybe you get ahead of yourself." He looked at her meaningfully. "Like maybe you make up some stories about people you don't even know, and get so wrapped up in them you can't see the truth when it's right in front of you."

Hazel kept patting the ground even though it was perfectly flat. She had always thought that she was exceptionally good at seeing the truth of things even when no one else could—*especially* when no one else did.

"But it's that first part that's important. You're smart, Hazel. Use that brain of yours. Think before you act." He stood up and brushed his hands off on his pants. "Like this. This is thinking."

"Really?"

"I wish someone'd done something like this for me and

Alice, I can tell you that much," he said. "Now go get changed; you have a funeral to run."

Hazel's invitation list had started small: Samuel, Mrs. Sinclair, Miss Lerner and Mrs. Angus from the library, and her parents. Plus Samuel's grandmother, but that was just out of politeness and she felt certain Mrs. Switzer wouldn't come. As she'd made her preparations, though, her list had grown. When she emerged from the cottage wearing a black skirt and white blouse, the whole group was gathered by the cemetery gates, dressed in black as she'd instructed. As she'd expected, though, Mrs. Switzer wasn't there. Samuel stood in the center, dwarfed by all the adults, looking small and alone.

"Follow me," she said. Miss Lerner gave her a warning look. If her eyes were telegraphs, they would be signaling, "He doesn't need this silliness." But Hazel ignored her and led the group to the grave where Mr. Jones stood next to Father Paul. Mr. Jones, too, was now dressed in black. In his suit, Hazel thought he was almost handsome, in a Humphrey Bogart sort of a way.

"Dearly beloved," Father Paul intoned. The adults shifted their feet. Hazel glanced at Mr. Jones, who nodded in encouragement. "We are gathered here today to say good-bye to Randy Butler."

Samuel blinked rapidly.

"Randy was taken from us many years ago, but those of us in Maple Hill who knew him never had a chance to formally mourn his passing. Thanks to Hazel, we now have that chance. I'd like to begin with a passage from Psalms. 'The Lord is close to the brokenhearted; he rescues those whose spirits are crushed.' As we pay our respects to Randy, his family—both those who are here and those who cannot be—they should know that the Lord is always with us, especially in times of sorrow. We cannot always see him, but we can see those who do his work." He turned to Hazel. "I believe you've arranged for some eulogies."

Hazel pulled out a sheet of paper, the results of her investigation. Some people remembered him as Miss Lerner had, but others had different stories. The paper rustled in her hands as she began speaking. "Randy Butler was a good man," she said. "He liked to work on cars with his best friend, Charlie Wall." Mr. Wall nodded. Hazel turned next to Mrs. Buttersbee, who was holding on tight to Mr. Jones's arm. "In the winter, he would shovel the driveway for his neighbor Mrs. Buttersbee. In the summer he'd pick the blackberries from her bushes and she'd make him jam."

Mrs. Buttersbee said, "He always said it was the best jam he'd ever tasted."

"He liked to drive out to the quarry and go swimming in the summer, too, and he was never afraid to jump from the highest ledges. He liked to go to the library and read books with Mrs. Angus about folks caught out in the wilderness."

Mrs. Angus stepped forward. She had a book wrapped in

brown paper. "This was one of his favorites," she said, and handed it to Samuel. Samuel took it and held it close to his small body.

"He took care of his dad, who couldn't take care of himself." Hazel was afraid to look at Samuel. She thought she heard him crying. "And he loved Lacey Switzer. And Lacey Switzer loved him." Hazel turned then to Mrs. Rushby, who had tears in her eyes. The smell of smoke from the chimney of the house filtered out to them.

Mrs. Rushby cleared her throat. "I lived next door to Lacey Switzer and she was like a little sister I never had." She looked at Miss Lerner and at Hazel's mom. "I still remember the night Lacey came and told me she'd kissed Randy. I thought she was pulling my leg because they were so different. But then she started talking to me about his eyes, and his hands, and a poem he had read to her, and I knew she was in love." Mrs. Rushby rubbed her eyes. "They planned to get married, even before you were in the picture, Samuel. You need to know that your parents loved each other. They were excited to get married. Lacey was excited to have you, and I'm sure your father would have been over the moon. I didn't know your dad well, but I do know that he didn't mean to leave you behind. That if he could be here, he would. And so would your mom. If she could."

As Mrs. Rushby spoke, Hazel heard someone crunching through the leaves behind her. She turned and there was Mrs. Switzer, dressed in black and holding a white carnation.

Samuel stood at the foot of the grave, his head tilted down, but Hazel could still see the tears on his face. His body shook but he made no sound. Maybe she had made a terrible mistake. Maybe this was all wrong.

Mrs. Switzer stepped forward then. She leaned over, shaking a bit, and placed the carnation on the grave. Then she turned, and Samuel fell into her arms and she hugged him close.

Hazel's parents walked around and held Hazel to them just as tightly. Her mom was crying. This was not how she had pictured it at all. All this crying, all this emotion raw on people's faces. She wanted it to be a proper funeral, just like Samuel had asked for. "I'm sorry," she said. "I'm sorry, I thought this would help. I thought—"

"I know," her mother said. "You did good."

City of the Dead

From her perch in the tree Hazel could see the site of Samuel's father's grave. The chrysanthemums stood out against the grass like bright bits of confetti, and Hazel wondered if she had made the wrong choice in the yellows, oranges, and purples. She should have done something quiet and sophisticated, like white snapdragons.

She pulled one knee up and put her foot flat on the tree branch, then she put her cheek on her knee. She figured if someone saw her from afar, this position would show them just how melancholic she was. But there was no one to see her. Everyone had gone home.

The funeral had seemed like a terrific idea. She had wanted to give Samuel a chance to say good-bye. A funeral with folks talking about his dad, just like he had said. She'd wanted him to be able to see his father as others had seen him. But instead she had just made him sad.

She heard a rustling and looked down to see her father climbing the tree. The top of his head was shiny and pink where he didn't have any hair. "Dad?" she asked.

He looked up through smudged glasses. "Just a sec," he grunted. In a moment he was sitting on a branch opposite her, his arm wrapped tightly around the tree trunk. "This used to be my favorite tree to climb, too," he said.

"It's a good climbing tree," she replied.

He nodded. "It is."

They looked out over Memory's Garden, at all the headstones and the statues, at the paths and the ponds.

"When I was about your age, I used to imagine this place as a city. All the headstones were like the homes. The mausoleums were apartment buildings. And at night, I thought, the people would all come out and mingle and play games."

"You always said there's no such thing as ghosts."

"I wasn't imagining them as ghosts so much. It's hard to explain. I thought of them as people. Real people who came back to life at night."

"Like zombies?"

"No, not zombies. It's more that they got to resume their lives just as they were."

"That doesn't make any sense."

"I'm afraid my imagination was not quite as vivid as yours is. The point is, I used to see things that I took as evidence. I found a baseball once, over by the reflection pool, and was sure that there'd been a ball game the night before. Once I found a woman's necklace. Or I'd see the ground all trampled. Sometimes I'd even hear them when I was lying in my bed. I was sure that if I could just get to the window fast enough I'd spot them, but I never did."

"That's sad," she said. She could feel just how disappointed he must have been.

"Sometimes we want to believe something so badly, we see what we want to see instead of what's there."

Hazel scowled. This sounded like it was coming around to be some sort of lesson. If someone wanted to teach her something, she preferred they just came right out and said it instead of making her puzzle over a story and its deeper meaning. "Sure, Dad," she said.

"Then again, maybe if we believe in something enough, maybe it is real."

Hazel didn't reply. She looked down at her foot on the tree branch. Her sneaker was dirty, stained with grass and the root beer she'd convinced her mother to let her have one summer afternoon. She was never able to keep anything neat and clean for long.

In the neighborhood behind them, a mother called her child home, and the boy replied, "Coming!"

"You did a nice thing today, Hazel. Your mother and I are both proud of you."

"Samuel didn't like it."

"I don't know about that. He may have just been a little overwhelmed." He pushed his glasses back up the bridge of his nose.

"Everyone told me he was fragile. I should have been more careful."

Her dad shifted his weight on his branch, and all the leaves on the end shook like they were waving good-bye. "I think maybe everyone else has underestimated him. Everyone but you."

Hazel lifted her head to look at her dad. He was staring right back at her with his dark brown eyes. "You think?" she asked.

"I do," he said.

They were silent for a moment and then her dad laughed and shook his head.

"What?" she asked.

"I have no idea how I'm going to get down from here."

"Don't worry, Dad. I'll show you."

Simple Gifts

Samuel didn't come to school for most of the week after the funeral, and she could feel the space between them opening like a huge mouth ready to swallow her up. As Mrs. Sinclair talked to them about the solar system, and what made a planet, she wondered if she would ever see him again. Maybe he had run away, back to his mother, or to someplace new altogether. She could see him with his satchel and his strange clothes standing at the side of the road with his thumb out, hitching a ride to a new town, one where people didn't open up your wounds and pour salt in them.

He appeared, though, the night of the music concert. They sat backstage, side by side, while a first-grade class sang "John Jacob Jingleheimer Schmidt" onstage. Neither of them said anything and Hazel felt like she was being pulled into the chasm between them. She never didn't have something to say.

Maryann and Connie sat by their glockenspiels. In the end, Mr. Short had caved in. He'd answered the committee's questions, and given up the names of a few fellow workers who had once been in the Communist Party, and so he got a transfer to a plant down in Georgia. The investigators had packed up shortly after without finding anything or giving out any more names. Hazel thought that the other moms ought to have apologized to her mother, but of course they didn't. It was like Miss Lerner had said—whispers and rumors with nothing to them.

Now that Connie's family had to leave, she and Maryann were friends again, with Maryann declaring it a huge injustice that her best friend be taken from her. They cried daily, it seemed. For the concert they both had their hair pulled back with ribbons and wore brand-new dresses. Hazel was wearing last year's party dress again, and it pinched her under the arms. Timmy sat next to Maryann, pink and quiet, as Maryann babbled on. So even though the spirits hadn't spoken, Timmy had gotten the message. And even though Hazel had no interest in Timmy, she was jealous. Because Maryann got exactly what she wanted. Because everything with Maryann was easy. Because Maryann wasn't sitting next to her best friend paralyzed and afraid to say the wrong thing.

Timmy said something, and then Maryann turned and glared at them. "What are you staring at, triangle girl?" she hissed.

Connie added, "Ding, ding."

Hazel tightened her grip on her triangle.

"Ignore them," Samuel said. "They're stupid."

She nodded. She wanted to say something else. She wanted to say anything, but the words all died on her tongue. Mrs. Ferrigno came back and began ushering them onto the stage, and it was the only time in her life that she would ever be grateful to see Mrs. Ferrigno.

The lights were on them, and there was a hush all around. Hazel hadn't realized how hot it would be, how the lights shimmered off the metal on the instruments, so it looked like camera flashes were going off all around her. She tried to see her parents, but couldn't find them among the blurry faces in the crowd.

Mrs. Ferrigno stood in front of them and began conducting. It was the best they'd ever played, even Hazel could tell that. Her heart beat faster as they got closer to her part. Samuel elbowed her, they dinged, and the song went on. She let out her breath. Just one more ding and this all would be over. No more triangle people.

Samuel's foot was twitching and he shifted in his seat. Hazel wondered if he had to go to the bathroom. Mrs. Ferrigno had warned them to go before they got up on the stage. Twice. "You never know how nerves might pluck your strings!"

Hazel tightened her grip on her rod. Their next ding was coming up. She counted the measures. One, two, three, four, then another measure, one, two, three, four, and—

Samuel stood up. "Triangle solo!" he yelled out, and began banging on his triangle.

Hazel, flabbergasted, stared up at him. *Come on,* he mouthed. So she stood up, too. There are only so many notes that you can play on a triangle, and Samuel and Hazel used them all, dancing around as they hit the different parts of their triangles. Hazel felt her mouth stretching into a grin so wide it hurt her lips. Together and in perfect sync, they dinged out the entire song. She wished she could see the crowd, their reactions. She looked at Samuel, and he was grinning, too. They probably looked like a couple of lunatics. He nodded at her, she nodded back, and they sat down.

The class stared at them, mouths agape. Mrs. Ferrigno, though, tapped her music stand, brought the eyes of the class back to her, and picked up where they'd left off, all the while glaring fire at Hazel and Samuel.

When the song was done, the crowd clapped and Hazel couldn't be sure, but it felt a little more enthusiastic than it had for the other groups.

As soon as they got off stage, Samuel grabbed her hand and pulled her into the hallway. They hid in a little nook under the stairs.

"We can hold off our execution until tomorrow," he said.

"Why didn't you tell me?" she asked. "I could have prepared something."

"I wasn't sure if I could go through with it. I didn't want to disappoint you again. But then Maryann said that triangle people thing, and I knew what I had to do."

Hazel smiled and leaned back against the wall. "Triangle solo," she said, shaking her head. "It really was more of a triangle duet."

"It takes two to triangle," Samuel said.

"Did you just make a joke, Samuel?" she asked.

"I mustard a joke," he replied.

A silence fell over them, a tingly kind of silence that seemed to anticipate something that neither of them was quite aware of. Samuel still had his triangle and he twisted his fingers around it.

"I wanted to talk to you about the funeral," Samuel said.

Hazel's stomach sank into the toes of her navy blue Mary Janes, which her mother had insisted she wear. "Samuel, I—"

"I just wanted to thank you."

"Thank me?"

"It was the nicest thing anyone's ever done for me."

"I thought you hated it. You were crying. I thought you had left town and you were never going to come back and that would mean that in less than two months I would have lost two best friends and, frankly, I just don't think that's a very good track record."

Samuel was shaking his head. "It was just a lot all at once. I was sad. But I was happy, too, to hear how people thought of him, to see what he was really like. No one ever talked to me about him. He was just always gone."

The lights turned on and people began coming out of the auditorium. Parents were congratulating one another over how their children had done.

Hazel heard a booming voice. "Lydia! George! Quite a little star you have there!"

"Oh, well, now—" her dad began.

"Indeed," another voice said. "These things are normally a bore with a capital *B*. But your Hazel and that Switzer kid sure livened things up."

"She is a little spitfire," her dad said.

"That she is," the first voice said. "That she is."

Hazel and Samuel glanced at each other, which was all they could manage before they burst out laughing.

The Final Apology

Samuel arrived at her house on Saturday morning holding a thin package wrapped in brown paper. She wondered what kind of present he had gotten her. She thought perhaps it was just the right size for a nice magnifying glass. Before she could reach out her hands to receive it, he said, "There's one last thing we need to do to close this case."

"There is no case. It was a bust."

His hair had fallen down between his glasses and his eyes, and he pushed it away with his fist. "*Your* case maybe. Not mine. I researched Alice Jones in the library and found out all I could about her. It wasn't much. She won the spelling bee one year, and had a pig in the county fair another. I gathered it all in a book for Mr. Jones."

Hazel shoved her feet into her canvas sneakers. "Come on," she said. "I know just the person we need to go see."

She wouldn't tell him where they were going, because she liked to keep others in suspense, but Samuel figured it out when they started walking up Mrs. Buttersbee's street.

When they arrived at her house, Mrs. Buttersbee didn't seem confused or surprised. "Hazel! Samuel!" she said merrily. "You're right on time for lemonade. I just made it fresh. Folks think of lemonade as a summer drink, but I love it in the fall."

"Sounds great," Hazel said.

They followed Mrs. Buttersbee into her sitting room and sank into the floral couch. Mrs. Buttersbee tottered out, then tottered back in a moment later holding a tray with a pitcher and three glasses. She hummed as she poured. When she handed Samuel his lemonade she said, "You look just like him, you know. Spitting image, they say, though I for one have never cared for that phrase."

Samuel held his glass in two hands and looked down at his lap. "Thanks," he murmured.

Hazel took charge. "Mrs. Buttersbee, we're here on another investigation."

"I figured as much," Mrs. Buttersbee said.

"You did?"

"I was once quite the investigator myself, Hazel Kaplansky." She put her lemonade glass back on the tray and wandered over to her bookshelf. "Why else do you think I would keep all of this?"

Mrs. Buttersbee was making more and more sense the more Hazel got to know her.

"So what is it today, kids? More about your mother, Hazel?"

Hazel shook her head. "No. We're here about Alice Jones."

"Alice Jones?" Mrs. Buttersbee said. "That name isn't ringing any bells." Her fingers hovered over the spines of several scrapbooks.

"She died during the Depression. The flu outbreak."

"Ah," Mrs. Buttersbee said. She used two hands to pull out a black bound book. "That's this volume. Tough few years."

While Samuel flipped through the book, Hazel and Mrs. Buttersbee chatted about people in town. "Shame about that Short family," Mrs. Buttersbee said. "I always thought that Mr. Short was good people."

"He was just doing what he thought he needed to do in order to protect his family. Anyone could make that kind of mistake," Hazel said, glancing at Samuel. "It's understandable. Now, as for his daughter . . ." Mrs. Buttersbee cocked her head to the side, but before she could speak, Hazel said, "And don't tell me she's probably nice underneath, because I've looked underneath, and there's no nice there."

"Oh, I wouldn't dream of saying such a thing." She turned to Samuel. "Take whatever you want out of there. It's doing me no good." Then she turned back to Hazel. "I was a girl once, too, you know, and I knew my share of Connie Shorts."

Samuel transferred several articles from Mrs. Buttersbee's book into the one he'd made for Mr. Jones. "This is a wonderful resource," he told her. "It belongs in the library."

"Oh, no," Mrs. Buttersbee said. "Then why would anyone come to see me anymore?"

Hazel took a long drink of her lemonade. It was cool and light and tasted just like summer, which was perfect, she decided, for November. "I'd come, Mrs. Buttersbee."

Mrs. Buttersbee smiled and then ruffled Hazel's hair, which normally Hazel hated, but she decided that Mrs. Buttersbee was so old and so nice that it was okay. "Come back anytime," she said.

"Do you think she meant it?" Samuel asked as they walked down Mrs. Buttersbee's driveway.

"About the girls? Definitely. I bet there are girls like Mary-ann Wood and Connie Short going all the way back to ancient Greece. Aphrodite, for example. I bet she was all kinds of mean to Athena."

"No, I meant about going back anytime."

"Oh, sure. She loves company." Hazel bent over and scooped up an acorn cap.

"I'm going to find out all their stories. All the people buried with Alice."

"How are you going to do that?" She pressed the acorn cap onto her thumb, then wiggled it like it was a little person wearing a hat.

"At the library, with Mrs. Angus's help. And with Mrs.

Buttersbee's articles. Of course, I'll probably need someone to help me with interviews."

It didn't seem like the most exciting of cases. Then again, she'd made a bit of a mess of her first big, exciting case, so she thought perhaps she should try something a little more boring. "I'd be honored," she said. She reread the scrap of paper torn from her Mysteries Notebook. "This is his address."

It was an older house, small and green, with three steps up to a rickety-looking front porch. The curtains were drawn in the windows and there was a week's worth of newspapers on the welcome mat. Still, Hazel reached up her hand and knocked on the door. They waited, Hazel bouncing from foot to foot, but no one came.

Hazel bit her lip. "Maybe this isn't the right address." She flipped up the lid of the mailbox that was attached to the house next to the door. A Sears, Roebuck catalog was jammed inside. When she pulled it out, she saw that it was addressed to Mr. Paul Jones. "He has to be here. He's not at the cemetery."

"Maybe we missed him," Samuel said. "Maybe while we were at Mrs. Buttersbee's he left here and went to the graveyard."

"Maybe," Hazel said. But she wasn't really listening. She went down the stairs and around the back, where she finally saw a window without draperies. Standing on her tiptoes, she peered inside. Nothing. Absolutely nothing. No people. No pets. No furniture. Nothing. She dropped down onto her heels. This had to be his house, and yet he'd vanished.

She tried to remember the last time she'd seen him. At the funeral, of course. But had he been around after that? After noticing him so intently for so long, how had she been able to *not* notice him? Or to not notice that he was gone?

"He's not here," she said when she returned to the front of the house.

"Should we go back to the graveyard?"

"I don't think he's there, either."

"Well, where do you think he is?"

"Gone."

"Gone?" Samuel asked, gripping the package close to his chest.

"Gone, vanished, kaput. He split town. Now, why do you think he would do that?" She sat down on the steps, and Samuel sat down beside her, his satchel clunking onto the front porch.

"Maybe he's like Mary Poppins and once everything is sorted, he leaves."

Hazel thought that seemed highly unlikely, even if everything was sorted. Which it wasn't. Connie was leaving, but Maryann was still there to torment them, for one thing. And anyway, it seemed to Hazel that things always seemed to get unsorted and turned around, like the mess of thread in the bottom of her mother's unused sewing basket.

"Maybe he's a spy after all," Hazel said. "And he's been called back to Mother Russia."

"Hazel," Samuel said.

"He could be a double agent." Hazel liked that idea. "He could have been *pretending* to spy on us, but really he was spying on them and telling us all their secrets. He's gone back to Washington to tell them everything he knows."

"Hazel," Samuel said again. "Can't he just be Paul Jones? Isn't that enough?"

Hazel considered that idea, and she supposed just being Paul Jones was enough for Paul Jankowski.

But not, of course, for Hazel Kaplansky, star student, holder of knowledge, solver of mysteries, and future double agent.

Author's Note

After World War II, the United States and other Western countries entered into what is known as the Cold War with Russia and the Eastern Bloc nations. This was not a war in the traditional sense, but rather a series of threats and military flare-ups around the world, including the Korean War, mentioned in this novel. The United States and its allies were trying to fight the spread of Communism, a form of government that is supposed to allow for equality among all people but often gets stalled with an all-powerful dictator.

Senator Joseph McCarthy, who was elected to the United States Senate in 1946, took advantage of the fear of Communism. He claimed to know of hundreds of spies who had infiltrated the American government. He made a number of unsubstantiated accusations of Communism and disloyalty against those who tried to oppose him. Because of the atmosphere of fear—fueled in large part by McCarthy's accusations—many American leaders would not stand up to him, lest they be accused themselves.

One senator who did stand up to him was Margaret Chase Smith of Maine with her famous "Declaration of Conscience" speech in 1950. Though she never mentioned him by name, it was clear that it was McCarthy she was chastising when she said: "Those of us who shout the loudest about Americanism in making character assassinations are all too frequently those who, by our own words and acts, ignore some of the basic principles of Americanism—The right to criticize; The right to hold unpopular beliefs; The right to protest; The right of independent thought."

Most of McCarthy's accusations focused on those working in the government, but in November 1953 McCarthy began an investigation of the General Electric plant in Schenectady, New York. He claimed that secrets about atomic weapons were being leaked from the plant. Many of those accused refused to testify: they pled the Fifth. This was not an admission of guilt but rather a form of solidarity. Many believed they were not being targeted for their political beliefs, but because they were in the union. A labor union is a group of workers who band together in order to have more power and protections from their employers. Many union workers were former Communist Party members. During World War I, Communism was not seen as the evil it came to be known as. Instead it was seen as the party that best supported workers' rights. Even though most of the accused had left the party, they were treated as if they were still card-carrying members.

To learn about the fear of Communism in 1950s America, I spent a good deal of time reading and researching. You can find out more about that process on my website: www.megan frazerblakemore.com. At one point I wrote in my notes: *Joe McCarthy = ultimate bully*, for indeed that's what he was. He used innuendo, half truths, and fear to build his own power. In the end, though, Senator McCarthy was discredited. In 1954, the Senate formally censured him, and now his name is synonymous with a dark period in United States history.

However, the fear of Communism lived on through the 1980s, when I was a child. I remember the certainty I felt that the United States would be bombed by Russia. Like Hazel, I longed for a safe space to hide and made plans for the inevitable emergency. The Cold War ended with the fall of the Berlin Wall in 1989. Unfortunately the legacy of fear and turning against our neighbors did not crumble along with the Wall.

Although the Schenectady investigations really happened, there was not anyone involved named Alice Winthrop, nor did an investigation occur in Vermont. Given the time, though, anything seems possible, even an investigation in a sleepy Vermont town. In this culture of fear, neighbors turned on neighbors. In a 1954 poll, 78 percent of Americans thought that people should report their neighbors or acquaintances to the FBI if they suspected them of Communism. In one case in

1950, a customer reported the owners of a Chinese restaurant as Communists because they were Chinese.

History does not only take place on a grand scale, at the level of nations and world leaders. It happens in big cities and small towns, in neighborhoods and houses across the world. It is, of course, happening at this very moment. And while it's nice to think that in the future, looking back, we'll be able to say we acted justly, real life—and history—is rarely so simple and straightforward.

Acknowledgments

Thank you to those who shared their memories of growing up in the 1950s: Trish Poole, Carol Pikcilingis, Paulinda Oakes, Doris Bernstein, Kathleen Donegan, Sue Murphy, Cathy Haidorfer, and Ed Blakemore.

The time and space of the 2011 Kindling Words East retreat allowed me to finish the very rough first draft of this novel, and I owe deep gratitude to the organizers as well as to all the participants.

Thank you to the team at Bloomsbury, especially to Mary Kate Castellani, an editor extraordinaire: writing a novel can be like weaving in the wind, and you make sure no threads get away.

Thank you to my agent, Sara Crowe, for always working to find the best homes for my books.

A very special thanks to the middle-school book group at

Berwick Academy (ca. 2011–2013). You guys are the best, and I talk about you wherever I go. An extra-special thanks to Mr. Knight.

Thank you to the Blakemores for letting me be a part of your family, and for helping out with the kids so I can get the work done.

Thank you to my dad, Joseph Frazer, and to Susan Tananbaum for being both my champions and my supporters. Thanks also, Dad, for sharing your stories of growing up, though most of them were too wild for this tale.

Thanks to my mom, whose publicity skills are second only to those of the Bloomsbury publicity and marketing teams. Your stories of growing up with your brothers, and your friends Peggy and Kathy, provided a foundation for this story, not to mention the lovely detail about the sausage grinders.

And finally, thank you to Nathan, Jack, and Matilda for everything, always.